Yours Again

Quantity discounts are available on bulk orders. Contact sales@TAGPublishers.com for more information.

TAG Publishing, LLC
2030 S. Milam
Amarillo, TX 79109
www.TAGPublishers.com
Office (806) 373-0114
Fax (806) 373-4004
info@TAGPublishers.com

ISBN: 978-1-934606-58-2

First Edition

Yours Again

DEE BURKS

About

The Author

Dee Burks has been in the publishing industry for more than fifteen years. Dee has taught novel writing, ghostwriting and freelancing on the collegiate level and has an MBA with a special emphasis in international marketing. Introduced to the beautiful Northern New Mexico wilderness as a child, she often uses that setting for many of her historical and contemporary series.

www.deeburks.com

Chapter 1

Boston—1885

"Who invited him?" Samantha James directed her aunt's attention to a thin, well-dressed man who'd just stepped into the parlor of their Bostonian brownstone.

Mattie Eliot huffed an annoyed sigh. "I sure didn't, my dear."

John Lawson nodded in their direction, his smarmy gaze flitting over Samantha as if appraising a prize cow. It left her feeling filthy in a way even a good scrubbing in a big tub couldn't change.

"Do you think he suspects?" Aunt Mattie whispered, her small form ensconced in this season's latest fashion: a dark brown silk that set off pale green eyes to their best advantage. Even at the age of fifty-two she still turned heads, though none had turned hers since her late husband's death ten years ago.

"No, I made it clear to Gerald Farnsworth at the bank that John's access to our accounts and investments had been withdrawn but that he was not to say anything until I met with John tomorrow."

"Good, I'm not sure what he's up to," she whispered, "but I'd guess he's going to make another attempt to jump your knickers, the slimy bastard."

Samantha smiled. Mattie did have a way with words that would probably shock the other matriarchs of Boston society, but Mattie really didn't care what anyone thought and Samantha loved that about her. John had tried his best to get on Samantha's good side, but she found absolutely nothing to like about the man.

In his early thirties, John Lawson had worked in his father's investment firm for the past ten years. There was something about him that unnerved her. She couldn't really put a finger on it, and in reality it was probably a combination of things: the way he appraised every person he talked to as if assigning them a dollar value or how he constantly fidgeted with his clothing as if trying to hide something. Perhaps it was the lack of warmth he exuded from his eyes or the condescending way he spoke. The man had a coldness about him almost as if he weren't really human at all.

In contrast, his father was one of Mattie's oldest confidants and one of the warmest, kindest men Samantha had ever met. Ty Lawson had managed Mattie's investments both before and after her husband's death and had been very successful as they'd grown exponentially. He'd also managed the small inheritance Samantha received from her parent's death, and it, too, had grown to a substantial amount. She hadn't even known about the inheritance until three years ago, but knowing it was there relieved any pressure she felt to get married. She never wanted to be a stone around anyone's neck, especially Mattie's.

But everything changed a short two weeks ago. They got word of Ty's sudden death from John—the day after the funeral. It was extremely strange as Ty had been in his mid-fifties and in very good health. John had passed the hushed nature of the event off as family wanting privacy. But John was the only family and the fact that he hadn't told anyone or allowed them to pay their respects was very suspicious. Rumors had immediately flown all around Boston, and many families that trusted Ty with their investments weren't about to give John the same level of trust. Mattie and Samantha included.

The party was a relatively informal affair, which Mattie had for her close friends at the beginning of September every year before the official society season began. Many of the attendees were true Boston Brahmins who traced their families' lineage back to their arrival on the Mayflower, and even though Mattie had married into their circle and wasn't really one of them, she was very well liked. It certainly helped that her husband's death had also left her an extremely wealthy woman who was still beautiful enough to be mistaken for someone in her early forties.

The fact that John had shown up unannounced and uninvited to Mattie's party was just more proof to Samantha that he was after something—and that something probably included her. He'd made it very clear that he wanted his future attached to hers, but she had known from the beginning that he just wanted her money, and eventually Mattie's, since Samantha was her only heir.

While they both did their best over the next hour to avoid John, eventually he caught them boxed in by people where they couldn't discreetly get away. He sauntered up to Mattie, a glass of wine in each hand, "I thought you might be in need of refreshment, Mattie."

John held out a glass and Mattie had to take it to avoid a scene, "Thank you, John."

He stared boldly at Samantha while she pretended to watch something across the room. He refused to move away and stood in front of them, awkwardly blocking their escape.

Mattie took a sip and said, "I'm surprised to see you here, John." He knew he hadn't been invited, and hopefully pointing it out would at least produce some embarrassment or explanation on his part.

"Well, I'm sure the lack of invitation was just an oversight," he said smoothly. "It's hard to remember everyone once memory issues set in."

Mattie's face turned bright red and Samantha could almost count the seconds before John would be wearing that wine.

"I do not have any memory problems, John Lawson, and you damn well know it."

His condescending smile raked over both women, "Of course you do. Don't you recall discussing that fact with my father and that our firm would be exercising power of attorney over your investments?"

"What?" Samantha spat.

"We'll discuss this in the morning, Samantha, and know that I look forward to it." He gave a slight bow and strode from the parlor, still smiling. They heard the front door close a moment later.

Mattie fumed, "That greedy little piss ant! He wouldn't dare."

Samantha tried her best to calm her aunt, "He probably would, but he's not getting away with anything."

Mattie glowered at the door John had just exited and gulped the wine. "How that, that *thing* sprang from Ty Lawson's loins I'll never know." She fanned her face with one hand. "I'm so angry I could just melt."

Samantha glanced at her aunt just as Mattie's eyes rolled back in her head. She slid to the floor in a pile of brown silk and the party immediately descended into chaos.

An hour later Samantha glanced over at Mattie, lying peacefully in the large four poster bed. The doctor said she would be fine, but Mattie Eliot's collapse had surprised all the guests. Mattie was as vibrant as most women half her age, including Samantha. In the nine years since Samantha had come to live with Mattie she'd rarely seen the woman ill, let alone in a full swoon.

It was a mild early fall day, so heat didn't seem to be a factor, and even though Mattie had been more embarrassed than anything it was still highly unusual. Upon hearing that Mattie would be fine, the guests discretely departed and the household settled into the familiar quiet that Samantha loved.

The four-story brownstone on Newbury Street in the Back Bay neighborhood had been a sanctuary for an awkward fourteen-year-old girl who had lost both parents. Mattie and her sister Clair, Samantha's mother, were very close, but where Mattie had done the expected thing and married a wealthy Boston businessman almost twenty years her senior, Samantha's mother had followed her heart and married Sam James, a man who dreamed of striking it rich in the New Mexico Territory.

Though these days Samantha was the perfect example of an aloof, restrained, and educated young woman of good breeding from Boston, her childhood had been spent wild and free in the northern mountains of the New Mexico Territory. It seemed the last couple of years those carefree days crossed her mind much more often and lingered as a wistful longing. As one suitor after another attempted to impress her, she'd become more and more stoic. Samantha just wasn't interested in any of them—or anything else of late. A strange restlessness had settled in her heart and refused to budge.

Paul Creswell, Mattie's butler and the newest addition to her staff, fussed fluffing pillows and straightening the beautiful Baltimore quilt that covered Mattie's petite form. Boston society had recently become enamored of English butlers, so of course Mattie had to have one. Paul had more than twenty years experience serving as a butler in the great manor houses of England, but had only been in her aunt's employ for a few weeks. Samantha would guess him to be in his late fifties or early sixties with a full head of salt-and-pepper hair and steel blue eyes that were quick and lively. She had to admit Paul's formal dress and clipped British accent had certainly added something interesting to the household. Samantha saw his eyes twinkle when Mattie laughed, which was often, hard as he might try to hide it.

"Madam," he said addressing Samantha formally, "Should you need anything, I'll be right outside."

"Thanks so much Paul." She had to admit she already had a soft spot for the man. Mattie's whims weren't the easiest to deal with sometimes, but he'd been quite the sport—so far at least.

"Tea will be up shortly." He offered a curt bow, slid a worried glance toward the bed and then exited.

"That British accent still rolls over me like melted butter," Mattie's eyes popped open.

Samantha smiled and shook her head, "You know he was really worried about you." She sat on the edge of the huge bed, which made Mattie look that much smaller.

Her aunt scrunched up her nose, and rolled the covers down across her pink nightgown, "I know. I hope I didn't embarrass myself too much." Mattie squirmed into a sitting position and placed a pillow behind her head.

"No one thought anything about it," Samantha lied.

"Well, what are we going to do about John?" She asked.

Samantha sighed, "I think we should let your lawyer know what is going on immediately and even contact the police."

"Do you think he'd really try to enforce a fake power of attorney?"

"Well, he might, and I have to wonder if tonight's episode is part of something bigger," Samantha's suspicions had been immediately aroused when Mattie fainted so quickly after drinking the wine John gave her. It didn't take a genius to connect the dots.

"Surely he isn't that stupid," Mattie said.

"No. Whatever he is, he isn't stupid. I'm just wondering if he was sending some sort of message before tomorrow's meeting."

"What kind of message?"

"I have my suspicions, but let's cross that bridge when we get there. In the mean time, I think we should ensure all our assets are safe."

"Agreed. Do you think you should go see him alone?"

Samantha shrugged, "I can't imagine he'd try something in front of an office full of people, and he might be reluctant to reveal his true intentions if someone unexpected showed up."

Mattie stewed for a minute, then watched Samantha closely, "I noticed that you weren't really enjoying yourself much at the party even before John arrived."

Samantha shrugged. No, she hadn't been. *At all.* There were no conversations that held her attention. The last things she cared about were what was playing at the opera house this season and who was doing what to whom. Most of the women her age had young families and talked constantly about babies and husbands. At twenty three she was considered something of a spinster and the only other women her age who didn't have families were so wrapped up in shopping and voyages to Europe it was hard to get a word in. Not that she cared to.

"What is it dear?" Her aunt's pale green eyes pleaded. Mattie always knew when something wasn't right.

"I don't know. I just don't seem to be interested in anything anymore. It's like I'm waiting for something that never appears." The feeling had been growing for some time, and the worse it got the more annoyed Samantha became with everyone and everything in her life. "I don't know what's wrong with me."

Mattie spoke softly, "It's not something you are waiting on Samantha. It's someone."

She scoffed at the ridiculous idea and walked to the window. Though it had cooled some from the sweltering heat of August, it would still be a while before the leaves brought out their fall colors. Stately carriages rolled down Newbury Street, and she suddenly had the urge to jump into one and go. Where, she didn't know.

"Scoff if you will my dear, but I know what you are waiting on."

Samantha smiled, "And what would that be?"

"A tall, dark, handsome man to whisk you off your feet." Mattie grinned and bounced her eyebrows at Samantha.

She laughed, "Why is everything about finding me a man?"

"Well, not everything my dear." She thought a moment, "Of course if he had an amazing accent, that would be different as I honestly don't know how you'd help yourself."

Samantha laughed and shook her head, the woman was relentless, but she knew Mattie just wanted her to be happy— whatever that meant. "Well, don't worry about the appointment with John tomorrow. I can handle it."

At ten o'clock the next morning Samantha walked along Newbury and up a block on Dartmouth. Most of the buildings were new and construction seemed to be everywhere in this part of Boston. The Lawson Investment Firm was located in the ground floor of a three-story building with John and his father having lavish quarters on the upper floors.

She entered and was greeted by one of several assistants that occupied the outer office. He showed her into what had been Ty Lawson's office. The scent of expensive cigars permeated the room. The highest quality leather chairs and a massive oak desk perched atop a delicate silk carpet exuding wealth and success. Only now John sat behind the desk, a pretender to all his father had built. She perched on the edge of one of the leather chairs.

"You are a beautiful woman, Samantha." John stared at her with undisguised lust.

It was his father's desk, his father's office, his father's success, but John had taken over even before the flowers from Ty's funeral had wilted. John looked the part of an impeccable financial advisor but, as usual, had all the warmth of a headstone.

"We aren't talking about me," Samantha stressed, "We are talking about Mattie's accounts, and by my calculations more than two thousand has gone missing in the last week alone."

"Well you can't be expected to understand all the intricacies of finan-"

"Don't even," she growled. "I studied finance extensively—in fact much more than you ever have—and I am well aware of the investments in Mattie's portfolio, so don't think that just because my aunt and I are female, we are stupid."

John didn't react to her statement. He flicked an imaginary piece of lint off his immaculate jacket. A new, extremely expensive jacket, she noted.

"Perhaps once the accounts have all been settled and I've had time to recover from my father's sudden passing I'll be able to sit and explain things to you and your aunt."

Samantha rose to leave. "I'm more inclined to believe the rumors I've heard, and I'm quite sure you are not exactly mourning Ty's death."

"I'm surprised and hurt, Samantha." He turned his black eyes toward her and smiled, "Now surely you don't believe those lies. In fact, I was thinking about calling on you soon."

She stared at him for a moment. "What on earth for?"

"Well as a suitor of course." He arrogance oozed across the room. "You'd be lucky to have a husband of my stature and I believe your spirit could be channeled into worthwhile areas." His gaze flitted over her curves in appreciation, but felt like an assault.

She shuddered. "Mr. Lawson, I have no interest in you

whatsoever. In fact, you disgust me." She didn't notice the change in him as she rose to leave. "Whatever you are planning you absolutely will not get away with it." She glanced down at him. "I've already had your access to all our accounts removed and the bank alerted to possible fraud."

Lawson sprang to his feet.

Samantha continued, "In fact, my next stop is the police. I'm sure if there is money missing from Mattie's account, then others have been stolen from as well."

John came around the desk and grabbed her before she had time to react. A cold clammy hand slapped over Samantha's mouth from behind. She struggled to pull away until she felt the sharp edge of a knife push into her ribs. She froze.

"Not one word, you pretentious bitch," He hissed. "You have no idea who you are dealing with or what I can do, understand?" With that last word he shook her and she felt the knife slice her dress and rest against her skin. She didn't move a muscle.

He spun her around and violently pushed her back up against the door, her face within an inch of his. He held the knife at her throat. "There is nothing you can do to stop me from getting what I want."

John's gaze settled on the pearl buttons that ran down the front of her dress. He chuckled, his vile breath assaulting her, "And make no mistake. I will have what is mine, and that little fainting spell of Mattie's was just a show of exactly how dangerous I can be."

He popped off one button with the tip of his knife. It hit the floor and rolled a short distance. "I easily could have killed her, just like I can easily kill you right now."

Samantha willed herself not to panic. He had put something in Mattie's drink, just as she had suspected. He wouldn't think twice about killing Mattie or Samantha to get his hands on their money, and he was clearly unhinged. She had to find a way to calm him down and get out of this office.

"Not a peep," he whispered, "You will learn to respect me."

She nodded and he slowly lowered his hand from her mouth. Samantha forced her voice not to shake. "You are right John. I have underestimated your shrewd financial abilities. I apologize if I was disrespectful concerning your father."

He popped another button and it bounced across the rug. His eyes glinted as he twisted the knife in his fingers, his eyes on her breasts. John slid the cold edge of the knife into the new opening he'd made by removing buttons. The tip of the blade slid along her cleavage. He held her eyes and leaned down, flicking the tip of his tongue into the valley between her breasts. She cringed and stiffened.

A sharp knock on the door made Samantha jump.

"Yes?" His eyes never left hers.

"Mr. Lawson, you have a client waiting in the lobby," a voice answered.

"I'll be right out." He hadn't moved an inch. His steely gaze completely frazzled her nerves. "We will come to an arrangement."

She nodded.

"You will not say a word to anyone about anything you suspect. Otherwise, I assure you that you will be an orphan once again."

She had no doubt he would follow through on any threat he made. Of all the times she had let her thoughts flow right out of her mouth, this time it was serious.

"Of course, I was merely speculating. I can admit when I'm wrong, and clearly I was wrong about you." She managed a half smile.

"I would expect no less from my fiancée." Lawson loosened his grip, but the knife remained within an inch of her nose. "And when I come for you, you will see me. Understand?"

Fiancée? She really didn't care if he thought she was the next queen of England right now, although that was more likely than her agreeing to marry him.

"Of course, I'd be lucky to be with you." The words tasted like bile, but she had to get out of this office alive.

Lawson stepped back and slipped the weapon into his pocket. He yanked his vest down and tugged at his cuffs, once again cold and distant. "Please give your aunt my greetings and let her know we'll be setting a meeting to work out the details of our engagement tomorrow." He walked to his desk as if nothing had happened and dismissed her with a flip of the wrist.

Samantha ran.

Chapter 2

New Mexico Territory

The stage rocked along the mountain trail toward River City. Samantha was much more refreshed this morning following a night in the St. James Hotel in Cimarron. After four days on the train from Boston to Raton, New Mexico, and then another two on the stage to Cimarron, Samantha had been completely worn out. The stress of constantly looking over her shoulder had taken its toll.

This morning the stage was packed with five adults and two small children, all headed to River City. They started out before dawn, and thankfully both children slept soundly in their parents' arms. She'd not slept a full night since the meeting with John, and even now her mind was still in a daze. Mattie had immediately called her lawyer as well as the authorities the minute Samantha arrived back at the brownstone.

It was clear that Samantha was in the most danger as John's plan centered around her. She shuddered at the thought of his vile tongue on her skin and rubbed her knuckles against her chest to try and remove the memory. None of the other passengers in the coach noticed or paid her any attention. She was grateful to have her thoughts to herself for a while. Just the thought of his touch was enough to risk life and limb to get away.

The stage swayed rhythmically as the sun peaked over the mountains and highlighted the small but rapidly flowing stream next to the trail. She'd forgotten how incredibly beautiful this part of the country was, and somehow it seemed so much more vibrant and wild than she remembered. The overly civilized atmosphere of Boston was a far cry from this wild territory, and she liked this place. She liked it very much.

The decision for her to disappear until John could be dealt with was an obvious choice. Without Samantha, John couldn't get his hands on Mattie's money even if he tried; Samantha was the only heir. But if she stayed in Boston, everyone was in danger. If he could kidnap Samantha—and she had no doubt he would stoop to that—then he could easily do away with Mattie. They all decided that Samantha would immediately leave until the authorities could be apprised and John dealt with.

Only Mattie knew she'd come here. No one else had been told in case John had eyes and ears among some of Mattie's other confidants or friends. At this point they couldn't afford to trust anyone, and they agreed that there would be no communication between them that might tip someone off as to her whereabouts until their suspicions could be proven and John was no longer a threat.

She hadn't wanted to leave Mattie, but her aunt insisted she go. The Williams' didn't know she was coming, but Mattie assured her they would have no problem with a sudden arrival. At least she would be completely safe with three grown men to protect her. It might be a month, maybe longer but she had to get away from Boston and from John. She knew he could follow and was completely paranoid the four days on the train jumping at every loud noise or unexpected sound. After she arrived in Cimarron, she was reasonably sure he hadn't followed. At least not close enough to catch her before she reached the ranch.

The stage from Cimarron to River City today seemed to plod along the ever steeper terrain, and though she relished being in the mountains once again, she was anxious to reach her destination. There was so much she'd forgotten: the crisp clean mountain air, the streams that gurgled and bubbled their way along, and the wildlife that seemed to be everywhere along the trail.

She breathed deeply and enjoyed the peace for a short time. But once the children arose, the ride through the mountains grew much more tedious. As the hours dragged by, the day warmed the inside of the stage to an almost intolerable level, making the children and adults uncomfortable and moody.

Large rocks jostled the passengers until Samantha almost landed in the lap of the man across from her. He was older, but distinguished and looked at a large pocket watch frequently. He winked at her and she looked away, not wanting to make any connection with anyone. Her hands strained and cramped trying to hold on until suddenly the trail opened up into a wide valley and the road smoothed. They picked up speed and she smiled, only a few more miles now. Her heart raced with anticipation.

They finally pulled into River City by late afternoon. She disembarked and nodded a farewell to the other passengers. Grabbing her small valise, Samantha walked along the main street of a town she hadn't seen in more than nine years. River City looked so different from when she'd left, although she recognized a few stores. When she was a child they were newly built and full of patrons. Now most were either empty or abandoned, a mere shadow of their former selves. Back then the town had bustled with people everywhere and more than a hundred homes crowded below the bluff at the end of Main Street. She'd played with other children outside the small schoolhouse and had even thrown rocks off the bluff into the creek below. The schoolhouse looked to be in disrepair, and it was much smaller than she remembered. The weathered logs of the building sank toward one corner as if it was someone's forgotten project.

The River City of her childhood was now part ghost town, part boomtown with the saloon, hotel, and Miss Sadie's Gentlemen's Club being the most prominent buildings. There were still barely visible foundations from homes that had been moved elsewhere, but she refused to allow it to dampen her spirit. She clutched the small valise that Mattie insisted she take a little tighter. Traveling light meant she could go quickly and mostly unnoticed as she traveled and now, after days of getting on and off trains, up and down on stages and back and forth to a hotel, she was exceedingly grateful she hadn't brought anything larger.

Samantha walked all the way to the end of Main Street and up along the road that circled around the bluff to the top, her breath now coming in short gasps. The elevation was affecting her, but she continued on despite the protest of burning lungs. Once at the top of the bluff, the cemetery took up some of the flat ground, but the rest was still vacant. Samantha took in the view from all directions: the mountains to the west, Baldy Peak to the north, and the valley stretched out to the north and south. The river flowed right beside the trail that led to the pass. The feel of this place was so much bigger, grander than she remembered, no matter how the town appeared, and she felt excitement welling up in her throat.

She was home. Really home. Samantha reached out her arms and pointed her face to the sun. She breathed deeply and spun around, still not quite believing she was really here. Something in her heart lurched into motion once again. As if some clock that sat dusty and forgotten had suddenly chimed once again.

A rumble in the distance got her attention. Clouds darkened the western sky behind the peaks and she remembered the stage driver say that rain might be expected later. It didn't give her much time. She could wait in town another night, but now she was almost within sight of the ranch. She refused to wait another minute.

Dee Burks

Yours Again

Chapter 3

Taos Williams rode into the tiny mining town of River City in the northern mountains of New Mexico Territory. His body tense, he scanned the buildings for any sign of threat as he slowly rode his large chestnut gelding down the main street. River City had, as short as ten years ago, been the county seat and biggest settlement in Northern New Mexico. But now, with the initial gold boom a distant memory, it had shrunk to only a few hundred residents. There were one or two companies still mining some productive veins, but everything else had mostly petered out.

That was until a couple of months ago. Discovery of new placer deposits in the Placer River and a new vein of lode gold up on Baldy Peak had people streaming in again, but not nearly at the volume they had been coming a decade earlier. Still, the town was shifting into boom mode again.

The good news is that it meant higher prices and a larger market for their cattle close to home. Driving them through the mountains to the railroad wasn't the most efficient as far as time or revenue was concerned. But he and his two brothers, Charlie and Darren, had done what they had to do the last few years, which is why they survived the post-boom downturn when so many other cattlemen had to pack it in.

Taos noted a few men he didn't recognize leaning against the railing of the saloon, but that was a regular occurrence these days. New people arrived with every stage, and there was no way to keep up with who was who, especially since he didn't come to town unless he absolutely had to.

The men eyeballed him as he rode past but none made a move. Used to be this town was a happy go lucky old fashioned boom town, but this year had turned neighbor against neighbor, friend against friend. An extended drought dried up creeks and springs all over the valley, and now with miners competing with ranchers for what little water remained, things had reached a fevered pitch. Last week's incident down at Bear Creek had brought things to a head as several cattle had been found shot dead, presumably by miners.

The whole town was a cinder box waiting on a match—both figuratively and literally. One shot could potentially start a full blown range war that would put the Lincoln County war to shame. While the timber and forage pastures were so dry right now that even a wayward spark or lightning bolt could start an inferno that would sweep through the valley destroying what little remained of the town or the livestock. Every single person seemed on edge and with very good reason.

Some of the best water in the valley was on the Williams' ranch and Taos was under no illusions that there were some who would use just about any means to get their hands on it. He'd had offers from other ranchers and even mining companies to divert some of the water on their ranch, but he'd turned them all down. Water was life in this valley and once it was gone, you were done. He had to protect what was his, and he'd do it at any cost.

Taos reined up at Hardin's Mercantile and tied up his horse. The nervous atmosphere of town made his horse dance a bit in front of the hitching post. He stroked the gelding's neck and spoke softly, calming the animal. He didn't really blame the horse; having to be around the people of River City made him just as jumpy.

Spurs jingled as Taos strode across the planks in front of the building. The bell above the door alerted everyone in the store to his presence, and as usual when he went anywhere in this town, conversation stopped and they all stared. It's not that he wasn't used to it, but it was still a little awkward. He ducked into the store, feeling much taller than his six-foot-three frame and completely out of place among the women shopping.

Taos had never been overly popular with people in town and that certainly included the women. Even when he was younger he had kept to himself and didn't mix much; his height had made him an uncoordinated and abnormally skinny teen. He'd put on a good sixty or seventy pounds since then, all of it muscle, but that had only made him feel like a hulking beast. Then he'd married and when that went south, a terrible image was planted forever in people's minds, courtesy of his wife.

Even now, years after his she had fled the territory, people still treated him like a leper. He learned years ago that there was no way of convincing anyone that his wife had lied about everything that had happened in their short marriage. The story was just too juicy for the townspeople to drop.

Mr. Hardin greeted him with a nod and took the list Taos offered, gazing at it through the half glasses that sat on his nose. The man's wife smiled, "It's a fine day today, isn't it Taos?"

He nodded, "I suppose it is."

"Might even rain if we're lucky," Mrs. Hardin smiled at him while her husband gathered the items in his order.

The Hardins had known Taos's father for years before he died and had gone out of their way to let Taos know they didn't give a hot mouse turd what anyone said about him. Mrs. Hardin always made a point to speak to him even if no one else in town did. He appreciated her effort, but he knew it was no use. She probably did, too, but it was still nice to at least see a friendly face.

Once his father had died, there had been nothing to stop the rumor mill from working overtime. Jake Williams had been larger than life and had the kind of personality that could win over anyone about anything. Taos often thought the man should have run for office, but Jake was content to stay on the ranch after his wife died and raise his three boys. Taos only hoped he'd be as good a father to his son, Tommy.

Taos's brother Charlie had the same personality as their dad, and as annoying as it was sometimes, it certainly came in handy on occasion. He wished Charlie had been around today to take care of this little chore, but he'd been escorting a prisoner over to Taos for Sheriff Blake as he often did, and wasn't due back until late this afternoon.

"Taos! Taos Williams!" a female voice squealed.

He groaned inwardly and pretended not to hear. It was one of Mertie Mae Morrison's daughters. He wasn't sure which one, but it really didn't matter; they could both scare off a whole flock of crows with their screeching.

"Mr. Williams?"

He turned toward the girls' mother. Mertie Mae Morrison was never far from her precious offspring and she looked ready to pounce on Taos today. A tall hawk-beaked woman with an abnormally long face and teeth too big for her mouth, Mertie Mae's face closely resembled that of a horse. Taos had no idea how a man could kiss a woman like that and not have his horse look at him funny every day afterward.

"Mr. Williams, I'd like to discuss some business with you, if you don't mind."

Oh boy. He knew exactly what kind of business she wanted to discuss, and he absolutely did not want to hear it. Mertie Mae was determined to foist off those girls of hers on someone and if she could get some water for her parched farm out of the deal, he was sure she would consider that a win.

"Uh, I'm just picking up a few things. I've got to be on my way."

The woman gave him a disbelieving glare. "It won't take but a moment and I'm sure you have time to spare in your social calendar."

The comment drew a few whispers from the handful of spectators and instantly pissed him off. She couldn't resist pointing out he had absolutely no social calendar and preferred it that way. The last thing he wanted in his life, or his son's life, was a meddling woman.

"Actually I don't, Ma'am. I have a meeting. "

She didn't budge.

"At the saloon," he leaned forward for emphasis and saw her twitch. Mertie Mae was a bible thumper and wouldn't dare follow him into the saloon. He didn't really have any business there, but if he had to hide out and have a shot of whiskey to get rid of her while Hardin filled his order, then so be it.

"Fine, but I intend to discuss this business with you as soon as possible."

Taos never ran from confrontation. In his mind it was better to get it over with than have to face it another day. "Look Mertie Mae, I'm not interested in your girls," he cast a glance at their embarrassed faces and instantly softened his reproach. "I'm sure they will find someone who cares for them and settle down, but I am not going to marry one of them. Ever."

Mertie Mae lowered her voice, "Well, perhaps we can come to another arrangement. No need for you to get into the same situation as before."

Taos actually thought about popping her one right on that hawk-bill nose of hers. Not that it would do the rumors about him any favors. What kind of mother basically sells off her children to save livestock?

Taos towered over the woman, purposely crowding her, "If you are planning to sell your daughters' virtue to the highest bidder that is your business, but don't expect me to be one of those bidders."

Mertie Mae sputtered, "Well, I never! I had no such thing in mind. Come on girls." She stomped out of the mercantile and he turned back to Mr. Hardin, who had a hard time concealing his grin.

Mr. Hardin winked, "I added a few of those lemon drops Tommy likes so much, if that's okay."

Taos nodded and picked up his order, leaving without another word. He packed the items carefully in his saddle bags and grabbed the saddle to swing up. He glanced up at the bluff that rose about fifty feet above the town at one end of Main Street.

The bluff had the best view in the whole valley of the surrounding mountains. He'd never understood why the town had decided to reserve that prime spot for the dead, but they had. The last time he was up there was his father's funeral. The old man wanted to be placed next to his wife instead of on the ranch, and they'd honored that request. Taos hadn't been back up there since.

Taos thought he caught a movement or glint of something on the bluff, but as he stared he didn't see anything. Another moment passed and suddenly a small woman came into view.

The sun glinted off golden hair the color of spun silk. That was what he'd seen. He didn't recognize her as someone from River City, but with all the new people coming in, it could certainly be someone he just didn't know yet. *She must be paying her respects,* he thought until she spread her arms wide and twirled around, an angelic expression on her face.

His breath caught for a moment as he stared trying to make out her face. Whoever she was, she'd put old Mertie Mae's girls to shame, not that it was all that hard. That woman had gotten more desperate with each passing week as more people came to River City. While it expanded the available pool of possible suitors, most were dreamers still looking to make their fortune, not landowners who'd already made theirs. And that was what Mertie Mae had in mind as son-in-law material.

He frowned. Pretty women coming to town would not be good news for Mertie Mae's matchmaking, but it also made Taos very wary. He'd been the victim of feminine wiles before and he'd be damned if he fell for it again even if the woman looked like an angel straight out of heaven.

Yours Again

Chapter 4

Samantha walked back to town and quickly rented a horse from the livery, setting out to the north. She hadn't ridden astride in nine years, but it felt good to feel the horse beneath her body as it ran. She yanked the pins from her hair and tossed them into the wind, allowing her hair to flow in the breeze.

They raced across the valley as the last rays of sun dipped behind the clouds and shadows crossed the land. Just the feel of wind rushing past her body filled Samantha with a sense of freedom and control. It was a remembered feeling that she only now realized she had missed.

She reined the horse to a stop at a creek bed that crossed the valley, surprised that it was dry. She'd never remembered this creek being dry, and certainly not at this time of year. She looked around and realized the grass the horse ran through was dry and crisp as if there hadn't been rain in a very long time.

A loud clap of thunder snapped Samantha into action. She urged the horse down the side of the bank and across, quickly climbing the other side. A creek bed was no place to get caught in a thunderstorm. As a child, she'd witnessed the terror of flash floods racing through the valley and knew the danger well.

The ranch land was remarkably unchanged with rolling hills escalating into the tall peaks in the distance. There were fewer homes than she remembered, and some of the cabins she passed seemed abandoned. Not surprising, given what she'd seen in town. The pastures rolled up to the tree line part way up the mountains that sported tall pines and beautiful aspens in full summer greenery. Cattle dotted the range in some areas but they were sparse.

As Samantha rode toward the upper end of the valley that led to the western mountain pass, she could see several areas that had been mined and old mining equipment that looked as if the workers had just dropped their tools and walked away. She wondered what had happened on the Williams' ranch and on her ranch which bordered theirs to the south.

The Williams brothers had looked after her property for nine years, and hopefully at least the house was still standing. She didn't want to impose on them forever, but for the time being it was probably better she stay at their house just as she had the few months after her mother died.

Samantha's father had built their cabin by hand, but thinking about standing in it once again made her uneasy. It held some wonderful memories but had also been witness to all the grief and heartache she'd experienced at such a young age. She didn't relish the idea of digging up all that pain again.

The sky darkened and rolled with unspent fury like a cauldron waiting to boil over. The man at the livery had been right. She should have waited for the storm to pass. The weather hadn't looked that bad an hour ago, and after days of confinement on the train and stage coach, she'd needed to breathe deeply of fresh air.

The horse's hooves slid sideways a short distance, jolting her attention back to the trail. Samantha gripped the saddle horn tightly. Sandy mountain dirt became a river of muck very quickly and if the horse lost its footing not only was it dangerous, but it could be deadly. Now splattered with large round wet spots, the once beautiful periwinkle silk of her traveling dress looked like a ridiculous polka dot. She hadn't had time to buy something more suited to this wild, rugged country when she fled Boston, and it was clear that this dress had seen its last ride. Not that she cared much, but it had been one of Aunt Mattie's favorites.

One quick flash of lightning brought a torrent of rain and silhouetted a lone rider at the top of the ridge she'd just passed. Samantha's back stiffened. With the next flash she looked again. No one. Her nerves danced, and she urged the horse faster, scanning the ridge repeatedly. Still no one. Maybe she had imagined it. But she couldn't shake the feeling that unseen eyes followed her every move.

Another bluff loomed just ahead and she exhaled her relief. Shelter was close. She shivered. Large drops pelted the ground and the aroma of sage permeated the air. Steam rose off the horse's neck into the rain cooled air as it galloped. The countryside now smelled like Aunt Mattie's kitchen on Thanksgiving.

A shout in the distance sent a tremor of fear skittering up Samantha's spine. She dug her heels into the horse's side and leaned forward in the saddle. The beating of hooves and rumble of thunder drowned out the man's voice. The harsh reality of riding headlong through pouring rain with no help in sight constricted her breathing and made her heart vibrate erratically. If this stranger intended her harm, she would be at his mercy. The Williams' didn't even know she was on her way. They wouldn't know to come looking if she never arrived.

Samantha skirted the base of the bluff toward a small box canyon on the other side—a dead end. No one knew about the old mine opening but the Williams boys and maybe an Indian or two. A stranger, even a ranch hand familiar with the area, would not be able to find it. Jake Williams and Sam James had initially started out gold mining but quickly realized they could make more money selling beef to miners than actually mining. The mine had been abandoned long before she could even walk.

If Samantha could get far enough ahead of the rider, it would be easy to slip inside the old mine and wait out the storm. He'd go on thinking she had just disappeared. Now she was actually grateful for the rain. It held the dust down and quickly erased any tracks at the same time, making it very difficult for anyone to follow. She glanced behind her. Nothing.

If I can't see him, then he can't see me.

She pulled the reins across the horse's neck and veered toward her destination. The mine was at the very back of the tiny canyon beyond a small stand of thick brush. She nudged the animal forward with her ankles as its hooves slid on the steep terrain.

What did the liveryman say this horse's name was? Jerry, Jamie, no . . . Jessie, that's it.

Samantha reached up and patted the overheated flesh, "There you go, Jessie. Come on, just a little further." He responded to her voice, bobbing his head and trudging a few more steps up the hill. When it seemed they could go no further, Jessie stopped and she climbed off.

Intent on finding the mine entrance, she tripped over a rotted log and slid to her knees. Cold mud soaked through her dress to her legs sending a shiver up her spine. The sticky dirt clung to everything that touched it. She stood, her skirt straining at the waist, weighed down now by thick muck. She concentrated on lifting her mud-caked feet one by one as she trudged up the hill, the earth threatening to suck each shoe off in turn.

Samantha finally found the mine entrance and hurried forward. Jessie hesitated. A sharp tug on the reins, and they were both engulfed in inky blackness. Only shadows filtered through the long narrow opening, even though the lightning flashed nearer now. Shivering almost uncontrollably now, Samantha rubbed her upper arms, trying to get some warmth going. She listened intently for any hint that the man still followed. The pounding of raindrops and the gurgle of water flowing down toward the bottom of the canyon were the only sounds.

Jessie huffed hot breath into the darkness. She rubbed his nose, then placed icy hands on his hot neck, trying to borrow some warmth. They waited for what seemed an eternity but was probably no more than a few minutes. Samantha edged toward the opening, groping her way along the wall. Gingerly she stuck her head out and squinted through sheets of rain. She seemed to be alone, but couldn't really tell.

Minutes passed as she strained to detect any movement in the canyon below. Still nothing. Her heart calmed a bit, and she walked blindly toward her horse. The animal nudged her outstretched hand. She ran her palm along its mane and back to the small bag tied to the saddle. The valise contained only two dresses. Hopefully something would be dry. As she reached to untie the bag, a rock tumbled into the entrance. Jessie nervously stepped back a pace. Samantha stood frozen and held her breath.

"I know you're in here, lady." A deep voice echoed off the walls of the tiny mine and reverberated in her ears. His presence filled the space and seemed to take up what little air remained.

The stranger shuffled forward and his boot clunked against a rock. Samantha heard pebbles shower the mine floor as his hand brushed the wall. She could hear his breathing as he moved closer—almost within reach now. Ducking low, she crept quietly along the opposite wall but was still no more than a few feet from the man in the tiny space of the mine. She hoped his horse would be agreeable to a different rider if she was lucky enough to make it outside. Samantha felt the air swirl as a sleeve passed over her head, and she dashed for the entrance. Gloved fingers clamped around her wrist like bands of steel, jerking her to a halt.

"Gotcha!" His tone was triumphant, "You need to come along with me."

"I'm not going anywhere," Samantha scrambled for footing, trying not to fall headlong into the dirt. "I'll be fine right here." She squirmed and tugged against his grasp.

"In a mine?"

Samantha was both panicked and annoyed at the sarcasm in his voice. "I can take care of myself."

"You think so?" His tone indicated that he was smiling. If he thought she was some wilting wall flower, then he was in for a surprise

"I know so."

"Do you have any food?"

"Well, no."

"Any water?"

"I'm dripping wet." She heard him grunt and continued her struggle against an iron grip. "I'm not hungry or thirsty, so it's not a problem."

"Your *horse* is hungry and thirsty, and I know you're wet and cold. Do you have any way to build a fire?"

"No."

"Look lady, this ain't some big city back east. It's dangerous out here. This storm doesn't look like it will let up anytime soon."

Fear contracted her chest. How did he know she was from Boston? Had he followed her from town? She tugged harder and moved one foot in a large circle feeling for something solid. She needed a weapon, maybe a big rock. "I said I'd be fine right here. Go attack some other poor woman." She gave him a look that would have withered an entire forest if he'd been able to see it in the darkness.

"I'm trying to help you, not attack you." He flicked his wrist and she lurched forward, slamming into him. "If you had half a brain, you would know that."

She could feel his voice rumble through his massive chest. "Well, excuse me for not being able to tell the difference." Samantha's head came no higher than his shirt pockets. The man was a giant and obviously used to getting his own way.

He leaned toward her. The warmth from his breath touched her cheek. "I'm not going to stand here and argue with you. You are coming with me whether you like it or not, and we are leaving right now."

His voice was soft, but it sent an uneasy tremor down her spine. *Keep him talking and think of some way out of this!* "I am not going anywhere with you." She slid one mud-clumped foot back behind her. What kind of mine had no rocks?

"Yes, you are!" His voice echoed off the walls and rang in her ears.

She stamped her foot in frustration and tried to peel his fingers off her wrist with her free hand. It was like trying to move granite with a toothpick. "Do you spend all your time harassing unsuspecting women?"

No answer.

She squirmed like a trapped rabbit. Her panic forced a false bravado. "I will not be held captive by some lonely, love-starved cowboy."

He chuckled, "Lady, if I was lonely, I could do a damn sight better than some half-witted piece of fluff too stupid to come in out of the rain."

Half-witted piece of fluff? Her fear transformed itself into anger in the space of a heartbeat. "You obnoxious, cocky . . . um,"—expletives weren't really her forte, and she couldn't think of one vile enough for this situation—"cowhand! Do you think you can bully anyone who comes along?" The mine echoed her rage. "First of all, I happen to be out of the rain and you're trying to drag me back into it. You act like your mother never told you 'no' your whole life. I bet you just smack anyone around who doesn't follow orders. It's no wonder you're so desperate. You just wait until the Williamses hear about this!"

Samantha sensed the change in him as his grip tightened on her wrist. She had pushed him over some unknown precipice. The air inside the mine crackled with more electricity than the air outside. Her heart filled with dread and she braced herself, closed one eye, and cringed, waiting for the blow. It would certainly not be the first time her mouth had attracted more trouble than she could handle. She flinched as huge hands grabbed both her shoulders.

"Who are you lady, and what do you want?" he growled

Her mind went blank as fear washed over her anew. He shook her once and her head snapped back. She saw stars for a moment. Samantha instinctively kicked out and connected with his shin. He didn't even seem to notice. The man bent over, picked her up, and slung her over one shoulder. Samantha beat his broad muscular back as hard as she could with both fists, unleashing the fear and panic she'd tried to contain. One strong hand held the back of her thighs and kept her from kicking as if she were no more than an annoyance. The man grabbed Jessie's reins with the other hand and walked out of the opening.

The rain was now a torrent and immediately seeped and soaked through every layer of fabric Samantha wore once again. The stranger led Jessie slowly and carefully down the incline toward his waiting horse. The raindrops streamed down Samantha's back and around her neck, dripping off her chin. She sputtered and tilted her head up to keep water from running up her nose. Maybe if she were lucky she would drown before he attacked her. Without warning he plopped Samantha on her feet and quickly tied her hands together with a piece of rope, looped the long end around her waist, and pulled it snug.

Her confidence waned sharply at this turn of events. Being slightly manhandled was one thing, but being tied up and helpless was quite another. "I do not appreciate being treated like some convict."

He grunted, "And I don't appreciate having my back pounded like some steak you're getting ready to fry."

It was too dark to make out his face, especially with his hat pulled so low, but he was indeed a giant; almost six-and-a-half feet tall if she were guessing. And judging by the pain in her fists from pounding his unyielding back, he was almost solid muscle. He stepped away and tied Jessie's reins to his saddle.

A gush of water flowed down the small canyon past Samantha's feet. She swayed as she tried to keep her balance. Another gush and both feet slid out from under her. She fell backward into what was now a small torrent of water. Cold, sticky mud soaked the back of her dress.

"You are nothing but a handful of trouble!" The man shouted over the thunder.

"I was *fine* before you came along."

He ignored her as he re-secured her valise to her saddle.

"Aren't you going to get me out of this mud?"

No answer.

"You have no manners at all! You can't just leave me laying here! Where are you taking me?"

Silence.

"When the Williams find out how you've treated me, they will probably kill you!"

He walked a few steps up the incline and stood over her in the semi-darkness. Rain streamed off the brim of his hat onto her face.

"You're already muddy, lady." He spoke carefully, like she was a slow-witted child. "If I pick you back up, you will just fall down again. If you'll be still, it won't be so bad."

"How can you be so cruel? I can't just lie here quietly in the mud until you get ready to carry me off to God knows where."

"I don't doubt that." He dug into his back pocket.

Samantha smelled it before she saw the handkerchief he stuffed into her mouth.

"There may be hell to pay for this, but at least you'll be quiet."

Samantha's stomach churned as she tried not to imagine how many kinds of vile filth covered the crusty piece of cloth. Her fingers flexed involuntarily with disgust, and she yanked on the rope. If she ever got half a chance she would scratch his eyes out or at least leave some very satisfying claw marks on his cheeks.

"I am taking you to the *Williamses'*, and we'll just see how they feel about this."

He didn't sound the least bit scared. He must be a friend of theirs, or one of their ranch hands. *Of course.* Relief filled her heart. This small canyon sat on the border between her ranch and the Williams ranch, which took up most of the ridge to the north and countless acres of grassland in the valley below. He would have seen her riding across the valley and followed. She relaxed a little. At least he probably wasn't about to ravish her, though being tied up wasn't a good sign.

The giant walked over and hauled her to her feet again yanking her toward his horse. Mud oozed down her back like cold, lumpy gravy. The horse shifted as the man settled his weight in the saddle. Dragging her up by the armpits, he sat her sideways in front of him. Opening his coat, he wrapped it around her, pinning down her flailing elbows.

The man kicked his horse into motion, and Samantha bounced roughly in front of him. Though she seemed to be in no immediate danger, his nearness made her uneasy. She bounced harder as they picked up speed and her body stiffened. The bruises on her backside would be as big as apples tomorrow.

She leaned as far away from him as the confines of the coat allowed. An involuntary tremor shook her body. She squeezed her arms to her side in an effort to control the shaking. He pulled her gently toward his chest, but she instantly pulled away.

"Thought you might be cold, lady, but that's fine. I wasn't looking forward to getting covered with mud anyway." She glared at him in the darkness for a minute, then twisted and slammed her full back into his chest. The mud made contact with his chest with a satisfying thwack. Samantha wiggled her back a little. The sticky mud fell off her back in clumps and onto him.

There you go, cowboy, get nice and filthy.

His arm tightened against her ribs and she felt a chuckle rumble through his chest. She fumed in forced silence as the warmth from his body slowed her shivers to a halt. *How dare he tie her up and carry her off? This wasn't the dark ages.* She was too mad to think, and if he squeezed any harder she wouldn't be able to breathe either. Under normal circumstances she would be grateful for the warmth, but these circumstances were anything but normal. As they made their way up the ridge, Samantha saw the shape of a house in the distance.

The Williams homestead grew steadily out of the darkness. Her smoldering anger turned to excitement. She was finally within earshot of safety. She straightened her back and tossed her head triumphantly. Taos Williams would knock this cowhand clear into next week, and Charlie or Darren just might shoot him. That prospect filled her with smug anticipation. She had tried to warn him.

Her captor headed for the barn and slid off the horse, taking Samantha with him. Her sore muscles tried to adjust to standing again, but she was more than a little wobbly. He stood behind her still holding her close. After a few minutes he leaned toward her until she could feel his warm breath tickle her left ear. The sensation sent a warm tremor through her chest and she tensed, waiting.

When he made no effort to move, she brought her heel down sharply on the inside of his foot. He grunted and jerked his coat away from her, spinning her around. The sudden chill rippled goose flesh across her skin.

Hefting her over his shoulder, he walked the short distance to the house. The man opened the front door quietly, and deposited Samantha on the nearest piece of furniture. She winced as pain shot through her hip. He lit a lantern, tossing his wet hat next to her on the bench.

Samantha was stunned. *Taos Williams.* He was almost exactly as she remembered, only older and more tired perhaps. As a girl, she had run around with Taos and his brothers and they had treated her like a little sister. When she was fourteen, Taos had been twenty-one and every girl's idea of a dashing hero. She had looked up to him and even had a crush on him until her parents died.

Taos frowned as he loosened the rope and rubbed her red wrists. "There are people asleep here, so keep your voice down," he whispered.

He had the same wavy brown hair and ice blue eyes, though the rest of him had filled out somewhat. Broad muscular shoulders tapered to a lean and lanky torso. His face held deeply chiseled features set off by well-tanned, weather-worn skin. His eyes held hers captive, momentarily taking her breath away. Her emotions tumbled from surprise to relief to anger. Samantha batted his hands away and grabbed the handkerchief out of her mouth.

"When did you get to be such a bully?" Her voice was a harsh rasp; the inside of her mouth felt like it was coated with cotton. She coughed. Fine grit covered her teeth. She stood and a shower of mud pellets hit the floor.

Taos grabbed her arm. "Stay here while I tend the horses."

"Why would I leave?" she snapped. There wasn't any aroma of liquor on him, though he certainly sounded drunk and confused.

"I don't know and I really don't care anymore. Just stay put."

She smiled sweetly and stepped toward him, pointing a finger at his chest. "Taos Williams, I have had enough of your manhandling and threats for one night. If you don't remove your hand from my person, you will regret it."

He raised an eyebrow and tightened his grip at her challenge, silently calling her bluff. Samantha brought her knee up into his groin, connecting. His fingers loosened and she broke free, running for the stairs. She heard him mutter a curse and slam the door on his way out.

Yours Again

Chapter 5

How in the hell does she know my name?

Taos removed the saddle from his horse and brushed the animal in long strokes, but his thoughts focused on the woman. It would be one thing to know of him and even know his name, but she knew him instantly on sight.

She looked like hell, but she smelled like flowers. Roses maybe?

He shook his head. He had been out on the range too long. Most men were intimidated at first sight of him. Not her though. She'd stood her ground, even fought back when she had to know she had no chance of winning. She had spirit, he had to give her that.

It nagged at his mind that he couldn't place her. Something about her seemed so familiar. He didn't encounter many women as a rule. Usually they crossed the street to avoid him. Had he heard her voice somewhere? No, she had a bit of a Yankee accent, he would have remembered that. Her clothes appeared Eastern, and she obviously had means. Or had at one time.

So why was she riding hell-bent through a rainstorm? That's another thing that didn't make sense. She rode astride, like she'd been born to a saddle. And a Western one at that. The few Eastern ladies he had met wouldn't be caught dead without a side saddle and never got beyond a trot. He barely kept up with her when she took off for the mine. His brush slowed to a stop.

The mine.

A person would have to know its exact location to find it in broad daylight, let alone in a rainstorm at twilight. She had to be from around here. His mind drifted back to their ride. Her slim form pressed against his chest, one hip rubbing the inside of his thigh. He'd forgotten how good a woman felt and had to admit that he didn't ride near as fast as he could have just to feel her warmth against his chest a little longer.

Lilacs. Maybe she smelled more like lilacs.

He finished with his horse and moved to brush down her mount. The woman had looked at him like she'd seen a ghost when he'd lit the lamp. Then she went from happy, right to mad as hell. Maybe she was a little touched. That would certainly explain a few things. Although she seemed articulate, educated even. He sighed. She certainly had no problem expressing herself, that was for sure.

When he'd rubbed her hands, he'd stared into two eyes that glittered like great big emeralds. It almost took his breath away. If he'd come across a woman with eyes that green, he would have remembered. She could be younger than she looked. He'd guess her a few years beyond twenty, but these days some fifteen year olds looked twenty-five. A man couldn't be too careful trying to guess a woman's age, and it certainly wasn't something he was good at.

Still, someone that age would have a husband and family waiting on them somewhere. What was she doing out here alone? Only the locals who knew the land would attempt a ride like that, trying to beat a storm.

She has to be some rancher's daughter.

He looked her horse over. Nothing but a livery nag, not a horse a rancher would have. If her family did live around here, it would be hard to explain trussing her up and hauling her off. Especially since he didn't know why he had done it.

No one would believe a man his size had to tie up a woman and stuff a rag in her mouth to get her out of the rain. Well, they might believe his urge to shut her up if they heard her talk for five minutes. He chuckled. Sure, he'd left her lying in the mud on purpose. It served her right for fighting him when he had only tried to help her. Besides, it had to be the funniest thing he'd seen in months. After all that, she still fought him when he pulled her onto the horse. He shook his head and smiled. She was something, all right.

Maybe she just knew of him from people in town and planned this little charade to get to him.

A strange sense of foreboding snaked through his soul. He'd been played for a fool before, and everybody in town knew it. The possibility of looking down the barrel of some angry father's gun again filled him with dread. Once was one too many times. He'd learned that hard lesson well.

Times were tough and the drought had gone on for months now without so much as a hint of rain, not that they'd gotten enough moisture the previous two years. This storm was the first drop they'd seen in six months, and though it helped, it wasn't near enough. Other ranchers and farmers were getting more desperate by the hour; Mertie Mae's proposition in town today was proof of that. Marrying off a spare daughter to a man with land, money, and water might be too big a temptation—even if he was a virtual social outcast.

Taos's suspicions simmered. There weren't many reasons some damsel in distress would be riding across his land unless she was looking for him. This had all the hallmarks of a setup, and Miss Fancy Pants was in his house, probably crawling into his bed right now to close the deal. Slamming the brush on a shelf near the barn door, he stalked toward the house. Whatever she wanted, she would not get it. He'd see to that. He would never be a sucker twice.

The rain had slowed to a cool drizzle when Taos opened the front door and glanced into the parlor. *Gone.* She was probably already flipping over the china to estimate its worth and looking for the silver. He could imagine her disbelief when she found no such luxuries here.

After Sharisse, he had learned to live well below his means. No one would have any indication of the size of his bank account by appearances. It had been his experience that a show of wealth attracted the wrong sort, and this situation was yet another confirmation of that fact. He climbed the stairs as quietly as possible, skipping the seventh one that creaked. The door to his room was cracked open slightly, and a light shone from within. He crept toward the bright glow and peered inside.

A large pile of clothes lay on the floor and dried mud littered the hallway. The woman washed her face with her back to him; she wore one of his shirts. The denim sure looked a damn sight better on her than it ever had on him, and Taos struggled to pull his eyes from the shapely length of calf the shirt left bare. She put down the wash cloth and picked up his brush, leaning over to pull the golden strands of hair over her head. The color of her hair sparked some recognition. The woman on the bluff. It had to be her.

He caught a glimpse in the mirror as the shirt gapped open. She was naked to the knees. Taos tried to close his eyes, but they refused. He stared as she brushed in long strokes. His mouth went dry at the slight movement of her breasts with each stroke. The motion was hypnotic and he was instantly hard.

What kind of woman strips down and puts on a strange man's shirt in his bedroom? Not an innocent rancher's daughter, that's for sure.

Maybe she's one of Miss Sadie's girls.

He hadn't been by there in a long time, and Sadie did tend to have classy whores. That would explain everything. The fancy clothes, being out here alone, riding in the rain, running from some man. It made perfect sense.

She would have heard of him in town, maybe had seen him from a distance. That's how she knew his name! A slow smile spread across his face. This changed things, and for the better in his opinion. A whore that made house calls—how great was that? Relief combined with anticipation took hold. He might just benefit from this yet. He stepped through the door, closing it behind him.

The woman straightened and flipped her hair back. The strands floated over her shoulders like spun silk. She glanced at him in the mirror and continued like he wasn't there. Taos's eyes followed each brush stroke as he peeled his wet coat off and unbuttoned his shirt. She was sultry, tempting and he watched her gaze linger on his bare chest. He smiled as she forced her eyes back to his.

"What kind of *lady* are you anyway?"

She frowned, "I borrowed one of your shirts so my clothes could dry."

She wasn't a great actress. He slowly walked toward her, coming so close she stepped back. "How do you know it's mine? I'm sure you know I have brothers."

"Of course I know you have brothers. This isn't Darren or Charlie's room. Besides, they are nowhere near as tall as you are."

That's it! How could she possible know who slept where in his house? He jerked off his shirt and tossed it aside in a shower of dried mud. He grabbed her arms. "Who are you, lady? How do you know so much? Have you been watching us?"

She stared at his chest like she'd forgotten her next line. He waited and could feel her grasp for another approach.

"You really have no idea who I am, do you?" She flashed him a blinding smile. "Didn't we already have one discussion about you not grabbing me?"

Fine, if she wanted to play, he could play too. He released his grip, but slid his hands slowly down her arms brushing the sides of her breasts with his fingers. Her eyes widened in surprise, but she didn't move away. She stared at his lips and he leaned down until they almost touched hers. "Who are you?" He whispered.

"Who do you think I am?"

He brushed his lips across hers, moving slowly toward her neck. He felt her lean toward him almost begging his lips to go farther. "I'd say," he whispered, "you're one of Miss Sadie's girls and doing a damn fine job so far."

She placed both palms against his naked chest and he smiled to himself knowing he was right about this one. She shoved hard and Taos fell backward on the bed, scooting it an inch or two across the floor with his sudden weight. She paced barefooted in front of him as he sat up on the edge of the mattress.

"Let me see if I have the facts straight."

He wasn't sure but he thought he detected a smile. *Why was this funny?* What was she trying to do, make him work for it?

"I try to get to . . . let's say, a friend's house."

He snorted, "Friend my ass."

She ignored him and continued, "And I get caught in a rainstorm. I am then chased by a very strange man." She paused to stare pointedly at him then resumed her march. "When I finally find some shelter, this same barbarian insists on rescuing me. To prove it, he scares the life out of me. Ties me up. Rolls me in muck. Then proceeds to drag me to his home like I'm some *criminal*."

The beginnings of a fine sheen of nervous sweat popped up on Taos's forehead. There was something about the way she said the word 'criminal' that unnerved him. What if he was wrong? Because if he was, this could turn out very badly. "I was just trying to—"

"I'm not finished yet." She continued to pace, "As if all that weren't enough, while I'm trying to clean up and dry off, he has the nerve to call me a woman of questionable morals." She stopped in front of him. "Is this the series of events as you remember them, *Mr.* Williams?"

"Uh, well," His mind searched for a way out of this. "What was I supposed to think with you taking off every stitch up here?"

"Well, let's see," The woman crossed her arms and tapped a finger on her cheek. "You could have thought that maybe I preferred not to drip on the floor all night. Or you could have thought that I needed privacy as opposed to wandering around the parlor naked. Both of these seem logical assumptions, yet for some reason you chose to conclude that I was . . . Hmm, here for your enjoyment shall we say?" She leaned toward him, "Why is that?" She arched a brow and slid a glance toward his trousers. "Been a while has it?"

Taos was at a loss for words and the silence dragged as she waited for an answer.

She narrowed her eyes. "How do you know that I took *all* my clothes off? Were you watching me?"

"I didn't watch you undress." His eyes involuntarily flicked toward the opening of her shirt and she clamped a hand against the fabric.

"What do you want from me?" He was tired of this little game and it was time to end it.

She grinned. "What do you think I want?"

"If you have a father, or anybody else, with a shotgun waiting downstairs, you better tell me now. I'd hate to kill a man unnecessarily." He watched her carefully waiting for her to reveal whatever plan she had cooked up.

She laughed, "No, there is no father or anyone else downstairs."

He smiled. She was here alone. "Good." He grabbed her waist and slammed her against his chest. "I'm tired of playing games." His mouth came down hard on hers.

She pressed her lips closed and tried to push away. He moved one hand to the middle of her back and pulled her closer. After a moment, she relaxed and arched her body toward his. His lips molded to hers and gently coaxed them open. He could tell it had just been a token resistance. She followed his lead cautiously at first, then with more confidence. She had to be stringing him along. Her open palm slid along his rough cheek and into his hair, leaving a trail of heat that electrified his body.

As the kiss deepened, his hands slid over her butt and down the backs of her thighs. He slid them under the shirt and up her hips. Smooth fleshed molded to his hands as he glided them over her body at will. He trailed hot, wet kisses from her mouth to her neck, nibbling until her breath came in short gasps. She let out a small moan as his hands crept up her ribs toward her breasts.

He chuckled, "Miss Sadie would be proud. I haven't seen a performance like this in ages."

She went from passion to white hot fury in a heartbeat.

"Let me go you . . . you!" She struggled backward pounding her fists on his chest until his hands fell away. She gathered her wet things in a huff and headed to the door.

"Scare you off, sweetheart?"

"Not on your life, *mister.* You can deal with me *and* your brothers in the morning. I hope they beat the snot out of you for this." Her irritated steps echoed down the hall.

Taos lay back across the bed. *Why would his brothers care how he treated her?* The past hour hadn't lessened his confusion one bit or offered any hint as to her identity.

He stared at his hands, still warm from the feel of her soft skin. They trembled as he balled them into fists. Another few minutes and he might never have stopped. Going without for so long must have affected his self-control.

That's all it was. He nodded to himself. Just a normal man's reaction to a half-naked female. A very dangerous female. She had been much more beautiful than he'd imagined during their ride and there was no way she could hang around here. He had to get rid of her, and soon.

The long day and frustration of dealing with the mysterious woman finally caught up with him. Sleep clouded his mind as he drifted off.

Honeysuckle. She tasted like honeysuckle.

Yours Again

Chapter 6

The sun had yet to make an appearance as Samantha pulled on her wrinkled yellow dress. It didn't look like much, but at least it was clean. Thank goodness Darren had recognized her immediately, and he'd gladly given her his bed for the night while he slept on the bench in the parlor. She hadn't had to wake anyone else. Not that she'd slept much.

She couldn't believe Taos hadn't recognized her, and she had no idea how to explain what happened between them. She'd had her share of suitors in Boston so it's certainly not like she'd never been kissed, but she'd never felt anything like that before. Just thinking about his hands roaming over her naked skin vibrated warmth through her body. Her face flamed. It was as though she had no control over her own body and it molded to his as if she'd done it hundreds of times.

Why wouldn't he think she was a whore? She'd certainly acted like one. She should be embarrassed, but the truth is she'd liked it. Not that she'd ever admit it to anyone, or even say it out loud, but as soon as Taos figured out who she was that would end it, and he'd go back to treating her like a little sister again. It gave her a twinge of wistful sadness.

Darren had been thrilled to see her, so at least one brother was glad she was back. The sun would be up soon. Samantha quickly ran a brush through her hair, then stuck her head out the door. In the predawn shadows, only the faint sound of snoring reached her ears. Hunger rattled restlessly in the pit of her stomach as she crept downstairs. The last thing she'd eaten was a piece of crusty roll and some cheese when the stage stopped for lunch on the trail yesterday.

Quiet stillness permeated the kitchen. It was exactly as she remembered it. In fact, she'd bet not one thing had been changed in the last nine years. A long table with five chairs took up most of the room. It may have been a little more worn, but it was the same one she remembered.

She'd spent months in this house, in this kitchen, after her parents died. Somewhere in her fourteen-year-old mind she'd thought that Jake Williams would let her stay with them instead of being sent to Boston to live with an aunt she'd never met. Now she could see how silly that idea was. There was no way Jake could handle a girl on the edge of puberty when he had three boys himself, two still in their teens. It had been the right choice, though she sure hadn't thought so at the time.

Samantha rummaged around in the cabinets and quickly found the coffee, flour, milk, and some bacon. Within fifteen minutes, bacon and flapjacks sizzled in the hot skillet, the enticing smell mingling with the aroma of freshly brewed coffee.

In the kitchen she felt at peace. At Mattie's, the kitchen had always been a place where she could collect her thoughts and prepare for the day. Many of Mattie's friends had frowned on Samantha's love of cooking. The ladies of society considered it a serious contest to see who could employ the most desirable cook. Most viewed the art of cooking as a lower-class function, not fit for a young woman of means. Thankfully, Mattie ignored them and encouraged her niece to do what made her happy. Samantha spent years perfecting her skill, covered head to toe in flour most days and she longed to be able to feed more than just herself and Mattie.

She stared at the flapjacks, mesmerized by the tiny bubbles that rose and then burst in the batter as they cooked. Last night refused to leave her mind, even for a minute. Well, not the whole night, just that kiss. Pinpricks rolled up her arms and she shivered, remembering his touch, his lips, his heartbeat under her fingertips. Heat rose to her face yet again. She had to stop this or everyone would think she had a permanent sunburn from blushing so much.

Most of the men who came to call on her in Boston lived a life of luxury, their days spent in mindless pursuits. To her, they seemed shallow and petty; none held her interest very long. Mattie had never pushed her into a relationship; she always said when the right one came along she'd know. Taos had a rugged strength about him, as wild and untamed as a river flowing wherever it willed—something that scared and excited her at the same time. He was definitely out of the ordinary.

Samantha sighed, it wouldn't take him long to figure out her identity this morning. How would he react when he did find out? Would he be intrigued, or irritated? Would he still see her as the same annoying pest she had been as a kid? He might push her aside and ignore her. Could she handle seeing him every day after that? Never getting close enough to touch again?

It was just one kiss for heaven's sake! It didn't mean anything. She flipped the flapjacks over to brown the other side and glanced out the window next to the stove. The warm glow of dawn splashed across the ground. The grassland glinted like polished marble from the rain. The mountains glowed pink and orange, the tall pine and aspen cloaking their slopes. It made her breath catch. She'd seen this same scene everyday growing up, but it was easy to take it for granted when there was nothing else. Nine years in Boston had taught her that. Even though the ocean was beautiful in its own way, it still didn't instill the majesty and inspiration in her heart that the mountains did.

Out of the corner of her eye she saw a small head peek around the corner then disappear.

"Good morning, Tommy," she said.

The head appeared again. Darren told her that Taos's son was the spitting image of him, and she could certainly agree. Already tall for a seven-year-old, he had wavy brown hair that bordered on unruly and piercing blue eyes. The boy inched toward the stove.

"What are those?" He asked as she lifted the hot, steaming flapjacks onto a plate.

"Flapjacks. Would you like some?" She held out the plate and smiled as the boy licked his lips.

"Uh, thank you ma'am, but no. Pa says we all gotta fend for ourselves in the mornings. Can't depend on nobody to do it for ya."

She frowned as he pulled a heavy chair across the floor toward the cabinets. *Stubborn must be inherited.* Samantha watched him reach for the oatmeal and fill a small pot. One of Mattie's old sayings came to mind.

There are four words a woman can say that a man can't resist: Can you help me? If it works on a man who is thirty, why not one that's seven?

"Tommy?" She watched him while she poured more batter into the skillet.

"Yes, ma'am?"

"Does your father let you waste good food?"

The boy looked at her like she'd just bit him. "No ma'am!" He shook his small head. "He'd whoop my hide for sure!"

"Well, I cooked too many of these for myself, and they'll just go to waste if someone doesn't help me eat them." The boy stole a glance at the flapjacks Samantha set on the table.

"Can you help me, Tommy?" she asked softly, "Please?"

The boy jumped down and ran to the table, the oatmeal already a memory. "As long as you're sure they'll just go to waste." Nearly drooling, Tommy proceeded to stuff his mouth as full as possible. She watched in absolute amazement at how much food he could get into such a small space.

Noise and heavy footsteps announced Charlie and Darren's arrival.

"Sammy!" Charlie gave her a big hug, lifting her off the ground and spinning her around. "I told Darren I wouldn't believe it 'til I saw you for myself."

Breathless and laughing, Samantha kissed his cheek as Taos walked in.

"Well, you seem to be making the rounds this morning," Taos's eyes narrowed at her.

Samantha gave Charlie an exasperated look and shrugged her shoulders. He grinned at Darren, who winked back. She'd told Darren about Taos not recognizing her. It looked like they were willing to play along and have some fun at his expense. Taos certainly deserved it.

Charlie put her down and headed to the stove. "What smells so good?" He poked a finger at one of the bubbles.

Samantha nudged him out of the way with her elbow and turned the flapjacks. "Remember your manners, or I'll starve you."

He held his chest like he was dying. "You'd let me wither away to nothing?"

She smiled, "Maybe."

He pecked her on the cheek and winked at Tommy. "At least it's a maybe."

Taos poured a cup of coffee and sat at the table. Samantha glanced at him under her lashes. His scowl indicated he hadn't slept any better than she had apparently. His eyes strayed to Tommy as his son stuff half a flapjack into his mouth. The boy grinned at Taos as best he could. Pieces of flapjack stuck out between the gaps in his teeth. Samantha's heart melted. Tommy was adorable.

"Where'd you get those, son?"

The boy pointed at Samantha with his fork, his eyes wide at the tone of his father's voice.

"You know we all do for ourselves in the morning."

The boy nodded and tried to swallow.

"He was helping me." Samantha glared at Taos as she heaped bacon onto a plate. "I cooked too many for myself and didn't want them to go to waste."

Charlie shuffled up behind her and inhaled the rising scent from the stove. "You gonna eat all those, honey?" He nodded toward the second plate of flapjacks.

"Oh my, it looks like I cooked too many again." She feigned surprise. "I don't suppose you would be kind enough to help me eat them?"

"Oh yes ma'am, I would love to help." She served Charlie very generous portions of both bacon and flapjacks, then poured more on the griddle. She arched an eyebrow at Taos, daring him to object. He ignored her.

Darren prepared two cups of coffee and sat next to Charlie at the table. He pushed one of the cups in Charlie's direction.

"I hate that stuff," Charlie whispered.

Darren insisted. "You'll love this."

Charlie took a small sip and groaned as the rich brown liquid rolled down his throat. "I've died and gone to heaven," he said stuffing the better part of a flapjack into his mouth. He poked the back of Darren's hand with his fork, defending his pile of bacon. "Get your own," he mumbled.

Taos studied her as she prepared a plate for Darren. She was obviously at home in the kitchen. She caught him staring and he immediately shifted his gaze away . . . for a moment. A return look revealed a slow smile spreading across her lips. Taos stared at her. As tired as he'd been last night, he dreamed of those lips and that smile. He'd awakened, wondering where she had spent the night—besides in his dreams. Curiosity finally got the best of him.

"So where'd you sleep last night, *honey*?" He just realized he'd never even asked her name.

"In my bed," Charlie said between bites.

Taos's cheek flinched as he ground his teeth together.

He saw a strange look flow between the woman and Darren. Darren shrugged at her.

"You know, damsel in distress and all that," Charlie continued. "I'm sure you would have done the same thing." He beamed as Taos's face heated. "Course I didn't have to tie her up first." Darren and the woman snickered. Taos thunked his coffee cup on the table and glared at Charlie.

She ignored the exchange and chatted as if she hadn't a care in the world. "I need to go into town and get a few things this morning. Could one of you take me?"

"How long you s-stayin'?" Darren asked, intent on his breakfast. His childhood speech impediment was barely noticeable, but Taos realized he wasn't the least bit embarrassed to talk in front of this stranger for once.

What the hell? Darren would hardly set foot in town at all anymore just to avoid people, and even when he did, he didn't utter a word. But Darren had no problem chatting with this woman.

"She's not." Taos took the plate she offered him and almost dropped it as she flashed him one of those smiles. She held a powerful attraction for a man. His brothers were already her slaves, but not him.

"Sure she is," Charlie piped up. "I'm not about to go back to your cookin' after this."

"She's *not* staying. We don't know anything about her, not even her name."

"Her name's Sammy," the boy piped up. Every person in the room turned toward him, except for Taos.

He stared hard at the woman and slowly picked out the features that should have been obvious: the straight blonde hair the color of golden silk, and those eyes. Those deep, emerald green eyes.

It couldn't be!

Taos scanned her appearance from head to toe. She was the spitting image of Claire. Why hadn't he recognized her? He continued to stare, his mouth slightly open. The skinny little girl he had put on the train nine years ago had grown into an extremely beautiful woman. His mind stumbled through his memory and settled on last night. He looked away quickly.

What was last night? Some kind of game to tease him and make him feel like an idiot? It had worked, and his brothers were in on it too. They obviously knew exactly who she was. He'd never hear the end of this. She had played him for a fool all right, and he fell for it. He should have known better. He had learned how dangerous a woman could be, even if it was Sammy. Nine years was a long time, and he really didn't have any idea who or what she was now. She hadn't even been here one day, and he'd already proved he was the same sucker he had been with Sharisse. His eyes stared at her lips. Her tongue darted across them and his gaze met hers. Heat built in his chest, part irritation, part . . . something else.

"Well, the cat's out of the bag now, isn't it?" Charlie polished off the last of his bacon as he watched Taos. Charlie nudged Darren with an elbow and nodded a head toward their brother. Taos realized that Samantha's face glowed red—probably a mirror image of his right now. Charlie wasn't stupid, unfortunately.

"Now this is interesting," Charlie waved his fork as he talked. "I mean, I think there's more went on last night than you let on, Sammy."

"Like what?" Darren stuffed more bacon in his mouth.

"This might be just what we need to liven things up around here." A half smile played around Charlie's mouth as he forked down another bite, ignoring Taos's hot glare.

"So what's the story with that guy that's after you?" Darren asked.

Samantha sat at the table and started in on a flapjack of her own.

"What guy?" Charlie's attention focused on her, as did Taos's.

"A couple of weeks ago, Aunt Mattie's investment advisor Ty Lawson died. His son, John Lawson, took over his father's business. But Ty's death was very suspicious, and I honestly think John had something to do with it. Anyway, he showed up at Mattie's saying that he was executing a power of attorney over her assets and he slipped something into her drink."

Taos watched her closely as she spoke. She seemed to fidget under his gaze. Was it because she was lying, or were her thoughts on last night too?

"Mattie doesn't trust John and has no intention of turning over her finances to him. I went through and balanced the financial ledgers for her and realized that there was quite a bit of money that had already gone missing. So I confronted John about it."

"By yourself?" Taos's sharp tone drew everyone's attention.

"Well, yes. I didn't realize how dangerous he could be."

"You thought he killed his father, but you didn't think he'd be dangerous?" Taos snorted in disbelief. "Are you stupid?" Samantha did her best to bore a hole through him with her glare, but he was unimpressed.

"Did he h-hurt you?" Darren's concern was genuine, of course, and she gifted him with a smile. Darren would believe anything she said. Taos knew all Darren remembered was the friend he grew up with. He'd had zero experience in how manipulative women could be.

"No, not exactly." Samantha said, "He just threatened me and basically told me that I was going to marry him. But he just wants to get his hands on Mattie's money and the second he has me I know he'll do away with her and probably me too . . . eventually." Her words hung in the air a moment.

Taos knew exactly what an unscrupulous man would do with Samantha—pretty much what he wanted to do with her last night. He clamped his teeth together, pushing that image out of his mind, and observed her closely. She didn't seem all that upset, so was this story the truth? A half-truth? A complete lie? Why had she shown up unannounced, and with this wild story? Why had she kissed him instead of telling him exactly who she was? It seemed like a little game last night, and now this morning she was in some kind of mortal danger? *Bullshit.*

Charlie pushed his plate back, angry. "Why would he think you would agree to that?"

"Maybe she encouraged his attention." Taos stared evenly at her.

"He threatened me! I have never *encouraged* anyone!"

"Now I know that's not true." He pinned her with his stare.

"Where did that come from?" Charlie snapped.

"Most men don't like a woman who's a tease." Taos continued to stare boldly at Samantha.

"I am not a tease!"

"Are too."

Samantha rolled her fork back and forth between two fingers and fumed. She'd never considered silverware a deadly weapon until this moment.

"You could have told me who you were." Taos sipped his coffee.

"After you tied her up and gagged her?" Charlie arched his eyebrows. "You deserve anything she dishes out and then some as far as I'm concerned."

"So then what happened, Sammy?" A little voice squeaked. Tommy stared with his big round eyes in rapt attention. "Did the bad guy chase you?"

The adults in the room had almost forgotten he was there. "Not exactly." She picked at the buttery flapjacks, reminding herself to leave out some of the more seemly details that weren't really fit for the ears of a seven-year-old. "Mattie thought I needed to get as far away as possible until the fraud could be investigated and John arrested."

"So you do want something from me?" Taos eyed her suspiciously.

She ignored him. "She suggested that I come here for a while. I thought I might check on things—you know, my ranch and all—while I was here. I really appreciate you all taking care of it for me."

Silence blanketed the room. Taos's coffee cup paused in midair, and Charlie and Darren exchanged a nervous glance.

"Who sent for you?" Taos growled.

The sharp demand brought Samantha's head up quickly. "No one. Why would someone send for me?"

"You know why."

Samantha's anger flashed. "Do you just wake up every morning and decide to be nasty, or is today special?"

"It's always special when I know someone is lying to me, *honey*."

"Lying about what? I told you the truth." She looked at Darren. "What exactly has been going on here? Why doesn't he believe me?" Panic seeped into her voice. They had to believe her, she had nowhere else to go. Charlie and Darren stared at the table. If they didn't believe her, what then? She couldn't go back to Mattie. And how would her aunt find her if she left? She wasn't about to stay at her ranch alone. She'd come here for protection, and now Taos couldn't wait to throw her to the wolves.

She stared at him. What happened to the hero she remembered? His gaze was unyielding and hard. She suddenly realized she had no idea who this man was now and she'd obviously been wrong to think he would help her. He didn't have an ounce of empathy in that oversized body of his.

"There's been a drought going on for a few years here," Charlie said. "It's gotten kind of ugly with some of the neighboring ranchers."

"Ugly?"

"There's been some livestock killed . . ."

"And a few shots fired." Darren said.

"It rained last night, I'm sure that helped." Samantha offered.

"Not really. Too little too late for a lot of folks. Many are selling out, and others are just doing without," Charlie glanced at Taos and continued. "'Bout the only decent water left is on our ranches."

"If things are that bad for everyone, I'm sure we can shar-"

"No." Taos slammed his empty cup on the table. "There's barely enough to keep our own head watered. It's none of your concern anyway."

His patronizing attitude felt like a slap in the face. She stiffened her back. How could she have kissed those lips or wanted his hands on her last night? What was she thinking? "What goes on within the borders of my ranch is my business."

"It's not your ranch, yet."

"Excuse me?"

"I'm sure you know the terms of you parent's will." Taos's voice was cool and even.

"What terms?" her heart pounded in her throat.

"You inherit the land and house that your parents had along with the profit the land has earned over the years." He watched her closely as if waiting for a reaction.

"So what's the problem?"

"You only get it if you marry or show up with an heir in tow. I'm assuming you plan on marrying soon. Maybe to the same man who sent for you?"

What? How could her parents do this? What were they thinking? She hopped up and paced the length of the table. Thank goodness her investments had done so well. That must have been why Mattie never pushed her to marry. She didn't need the ranch to live well. "I have to stay here, that's how we planned it."

"We?" He smiled and shook his head, "Like I said last night, you should be on the stage somewhere." He was so smug and sure of himself. Samantha stopped pacing and met his glare.

This man was a stranger to her. That safe feeling she'd had since last night crumbled. Taos couldn't protect her from John. No, he *wouldn't* protect her. She was already alone. An empty feeling crept across her soul. Tears stung the back of her eyes, and her lower lip quivered.

Charlie shook his head and reached for her hand. "Aw, Sammy, don't cry. We'll get this all worked out. In the meantime, you'll stay right here with us." Darren nodded his agreement and shot an angry look toward Taos.

"I want to see the will." Her voice was barely a whisper; hot tears rolled unheeded down her face. If she didn't have a right to be here, she knew now that Taos would never let her stay. He clearly thought nothing of her and wanted her gone as soon as possible. How ridiculous it felt now that she reveled in his touch last night; he would have cared more for her if she had actually been a prostitute. Charlie pushed her toward a chair and poured her some more coffee as Darren went to collect the papers.

Samantha captured Taos's gaze with hers and silently pleaded with him. He grunted and looked away. She stared at her fingers. How could he have changed so much? She remembered him kind and giving, not cold and heartless. She needed to think clearly.

Darren handed her a copy of her parents' will and Samantha stared at the words. Her mother's handwriting. Large loops with a perfect, flowing penmanship. Tears splashed on the pages as she turned them. There were only four, and the last one held both her parents' signatures. She ran a finger across the letters, desperately wanting to touch the hands that made them. She never felt as alone as she did right now.

Taos cleared his throat and tapped his finger on the table, motioning Tommy out of the room.

Samantha concentrated, scanning the pages until she found the passage concerning the transfer to her: *All aforementioned property, livestock, money and interest earned will be transferred to Samantha Kay James upon her marriage or directly to her heir.*

"You'll see that there is no room for any other alternative unless you marry." Taos stated. "I'm curious to know how quickly you were planning the wedding, since there is no other way to get your hands on the land."

Her irritation with this insufferable man grew in leaps and bounds. How could she have ever kissed those snarling lips?

"First of all, I don't need or want the ranch. That's not why I came here."

"Right," his sarcastic tone made her want to smack that chiseled chin.

"And just to be perfectly clear, it doesn't say here that I have to be married." She stared right through him, dashing away tears with the back of her hand.

He talked with slow and deliberate words like she was slow witted just as he had at the mine last night. "It is in black and white right in front of you. Just because you are pretending you don't want it that way doesn't mean it will change. Why don't we get down to what you've already planned and stop this little game?"

It took all her willpower to stay seated. She growled instead. "It says right here in *black and white* that I can either be married or have an heir." *Really?* Why did men assume a woman couldn't read a basic legal document? "It's an either/or statement, not a both/and requirement."

Confusion crossed his face, followed by anger.

"Do you mean you are planning to . . . You can't do that, I won't allow it."

Her eyes flew open as she realized that he thought she was planning to get pregnant! Ridiculous! She covered her mouth to keep from laughing out loud. He didn't know her at all, and that just might work in her favor. It really didn't matter what he thought of her as long as she could get the protection she needed for a few weeks. She had to think quickly.

He leaned forward and his voice shook. "I'll make sure no man comes near you."

She matched his angry stare without blinking. "How? You said I won't be staying here."

"Yes, you will. I'm not letting you out of my sight until I know exactly who is up to what." His voice vibrated around the room. "And until I find out, I run both ranches and everyone on them."

She needed to push him just a bit farther, make him believe she just might go to extremes. "Charlie, how many men would you say go to Miss Sadie's in a week's time?" She arched a suggestive eyebrow toward Taos.

"Uh, I uh," Charlie clearly wasn't ready for that kind of question. "Well, probably forty or more. Why?"

"Looks like you're going to be very busy, aren't you?" she dared Taos.

"You will not become a whore!" His growl rumbled through her, making the hair on her neck stand up.

"I have no intention of being a whore. Although you made it clear you thought I had some talent in that respect." She saw a blush creep up his neck as his brothers glared at him. "And I believe I would just need what you cattlemen call 'stud services.' Hardly the same thing."

Taos looked ready to explode.

She shrugged, "You're the one who suggested it."

"This is a ridiculous conversation," Taos's irritation was getting the best of him and he stood, clearly wanting to be done with this.

Samantha agreed this was ridiculous. It was so simple. She just needed to stay here for a few weeks, why was this so hard? Something in her wanted to give him another chance to believe her. Last night clearly wounded his pride and this morning they'd all had some fun at his expense as well. She walked over and stood right in front of him, her head tilted back so she could see his face. He was looking at anyone or anything in the room but her.

"Taos . . ." She waited. Finally he glanced down at her. "I told you the truth. I just need to stay here for a few weeks, then I'll leave. I don't want or need anything else from you, nor do I plan on doing anything with the ranch."

His expression told her he clearly didn't believe a word she said.

"Do you believe me?"

"Nope."

She hadn't expected a different answer, but still part of her hoped for one. She held his gaze. "Okay, if that's the way you want it, that's fine."

She stepped closer until she almost touched him. "But make no mistake. I am staying even if that means you spending every waking minute wondering what I'm up to, or *who I'm with*."

Yours Again

Chapter 7

"Went a little over the top, don't you think, sweetheart?"

Samantha ignored Charlie as the wagon bumped along toward town. Taos assigned Charlie as her temporary guardian with strict instructions not to let her out of his sight.

Taos's reaction didn't surprise her. She couldn't believe the words had come out of her own mouth. Stud services? Really! As if she would even have the nerve to mention such a thing in front of anyone else. It couldn't be taken back now, and it put her in a very awkward position.

She had to do something to make him think she was going to consider it just to stall him from booting her into the street. The man acted like women were the enemy. She crossed her arms and swayed in rhythm with the wagon. This predicament was entirely Taos's fault. If he had just believed her there wouldn't be an issue at all.

John was deadly serious about his treat, and she knew it. The farther away she got, the more worried she was about her aunt. Who would take care of her if John tried to use her as some sort of leverage? She was a tough, determined woman, no doubt—but John was a killer.

"You weren't really serious, were you?"

She looked over at Charlie. Apparently there was some doubt in his mind. Maybe she was more convincing than she thought. She squinted and looked hard at him. Same hazel eyes, dark thick hair, and devilish grin. Just as she remembered.

"What?"

"How can you still be the same person you always were, and your brother be totally different?"

Charlie gazed at the horizon as the first signs of town came into view. "He's not that different. He's just been through some rough times."

"Rough times?" They must have been horrible to make him this nasty. Maybe her ranch had been a hardship on him. That hadn't occurred to her. "You mean trying to run both spreads?"

"No. Now that he's good at." Charlie paused and shuffled the reins back and forth between his fingers. "Why do you want your ranch so bad right now?"

"I don't, I said that."

His head snapped around. "Then what was all that this morning?"

"Taos said I couldn't stay. The only other place I can go is my own ranch, but there's no one there to protect me. Mattie won't know where to find me if I go anywhere else. We agreed that I wouldn't contact her just in case John was intercepting her mail, and we highly suspect he has been." She stared into Charlie's incredulous eyes. "I thought I would be safe with Taos. What was I supposed to do, let him kick me out like a sack of rotten potatoes?"

"Taos wouldn't have kicked you out." He shook his head. "He thinks you just want the money and the land. All you have to do is convince him you don't. Problem solved."

"I tried that and he called me an out-and-out liar! How do you expect me to change his mind?"

"Hm. Got a point there." Charlie thought for a minute. "He's not one to back down easily when he makes a decision either."

"So I gathered. I do plan to convince him, but I wouldn't mind making him suffer a little first."

Charlie seemed worried. "You're not going to make me suffer too, are you?"

"Nope." She grinned. "Just him."

Charlie steered the wagon up and over the bank of the dry creek she'd crossed last night. It had been almost dark then, but now she could see the land was truly parched. The grass was thin and mostly dead. Large areas of what was once pasture were only dirt now. You could hardly tell there had been any sort of rain last night. The ground must have absorbed the moisture like a sponge.

"So what happened to Tommy's mother?" Samantha asked.

"That was the rough time I was talking about."

"Taos's wife?"

"Ex-wife."

"They actually divorced?" Samantha lowered her voice to a whisper. She knew of many estranged couples, but none would tolerate the scandal of divorce and she'd heard nothing of it at all in the few letters she'd exchanged with Darren in the last nine years.

"Yep. Sharisse was a piece of work alright. Her old man was after the land and the water from both ranches. He owns a spread downstream a ways. She never wanted a husband, only a lifestyle. They baited the trap, and Taos fell for it hook, line, and sinker."

"What kind of trap?"

"It happened at a barn dance. One like they used to have over at the schoolhouse."

She had watched her mother and father glide across the wooden floor of the schoolhouse in each other's arms all evening at those dances years ago. They'd loved each other so much.

"Her father arranged for them to be caught in a compromising situation, which was a complete set up." He shrugged at Samantha's raised eyebrows and lowered his voice. "She basically threw herself at him, and they were married on the spot. Her old man had the preacher ready and everything. By the time Taos knew what they'd done, she was expecting Tommy."

"He didn't love her at all then?"

"Oh, I think he tried to make the best of it. He humored her spending habits, which were unbelievable. I thought she was out to put him in the poorhouse, myself."

A vision of Tommy clouded her thoughts. "I don't understand how any woman could leave her child."

"She never wanted Tommy and she swore she wouldn't let Taos near her after he was born. It was pretty rocky."

Samantha's heart constricted. Tommy was the most adorable little boy she'd ever seen. "He deserves better."

"Tommy or Taos?"

Both. She couldn't imagine anyone not wanting Tommy. As far as Taos went, her temper still simmered. He probably deserved any nastiness his wife could dish out. But how could any woman not want him to touch her? Even she couldn't tell that big a lie.

While she knew it was never going to happen again, she also knew she would remember that touch for the rest of her life. "So what finally happened?"

"Things seemed to be smoothing out a little until she found out she was pregnant again, and they got into a big yelling match. She *said* it caused her to lose the baby and blamed him."

"Oh, how sad." Samantha held one hand to her chest.

"It seemed pretty far-fetched at the time to everyone around here. I mean, about losing the baby because of an argument. Sharisse was strong and healthy, and some people talked about how maybe she caused it herself."

"Do you think she would do that?"

"Yep, I do."

"So what does Taos think?"

"He never talks about it. Even to me and Darren. He just paid her off and she left."

"Paid her off?"

"I don't really know the details. I just know it cost him a lot, in a lot of ways."

She nodded, turning the information over in her mind. It certainly explained some of his demeanor, though it didn't excuse his treatment of her.

"Anyway," He paused as if gathering his thoughts. "I thought I better warn you before we got to town. Sharisse started a bunch of rumors before she left about how Taos abused her and beat her."

Samantha inhaled sharply.

"Now, not one of them is true," He rushed his explanation. "I lived in that house, Sammy, and I never saw him ever lift a finger to her, honest. Though if any man had a reason to, he sure did." He rubbed the leather reins with his thumbs. "People still talk though."

"Does she ever come around to see Tommy?

"Nope. Not once. I haven't seen her in more than five years now."

"That's too bad."

"No, honey, believe me it's not. That is one woman you wouldn't want to meet: all peaches and cream on the outside and stone cold ice on the inside. I'm glad Tommy doesn't really remember her."

They passed the first few of houses on the outskirts of town.

"So, were you?" He elbowed her playfully.

"Was I what?" She dodged his elbow.

"Serious or not about those 'stud services'?"

She smiled. "I haven't decided yet."

"I'm sure glad you don't play poker," he laughed, "Cause I'd be a real poor man by now."

Charlie pulled the wagon up to Hardin's Mercantile. Samantha surveyed the familiar scene. Her mother would have been amazed at how few people were left. Main Street was about the only place still muddy from the rain. Claire James had complained frequently about having to drag her skirts through mountain mud, and after last night's experience Samantha completely understood why.

A tinkling piano tune drifted down the street. Miss Sadie's looked like a worn-out Victorian home. Sort of. The lower level had clearly been a log cabin at one point, but someone had tried to change that by adding a second story, some white paint, and a few tattered looking gingerbread architectural accents. The paint on the building peeled off in several places, showing the dark brown logs.

A bright yellow sign out front announced it as "Miss Sadie's Place" and looked much newer. Still, it was the nicest building in town, which said a lot about the population. Mostly single men she'd guess as she'd seen very few women yesterday when she walked down Main Street. Unlike the other shops and businesses in town, Sadie's appeared to have plenty of clientele even though it was only mid-day. She was sure the building had been there when she was a child, but she never gave it much notice. She just knew it was a place where men went, like the saloon. But she wasn't a naïve fourteen-year-old anymore.

Charlie helped Samantha down from the wagon and escorted her inside the mercantile. The bell above the door chimed their arrival. Mr. Hardin's shiny head popped up from behind the counter and the rotund Mrs. Hardin bustled out of the back room.

"Charlie Williams!" Mr. Hardin's gravelly voice boomed toward them. The older man extended a hand and Charlie shook it vigorously. "Well, what have we here?" He tilted his chin to get a better look at Samantha through his half spectacles. "Mother, you better come have a look."

Charlie introduced Samantha and Mrs. Hardin's face lit up.

"Sam and Claire's daughter! I should have recognized you. Why, you're all grown up . . . and that hair! Just like your mother's."

Mrs. Hardin hurried Samantha off, plying her with questions. A tall, boney woman with dark brown hair streaked with grey stood next to the fabric counter. Mrs. Hardin touched her arm and pulled Samantha over. "Mertie Mae, here's someone you just have to meet!"

The woman looked Samantha up and down and sniffed as if she'd just stepped in a cow patty.

Mrs. Hardin continued on. "This is Miss Samantha James."

"Who?" The woman examined a bolt of denim like she was checking for fleas.

"You know, Sam and Claire James. She's staying with the Williamses."

Mertie Mae immediately focused her attention on Samantha. "The Williamses? Is she related to them?"

An awkward silence fell between the women. Mertie Mae pierced Samantha with suspicious eyes while Mrs. Hardin twirled her fingers nervously. Samantha felt compelled to say something, anything. "They are old friends of the family."

"But they are *not* family, are they?" The condescension in her voice matched her upturned nose. "You're not staying out there unchaperoned, I'm sure?"

Samantha had an instant dislike for this crow-like creature.

Mrs. Hardin frowned, "Mertie Mae, this town needs more fine young women from good families, like Samantha."

"What this town needs, Sarah, is respectable, quality women. Not the kind that turn every man's head and go about unchaperoned—and staying at the home of a notoriously violent man to boot."

"Mules in dresses, that's what she wants!" Mr. Hardin mumbled from across the room.

Mertie Mae pinned him with a glare and Mr. Hardin disappeared into the back room. The woman narrowed her eyes at Samantha and dropped the bolt of cloth on the counter, slamming the door on her way out.

"I didn't mean to cost you a customer." Samantha whispered to Mrs. Hardin.

"Don't think a thing about it. We're the only store in town." She patted Samantha's hand. "She'll be back. You pay her no mind. She's picked out the Williams boys as suitable matches for her daughters."

"Which one of the Williams boys?"

"Whichever one gets dumb enough to slow down!" Mr. Hardin tossed in, having reappeared at the counter near where Charlie stood. He and Charlie cackled at his humor.

Samantha bit her bottom lip and hesitated. She didn't want to look like she was sizing up the competition, but her curiosity was aroused. "Are her daughters pretty?"

"Mules in dresses." Mr. Hardin chimed in again.

Mrs. Hardin covered her laughter with the back of her hand. "Oh, Henry!" She half scolded her husband. "Let's just say they aren't very easy on the eyes." She nodded at the list in the younger woman's hand. "What can I get for you, dear?"

She gave the woman a long list of necessities, from clothing to writing paper, then wandered around the store as the items were wrapped and placed on the counter. Samantha amassed a large basket full of baking essentials, including some chocolate for cookies. Charlie's eyebrows crept toward his hairline as the number of packages grew. He separated her from an increasingly excited Mrs. Hardin and pulled her aside.

"Sammy, did you ask Taos about this?" He whispered, motioning to the mound of packages.

"Why should I? He doesn't have any say in what I do." She picked up a rag doll just like the one she used to have as a child. Black button eyes and red yarn for hair.

"He does when you're spending his money."

Samantha plopped the doll back down and opened the clasp on her small purse. She pulled out a large wad of bills and Charlie's eyes widened.

"What are you doing with that kind of cash?" He pushed her hand back toward her purse and glanced around to make sure no one else had seen it.

"Paying my own way. I won't be a burden to you if that's what you're concerned about." She slapped his hands away.

"It's not me, its Taos. He told me to take care of anything you need and put it on his account."

"I'll take care of myself. He is the last person I want to be indebted to." She turned in a huff and went to the counter to pay for her purchases. Both the Hardins looked at Charlie for an explanation, but he just shrugged.

Samantha stood on the walk and gazed down the street as Charlie loaded the wagon. For the most part it was a quiet morning. Two women walked by and nodded at Samantha, who smiled back. Potential friends. She could use a few. Miss Sadie's was hard to ignore as laughter drifted out into the street.

Samantha twisted her mouth as she thought, chewing on the inside of her lip. What she needed was education. If she knew one tenth of what those women knew, Taos would be convinced she was serious about following through with the idea of getting her ranch any way she could, even if she had no intention of going through with it. He'd have to guard her every second, which was the whole point of her hiding out in River City in the first place.

She stared at the building down the street. It's not like Aunt Mattie didn't explain the fundamentals of what men and women did behind closed doors, but fundamentals just weren't enough in this situation and she knew it. Besides, the feeling of being in Taos's arms opened up a whole new curiosity she just hadn't had before.

That's it. The idea made her stomach flutter with excitement. They're business women after all. The worst they could do is say no. Her pulse quickened. She waited until Charlie went inside for another load then disappeared down the walk.

She heard Charlie yell her name just as she disappeared down the alley next to the saloon. She'd come this far; she wasn't about to stop now.

Chapter 8

Samantha paused just inside the back doorway of Miss Sadie's, allowing her eyes to adjust to the darkness. Dark shapes slowly took the form of familiar objects: a table, chairs and a stove. She heard loud voices coming from the front of the building and the ever-present piano music. The kitchen she stepped into was just as deserted as the alley had been—so far. A bulky mass appeared from the hallway in front of her.

"Lordy! You scared ten years off me, Missy." The woman slipped into the dim light of the kitchen and looked Samantha up and down. "We don't allow no wives in here. Not good for business." She lit a lamp on the table. Samantha tried not to stare. Easily as wide as she was tall, the woman was dressed in some kind of tent- like garment in the strangest shade of orange she had ever seen. It almost made her want to blow the lamp out again.

"You better git or I'll have Adler toss you out."

"I'm here to see the woman in charge." At least Samantha's voice didn't shake as much as every other part of her body did.

"Sure you are, Missy. Like I said, no *wives*. Your man'll be home directly."

"I don't have a man."

The woman turned a more assessing gaze on her. "Lookin' for work? You'd make a real good living here with that hair and all." She waved a chubby hand toward Samantha's body and grinned, highlighting large gaps in what was left of a row of yellow teeth.

Samantha instinctively crossed her arms in front of her, feeling exposed. She stammered. "It's not like that. I mean . . . I have a problem and . . . I just need to see Miss Sadie." She reached into her purse, pulled out a few bills, and held them up. "I can pay for her time. It's strictly business."

"Well, that's different." A large hand reached forward to shake Samantha's. "The name's Ollie. Miss Sadie can always spare a few minutes for business."

Samantha followed the woman down a corridor and into what looked to be a parlor.

"Wait here, Missy. I'll get her."

The urge to run almost overwhelmed Samantha. She twined her fingers nervously and looked around the room. The furnishings were surprisingly normal. In fact, they were very tasteful. With its stylish furniture and conservative colors, this parlor might be in any home in Boston. She had expected something more . . .

"Trashy?" A slim, older woman dressed in a fashionable dark green taffeta leaned against the door jamb with one perfect eyebrow raised. Her black hair, with subtle hints of gray, had been pulled back into a knot at her neck. "You were expecting something gaudy and trashy?"

"Miss Sadie?" Samantha's voice croaked. Could the woman read her mind?

"No, I'm her Aunt Mavis." She crossed in front of Samantha and seated herself in one of the wingback chairs. "I'm not a mind reader either, dear. Your face gives you away."

She smiled warmly. Samantha was both relieved and drawn to her silent invitation, sinking into the opposite chair as the woman spoke. "Miss Sadie is more a title than a person. My niece has only been here a week, and she inherited the title from my sister." A rustle sounded down the hall. "Speak of the devil."

A small woman hurried into the room. "Did you send for me, Aunt Mavis?"

"Miss Sadie?" Samantha's shock gave way to concern. This woman couldn't be more than nineteen, twenty at the most. She had an almost nun-like appearance with every inch of skin covered in a black crepe dress that was conservative almost to the point of being unfashionable. Samantha's gaze traveled down the black fabric and was drawn to . . . it couldn't be . . . a string of rosary beads? Was this some kind of joke?

"The title is only temporary." The newcomer's lips drew into a thin line as she followed the path of Samantha's stare to the beads. "My name is actually Sage. And you are?"

"Samantha James."

Mavis motioned for Sage to join them on the small red settee. Samantha noticed the two women had the exact same shade of hazel eyes, both pairs of which were now fixed on her, waiting for an explanation.

What am I doing here? Samantha stared at the floor and rolled the fabric of her skirt between her fingers, trying to find a starting point for this conversation. She hadn't really had time to think about how to word her request.

Five minutes ago she was standing outside the mercantile, now she was sitting in an infamous house of ill repute as if she did this every day. Mavis's voice gave her a start.

"Just spit it out, dear, you won't shock us. I've heard just about everything over the last twenty-five years." Mavis exuded kindness and patience.

Samantha took a deep breath and opened her mouth. "I have this problem with my inheritance. I can't get it unless I'm married or have an heir, but I don't want to marry." The words spilled out bunched together. She paused. There was no reason to share the information about John or why she was really here. The fewer people who knew the better. Her heart pounded so loudly she could hardly hear herself speak. Both women listened intently but didn't seem surprised or shocked. She was unsure what to say next.

"So you need help in producing an heir?" Mavis's voice remained calm and reassuring.

Sage gasped. "You want a child, but no husband? Why would you do that?"

Samantha mentally calculated the time it would take her to dash from the room and away from this unbearable humiliation.

Mavis glared the girl into silence and turned her attention back to Samantha. "I apologize for my niece. She is new to this profession and still very naive."

The reproach was stinging, and the girl shrank back into the cushions.

"Your problem isn't a hard one to solve. Any cowboy could help you. Why come to us?"

This wasn't going well. Samantha bit her lower lip and stared at her hands then at Mavis. She seemed so kind, a little more truth surely couldn't hurt at this point. "Can I be completely honest?"

Mavis leaned back in her chair. "Please do."

"I just want a particular man to *think* that I would go through with having a baby on my own." The heat on her face intensified. "I don't know enough about it to convince him though, since I never, well, you know." Mavis nodded as Sage's eyes widened.

"So, what you need is education, dear?"

"Yes," Relief flooded over her. "That's it, and I would be happy to compensate you for your time."

Mavis stared intently at Samantha for several minutes before she spoke. "You're certainly different than the others who have come here."

"Others?" Samantha asked. Was it possible that this was a common occurrence? Surely not.

"Over the last twenty years I can count on one hand the number of times a *respectable* woman sat in this parlor. They are generally of two types: the tambourine bangers who come to save souls, or wives begging me to cut their husbands off. Figuratively speaking of course." Mavis chuckled at her own humor, which passed over Samantha and Sage completely.

"All of the women approach me in the same disdainful, emotional way as if I'm not fit to scrape bug juice off their shoes. You're different: honest, direct, and business minded. An unusual and potent combination, Miss James." She paused a moment. "I know there is much more to the story than you are letting on, but as far as I see it that is your business, not anyone else's."

Samantha had always been a terrible liar. If Taos could see that, none of this would even be necessary. She was relieved Mavis seemed completely uninterested in her real motives.

"Sage, go and get Cinnamon," The young woman leapt to her feet, glad to be leaving.

"So you'll help me?"

"I'd be happy to help. Cinnamon is about your age and quite skilled. I think you'll be comfortable with her."

"I can't tell you how much I appreciate this."

"Glad to help, dear. In fact, more than glad. Respect and dignity are in short supply in this profession. Your attitude and appreciation are a soothing balm to a long forgotten heart." Mavis reached over and patted her hand.

Cinnamon and Sage entered the room and Samantha was immediately struck with the thought that the two could almost be twins, though Cinnamon was about six inches taller and seemed a number of years older than Sage. Cinnamon certainly looked the part of a prostitute with her bright red satin dress, low-cut and fringed with black lace. A stark contrast to Sage's nun-like appearance. Sage turned to leave.

"Oh no, Sage. I think it's time you had a better understanding of what we do." Mavis's tone was insistent. Sage reluctantly resumed her place on the bench.

Cinnamon had her mother's calm and reassuring manner. She sat next to Sage on the settee and spent more than twenty minutes explaining most of the basics in a very direct and matter-of-fact way much as Mattie had years ago. As she spoke, Samantha slowly relaxed.

"Now that's most of it, but there are some variations," Cinnamon arched a questioning brow at Mavis, who nodded for her to continue. As Cinnamon talked, Samantha imagined herself attempting a few of the 'variations.' Some of the descriptions were intriguing, others downright repulsive.

Samantha looked at Sage, who seemed as mortified as Samantha felt. Well, at least she wasn't alone. *Surely people don't really do this? Or not all of it anyway!* At least she was gaining enough information to scare Taos.

Cinnamon continued on with the lesson. "Now, the first time, a man is going to be able to tell that you've never been with anyone else before." She looked thoughtful for a moment. "And for that you would need to find someone gentle that knows how to please."

"How would you do that?" Sage was as curious as she was.

"Well, I could give you a list." Cinnamon grinned. "Unfortunately, it's a short one. Most men don't care much as long as they get what they want."

Something just didn't fit. When Taos had touched her, he seemed to like it as much as she did. Could she have been wrong about that? "Why would women do this at all?" The question slipped past Samantha's lips before she thought.

Cinnamon and Mavis stared at her.

Cinnamon chuckled, "I explained how it works, but I guess I left out how it feels. When it's done right, that is."

Cinnamon's knowing smile had Samantha's full attention, but Sage looked like she wanted to crawl under the chair.

"Do I have to listen to this, it's disgusting!" Sage dropped her head to her knees.

"Oh this is the best part!" Cinnamon patted Sage's arm. She seemed to enjoy torturing the girl.

As Cinnamon described the kind of pleasure possible, Samantha's imagination took her back to Taos. She thought of the feel of his lips on hers, her hands on him, his hands on her. Her skin tingled in the strangest way. It was exactly what Cinnamon described, and the thought of feeling that surge of warmth roll through her again was intoxicating.

"If you don't mind my asking, dear, who is this man you're trying to convince?" She was startled from her thoughts as Mavis looked at her with intense curiosity.

"Taos Williams."

Mavis' eyebrows lifted slightly .

Cinnamon snorted. "He's definitely not on the short list!" She slid a long finger against her dark red lips. "But Charlie, now that's a different story."

"They both come here?" Mental images of Taos and Cinnamon doing the things she had just learned about tumbled through her mind, and Samantha had a sudden urge to scratch her eyes out. Mavis gazed at Samantha with a knowing look that made Samantha realize she must try to hide her emotions more. The woman *was* a mind reader.

Cinnamon, however, was oblivious to her discomfort. "They're not my regulars, so I only know what the others tell me. From what I hear, Taos hasn't been around in a very long time. When he is here, he just takes care of business and is gone. Not much to say about him."

Samantha cast a relieved look toward Mavis who smiled.

"Charlie is one of Raven's regulars. He would be at the very top of the short list. To hear Raven tell it, he's quite the lover."

Samantha noticed the time as the large clock on the mantle chimed. "Oh no, I have to go. Charlie is probably looking for me right now." She fumbled with her purse. "How much do I owe you?"

"Nothing." Mavis smiled.

"But . . ."

"You've already paid us back several times over just by coming here."

Cinnamon nodded her agreement, but Sage just dropped her head back to her knees.

A dusty cloud of frustrated fury burst into the room. All four women jumped to their feet and stared at Charlie.

"What in the hell are you doing in here, Sammy?" He grabbed her wrist and pulled.

Samantha was so surprised she tripped on her hem and nearly fell into him.

Sage rushed forward and stood directly in Charlie's path, "You will not come into my parlor and behave like an animal."

Charlie stopped short as he took her in. He caught sight of the rosary and cast a nervous look toward Cinnamon and Mavis. "Who's the nun?"

Cinnamon snickered and Sage's voice wavered a bit. "I'm not a nun. And if you have a question you can ask me yourself."

"Better watch it, Charlie, she swings some mean beads." Cinnamon received a reproachful glare from Mavis.

Charlie grinned at Sage, his anger temporarily replaced by his usual smooth charm. "I don't usually come here to be beat up by a girl swinging beads, sweetheart."

"I'm not your sweetheart."

He reached out to touch her hair.

She batted his hand away. "And the only thing you will ever get from me is a beating, or worse."

"We'll have to see about that." His eyes gleamed as they traveled down her body.

Sage stood her ground.

It had been better when she had no idea what men were thinking! Samantha tried to yank her wrist away but Charlie held tight, dragging her from the room and out the back door.

"Charlie!" She stumbled along behind him, trying to keep up as he hurried across the street.

He didn't answer until they reached the wagon. "I can't believe the amount of trouble one lone woman can stir up." He plopped her in the wagon seat and walked around to climb up. "It was bad enough at the mercantile," his voice dropped to a hiss as two women strolled by, "but Miss Sadie's?"

"I had to—"

"Taos will beat me to a pulp if he hears about this. What if someone had seen you? What then?"

"No one—"

"I would love to know what goes through that mind of yours! You damn near start a cat fight with the self-proclaimed one woman morality committee, then you end up in a whore house."

"I was just thinking—"

"What? What could you possibly have been thinking? You better tell me now, 'cause I don't think I can take any more little surprises!"

The vein on Charlie's forehead stood out just like Taos's, but it seemed ridiculous on him. It was all she could do not to laugh. "I was just thinking how nice it is that you're so quiet when you're mad."

He turned a frustrated look toward the sky as she lost the battle with her laughter. After a few minutes he joined in. He climbed into the wagon and sat next to her.

"So who was the nun?"

She shook her head. "You have a one-track mind!"

He winked and wiggled his eyebrows. "Yes ma'am."

Charlie slapped the horses into a trot and steered the wagon for the edge of town as fast as he could without causing too much notice. He slowed only after they passed the last house.

"What is the matter with you?" Samantha's hand still vibrated from holding onto the side of the wagon as it rattled through town.

"I didn't want to give you any opportunity to jump out and cause any more trouble."

"Honestly!" She turned away and stared unseeing at the countryside.

They rode in silence for a time, each immersed in their own thoughts. Samantha's mind was focused on Taos. She knew a whole lot more about him than she had this morning, but it didn't solve her problem. In fact it made it more complex. As rotten as he had been to her so far, she almost had the urge to go back and be nice to him. Almost.

She tried to imagine the kind of hurt he must have endured, living with a wife who tricked him into marriage, then left him to raise a child by himself. One child. He must have suffered horribly to lose a baby, then be blamed for it. According to Charlie, Taos hadn't trusted anyone since. How lonely he must be.

A familiar feature in the landscape drew her attention.

"Charlie? Will you do me a favor?"

"No."

"Why not?"

"Because I don't want a worse pounding than I'm already in for."

"That's ridiculous. Besides, this won't get you in any trouble."

He cast a skeptical expression at her.

"Or me either. Really." She pointed at a cabin partially hidden by a stand of trees. Her cabin. On her land.

Charlie nodded and turned the team toward the structure. As they approached, the house seemed much smaller than she remembered. The porch extended along the entire front of the house and a small barn sat just to the left. Samantha caught her breath at the sight of the yellow daffodils and bright pink tulips by the front steps. Her mother had them shipped from Boston the year before she died. Claire had worked so hard to make their home beautiful.

Charlie handed her down from the wagon and escorted her up the stone steps. The front door hinges squeaked, announcing their presence. Sunlight streamed into the room from the two large windows on the opposite wall. Few cabins had windows that large, and she remembered her father complained frequently about having to chop twice as much wood to keep the place warm in the winter because of them. But Samantha knew deep down he loved to look out at the mountain view as much as her mother did. Many nights she'd awakened and looked over the loft railing to see her parents snuggled together on the bench in front of those windows, gazing out at the beautiful snowfall.

Samantha walked around the room, running her fingers over each piece of furniture, the wide windowsills, the ladder to the loft she'd climbed hundreds of times. The table her father made for the three of them sat where it always had next to the small kitchen, the rocker that had been a gift from Aunt Mattie when Samantha was born remained on one side of the huge fireplace. The nails along the mantle where her mother hung flowers to dry were all still there.

She could almost feel her parents' presence, as if her father would burst through the door any moment and swing her into his arms, or he mother's lilting voice would ring out from the kitchen to let her know her favorite cookies were fresh from the oven. The whole cabin looked and felt as if they'd just left this morning to go into town and might be back at any moment.

The fact that they wouldn't be here again, ever, stung Samantha's heart and filled her eyes with tears. She heard Charlie shuffle over to the windows.

"Why is it so clean?" she asked. "Is someone living here?"

Charlie removed his hat and looked into one of the bedrooms. "We use it every so often. If we're branding on this place, it's a lot easier to stay here than ride back home." He leaned against the wall. "Taos pays an Indian woman to clean it and keep things in order. Darren stays here sometimes just to be alone, you know."

Samantha nodded. She did know. When they were children, Darren would sometimes go weeks or months without speaking because someone made fun of his stuttering. It was barely noticeable now, but people don't forget. Darren cherished his solitude. She pulled back a lace curtain on the kitchen window. Two white headstones reflected the sun from the small hill behind the house. Nine years had passed, but the pain crushed her heart with the same force. She breathed deep to keep the tears from overwhelming her.

"Do you want to go alone?" Charlie asked.

She shook her head and walked toward the back door. He followed a short distance behind. Small red tulips peeked out from the base of both stones.

"Who planted these?"

"Taos. He thought you would have liked them."

"I do." She crossed her arms and stared at the flowers. What kind of man would do something so kind, knowing she might never see it?

After a few minutes Charlie spoke, almost to himself. "Dad said it was a freak accident. The horse stepped in a hole and rolled with him. It could have happened it anyone." He paused. "She only lasted six months after he was killed."

Samantha nodded, remembering Jake Williams at the door, covered in dirt from the spring roundup just as she'd seen him and her father so many times. But that day he had her father's body wrapped in a blanket, draped over the saddle. She didn't hear what

Jake said, just watched from the window as her mother ran and pulled the blanket back. Clair stared into her husband's unseeing eyes, then slid to her knees, inconsolable.

Samantha looked at the dates on the stones. Almost six months to the day separated them. That six months was the longest of her life as she watched her mother waste away. Nothing she tried made any difference. "I'll never understand it. She just gave up. She wouldn't eat or sleep. She just sat in that rocker like she expected him to walk through the door any minute." Samantha picked a tulip and twirled it in her fingers. "How can you love someone so much that you would rather die than live without them?"

The familiar loneliness crept over her soul again. *How could she have chosen to die with him rather than live with me?* No amount of reasoning had ever provided an acceptable answer. She had stood here nine years ago, an orphan having just turned fourteen. She was angry. Very angry. Aunt Mattie had been so kind and tried her best to offer explanations, but nothing soothed the hurt. Finally Samantha became numb, and she stayed that way for a long time.

They spent a few more minutes at the small grave site then returned to the wagon for the trip home. Samantha picked a bouquet of daffodils and tulips from the front of the house to take with them. She also took the crazy quilt from her parents' room that her grandmother had made. Not that it was much, but it had been one of the things she missed the most when she left. It connected her to the women of her past somehow. Maybe it would give her a chance at the kind of love they had known.

Chapter 9

As the Williams house came into view, Samantha squinted against the warm sun of spring at the very large, black furry thing loping out to meet them.

"What is that?" She pointed hesitantly.

"Tommy's dog. Hey, Jimbo!" The animal leapt toward the wagon while the horses danced and snorted. "Tommy put him in the barn last night before it rained."

"That's a dog?" It was homely, hairy, and huge.

"Oh, don't worry. He's friendly." That seemed small comfort. The wagon pulled to a stop and Tommy rushed out of the house.

"How about helping me unload, Squirt?" Charlie asked as he lifted Samantha down from the wagon. The boy nodded.

"Where's your Pa?" Charlie hefted a large sack of flour and set it on the porch. Tommy climbed into the wagon and peeked into some of the other packages.

"He saw you coming up the road and went to help Uncle Darren move the herd to new pasture. He said for you to come help when you got back."

"You comin' with me?" Charlie asked.

"No. He said I'd just be in the way." Tommy's shoulders drooped. He plopped down on top of a bag of cornmeal. "I'm seven now, and he said I could help when I was seven." He scuffed his boot along the bed of the wagon. Large blue eyes stared off into the distance. "I guess he forgot."

Samantha pursed her lips. How could anyone disappoint this little boy? Hadn't he been through enough in his short life? It was a good thing Taos wasn't there; he deserved a swift kick. Her inclination to be nice to the man shriveled a bit. She walked into Tommy's line of sight and stood until he looked at her.

"You know the real reason he made you stay here?"

"'Cause I'm too little?" His soft voice shook with resignation.

"No, because someone needs to watch out for me. I get into lots of trouble when I'm by myself."

"You're gonna have your hands full too, Tommy." Charlie winked at her. "She's more trouble than a hundred mean steers in a stampede."

Tommy jumped off the sack and then bounced onto the ground. "I can do that!" His words came faster and faster as the excitement took hold. "I get into trouble all the time. Why, I could show you lots of things you shouldn't do."

"I'd really appreciate that, Tommy." She smiled, pulling packages off the end of the wagon for Tommy to carry as Charlie chuckled.

Samantha followed the boy inside and then motioned him upstairs, both of them struggling under a pile of bundles. He led her to the room that adjoined Taos's.

"Girls sure have a lot of stuff!" Tommy dragged off his straw hat and wiped sweat from his face.

Samantha looked around the room. "Yes, they do." Years ago this had been a large dressing room, but now it was definitely a woman's room, with lace curtains and a pink quilt on the bed. While it was tiny, it was still functional. She frowned as her gaze settled on the adjoining door to Taos's room. "Am I supposed to be in this room?"

"Yeah, Pa said. 'sides, all the others are full." He flopped down on the bed, waiting for her to open the packages.

"Maybe I could just switch with someone?"

"Why?"

Yes, why? Simple question, complicated answer. She tried to think of a reason a child would believe. Besides the truth, that is. "Um, I don't sleep very well, and I might wake your Pa up. Then he would get mad."

Tommy straightened to his full height. "Now that's one of the first things I can help you learn." He cleared his throat like a preacher instructing his flock. "When Pa says do something, it's better to just do it then hope he changes his mind later. He'll get lots madder if you don't do what he says first."

Hard to argue with the boy's logic—not that she was under any illusions that Taos might change his mind. She would have to talk to him about the sleeping arrangements later. She didn't think she could sleep knowing he was right on the other side of that door, and not because she didn't trust him. She didn't completely trust herself, especially after the instruction she'd received from Cinnamon. That could really complicate things. And things were already complicated enough as they were.

Samantha opened drawers in the dresser and armoire to find a place for all her purchases as Tommy sat back down on the bed. "Whose room did this used to be?"

"Nobody's."

"It had to be somebody's."

"Nope. Pa sleeps in there." He pointed toward the adjoining door. "And Uncle Charlie and Darren have rooms across the hall. My room's at the top of the stairs so I can make it to the outhouse fast."

She turned away to keep from laughing. *Well it's practical I guess, but who would have slept here? Sharisse.* Samantha shook off the strange feelings that name conjured up, a mixture of curiosity and irritation.

Charlie had said that Taos and his wife rarely shared a bed, so this must have been where she slept. What kind of woman had his mother been? The more time she spent with Tommy, the more the feeling turned toward disgust at the thought of her abandoning this child.

Samantha had purchased a few dresses to tide her over, and she pulled a lilac calico from the brown paper. She held it up. "What do you think?"

"It's pretty, and not as dirty as the one you have on."

"Thank you, I think. Why don't you let me change, then you can show me around?"

He stared at her and waited.

"Can you wait in the hall?"

The boy blushed deeply and darted from the room, obviously not used to having a female in the house.

Ten minutes later they were roaming the house's ground floor. Somehow Samantha remembered it being bigger too. Strange how everything shrinks as you grow up, everything except Taos.

Her memory of the Williams home rendered a tidier image than the present one too. Dust now hovered in every corner, beckoning a long absent broom. Cob webs dangled here and there, swaying with the occasional draft. She had difficulty determining the original color of a few of the rugs too, as they all seemed to be the same shade of dirt brown. Why didn't Taos have this house cleaned by the same person he had cleaning her cabin?

She placed the tulips in a large mason jar on the kitchen table. They were bright and cheery and made the rest of the house look that much worse.

Tommy talked, explaining the use of each room and adding other interesting information. Amused and intrigued by his narration, Samantha let him explain every detail to her. A doorway under the stairs was their next stop.

"That goes to my Pa's office." He stood aside, allowing her to enter first. "We're not supposed to be in here for anything 'cause he keeps important papers and special things in here."

The large, cluttered desk took up most of the room. Samantha strolled slowly around, absorbing every detail. Maybe there were clues that would hint at the changes in Taos. Walking behind the desk, she could feel his essence in the room, her skin rippled with goose bumps as she examined the books on the shelves. It was as if he were watching.

Gardening books, etiquette guides, and a variety of classic novels were among the titles—an eclectic mix to be sure. She pulled one of the many volumes on roses out and blew the dust off the top. The leather spine cracked as she opened the cover. The pages were yellowed, and inside the cover, in sprawling handwriting, "Elizabeth Williams, 1852" was written.

Taos's mother. Samantha had been very young when she'd died, and she couldn't really remember anything about her. She replaced the book, feeling a little like an intruder, and looked at the mess on the desk. Papers scattered across the entire surface and hung off the sides. There were even some papers littering the floor behind the desk and sticking out of a few of the drawers. If there were clues to Taos's behavior in that chaos, it would take her a lifetime to find them.

Samantha ran her fingers along the back of the leather chair. The room smelled like him, a combination of leather and spice, a scent uniquely his. Or at least this was the smell of the Taos she remembered. Very masculine, compassionate, and comforting. She longed for the old Taos. The one who carried her home after she fell off a horse and twisted her ankle when she was nine. He talked softly to her the whole way and teased until she was smiling again. He also comforted her when her parents died, sitting with her for hours while she cried. That person had to still be there, somewhere.

Tommy walked over to the small secretary adjacent to the door and opened a small drawer. "This is the 'mergency stuff."

Samantha peered in. There was a gun and a small box.

"The gun's loaded and we're not supposed to touch it. Unless it's a 'mergency, of course. Do you know how to shoot?"

"No, do you?"

"Yes, ma'am." His small face radiated with pride. "My pa taught me when I was five."

"Maybe you could teach me."

"Sure I could. Everybody needs to know how to shoot."

"What's in the box?"

The boy popped open the lid. "Money."

Her eyes opened wide. *A lot of money.* What kind of emergencies did Taos expect?

He snapped the box shut and closed the drawer.

"How about something to eat?" she asked, "I'm kind of hungry."

"Me too." Tommy disappeared down the hall.

She prepared a small meal for the two of them from left-over bacon and biscuits. They sat at the table together. "I bought some chocolate for cookies at the store."

The boy listened and chewed, his mouth stuffed.

"I thought I might make some this afternoon."

He swallowed. "I like cookies. Nate's momma makes some white ones that are really good."

"Who's Nate?"

"My friend in town. I stay with him sometimes and he stays with me sometimes."

They ate in silence for a while.

"I never had nobody that made cookies just for me. Maybe I could give Nate some."

The boy was very matter of fact, but moisture threatened Samantha's eyes. "I'll make some extra." She may not be here long, but while she was, Tommy would at least have someone who cared enough to make cookies just for him.

Once the food was devoured, the two spent the afternoon stirring and mixing, and then waiting anxiously as a heavenly chocolate aroma filled the kitchen. Tommy ate most of the first batch and several spoonfuls of dough out of the bowl for the second batch when he thought she wasn't looking. They piled the last survivors on a plate and covered them with a towel.

"There's still some stuff you haven't seen, if you want." He motioned her outside.

What she really wanted was a nap, but she didn't dare turn down the invitation. She ignored the dishes in the washtub and followed Tommy out the back door. The tour of the barn was uneventful and hot as the afternoon waned. Except that Jimbo apparently decided that he needed to smell every inch of her new calico dress. The dog almost knocked her down twice in his excitement. Friendly had been an understatement.

A short time later they neared the house again. Tommy said, "That's pretty much it, except for the flower garden."

"Flower garden?" The type of flower garden these men would have created conjured the vision of a single mound with one dirty daisy sticking out of the parched earth.

"I have to water it every day so they don't die, with the water being so low and all." He started off toward the creek.

They walked a few hundred yards along the bank, coming to a protected area with several trees surrounded on three sides by a small bluff. As they pushed through a row of low bushes; Samantha caught her breath and stared. She was surrounded by roses just starting their fall bloom. Some red, some pink, even a few yellow. Honeysuckle ringed the area, infusing the air with sweet freshness. Wildflowers bloomed in the open patches by the dozens. The air buzzed with the hum of insect wings as sweet fragrances wafted toward her. "Who planted this?"

"My pa."

"When?"

"When I was little."

"Why?"

"Don't know."

Why would he do something like this? It was beautiful. Taos couldn't have done this. Could he? She had a hard time even imagining the possibility. Her parents' headstones flashed through her mind. The tulips. Charlie said he had done that too. Why?

She walked around the small garden, stopping to smell the various roses. She admired each one, from the climbing vines, to the small bushes. Tommy followed her patiently, like a nanny with his charge. At the end of the garden stood a wooden cross and a small white statue of an angel.

"Tommy, what's this?"

He peered around her at the angel and shrugged. "An angel. Ain't you ever seen one of those?"

"Yes, but why is it here?"

"Don't know. Want to see the swimming hole?"

She nodded, still staring at the angel. Barely larger than a man's hand, it was beautifully carved out of a white stone. The intricate work didn't look like simple ornamentation, especially with the cross next to it. No inscription on the cross or on the angel statue offered any clues. Taos had to have put it here. She would ask Charlie about it.

Tommy had already started toward the swimming hole, and she had to run a few steps to catch up to him. He continued to chatter the whole way. "I don't get to come to the swimming hole by myself." He glanced back at her. "'Course, I ain't by myself today."

"I'm not by myself," she corrected.

"'Course you ain't. I'm here."

She laughed. They'd have to work on that. She glanced down at the boy. He seemed thrilled to have a temporary playmate.

Taos, Charlie, and Darren had done a good job. He had some manners and was polite. He just needed a little polish. They all did. Well, maybe a lot of polish.

The path was as familiar as if she had walked it yesterday. She and Darren had spent hours swimming here when she was little. As they entered the clearing, it was just as she remembered. The small pond was about fifty feet across with deep clear water, constantly fed from the creek. The largest tree leaned out over the water's edge. A long rope from one thick limb tempted even the most hesitant person on a hot summer day.

Small dark black tadpoles wiggled at the water's edge and the pointed nose of a turtle appeared then disappeared out of sight under one of the overhanging tree limbs. The pool drew a large number of animals, and three-toed bird tracks mingled with cattle hooves in the surrounding mud.

"I used to swim here almost every day with your Uncle Darren when I was little."

Tommy looked shocked. "You can swim?"

"Sure, can't you?"

"Pa always says he'll teach me every summer, but he never does." He hung his head.

Samantha thought for a moment. "Well, there's a reason he had to wait, you know."

"For what?"

She had his full attention. "For the magic of seven. I'm sure you've heard about it."

His small head shook no.

"Well, when a boy . . . er, *man,* is seven, there is a special magic that happens."

"What kind of magic?"

"The kind of magic that lets you float on the water. So it's easier to learn to swim."

"Really?" His voice squeaked with excitement.

"Really. I can prove it if you want to learn right now."

Tommy shed clothes, throwing them to the left and right until he stood in front of her in his underwear.

He's certainly not shy, she thought. Samantha grinned and caught the back hem of her dress, tucking it into her waistband. She pulled off her shoes and stockings and they waded out together to knee-deep water. The mud squished between her toes and the cool water lapped against her bare calves. She felt the slight tickle of a fish nibbling on her leg. It had been years since she waded into a pond, but it was tremendous. She stopped a few yards from shore. "This is a good place to start."

Tommy nodded, eyeing the deeper water warily.

She instructed him to lie back, and he followed her every word. She talked smoothly as she supported him in the water and gradually let go until he was floating on his own. "See, you're doing it!"

He popped up out of the water, splashing wildly. "I did it, I did it!"

They spent the better part of an hour going through the basics of dog paddling until he felt comfortable going in the deep water. Jimbo joined them, splashing and celebrating each of Tommy's accomplishments. As the sun slid toward the horizon Tommy dressed, and they walked back to the house hand in hand.

Samantha spotted Taos leaning against the porch railing. She had that urge to be nice again, but squelched it. She had a few words for him concerning Tommy first. The boy ran up the steps when he spotted his father.

"Why didn't you tell me about the magic of seven?"

Taos turned a confused frown toward Samantha. "What magic?"

The boy heaved a frustrated sigh that said grownups were a few bricks shy sometimes. "The magic that lets you float so you can learn to swim. She told me," he jutted a thumb at Samantha, "and sure enough I can swim just fine. Why didn't you tell me?"

"Uh, forgot I guess." Taos raised a questioning eyebrow and smiled a little when she shrugged.

"Old people sure forget a lot." The boy trouped through the back door. Charlie and Darren both dodged him on their way out.

Taos stared at her. How did she go and do in one afternoon what he had put off for two years? He was impressed, and a little annoyed. Teaching a boy to swim was something a father did. She didn't even ask if he would mind. Not to mention the fact that they had been missing for the better part of the afternoon. He had paced the porch for more than half an hour, wondering where they could be. Her nose had a little color and small wispy strands of hair floated across her face.

"What made you decide to take it up on yourself to—" His voice had an irritated edge, but he couldn't help it. Anything could have happened to them.

"What?" She climbed the steps and stood less than a foot away, intentionally crowding him. "Spend time with your son?"

He opened his mouth, but she cut him off again.

"The son you left here by himself so he wouldn't get in your way?" She poked a finger at his chest.

He backed up as she moved forward.

"The son you have made numerous promises to, only to welch on them?"

"My son is *my* business, and I don't welch on anything." He stopped his retreat and growled, "If I wanted your help—"

"You're getting it anyway." She whispered harshly, not wanting Tommy to hear. "Whether you want it or not, Tommy needs me. Even if I'm only his friend, it's more than you have apparently been lately."

Charlie and Darren stood perfectly still, and watched like spectators at a gun fight. Under normal circumstances, they would be the first to jump to Taos's defense. The risk of drawing that kind of female wrath, however, kept them both quiet.

"What makes you think you can just go off and not tell anyone where you're going?"

Samantha smiled and stepped closer. "Why, were you worried?"

"No," he lied. "It's just inconsiderate and irresponsible."

"Kind of like a man that makes promises to a boy and doesn't follow through?"

Darren finally offered the first olive branch. "S-So how was town?"

His attempt to change the subject was met with three glares of varying intensity.

"I found it highly *educational*." Samantha said saucily and brushed past Taos into the house.

Taos stared at Charlie, who refused to meet his gaze. The door banged as Taos followed her in.

"Wh-What did she mean educational?" Darren's question seemed to bounce off his brother.

Charlie looked out at the sunset and heaved a deep sigh. "God hates me today. That's what she meant." The back door slammed behind him.

Jimbo bounded up the stairs, and Darren bent down to scratch the dog's large ears. "Why is it I never know what's going on around here?"

Yours Again

Chapter 10

Tension battled with the mouthwatering aromas that soon filled the kitchen. Everyone waited with a combination of dread and anticipation, like spectators at a hanging. Tommy didn't seem to notice, and he babbled incessantly at Samantha.

"Tomorrow we can go fishin' if you want. I know where to find the biggest worms anywhere." He pulled a chair up next to her as she mixed up some cornbread.

"Where's that?" She asked, smiling at his excitement.

"Under the cow patties."

She laughed and glanced sideways at the table where all three men sat. The unasked questions were having an effect. One man simmered, one was confused, and one looked like he was headed to the gallows. Aunt Mattie always said that sometimes silence screams louder than words. Right again. *Let 'em stew a while.*

Samantha turned her attention back to Tommy.

"Did you really used to get into lots of trouble?" He waited for an answer.

"Oh yes. I was sent to my room all the time." She slid the cornbread into the oven and wiped her hands on a towel. "Sometimes it was worth it, though."

His mouth dropped open. "You mean you got in trouble on purpose?"

"Sometimes."

"Why?"

"Well, if I was doing something to help someone else feel better, or keep them out of trouble, that was usually worth the punishment." She paused for a moment then turned toward him to make sure that everyone in the room could hear her. "Of course, there are other times it's okay to get into trouble, too."

"Like when?"

"When it's the only way to make someone realize they're wrong about something."

Taos frowned, Charlie sank lower. Darren glanced back and forth between the brothers.

"Why wouldn't you just tell them they were wrong?" Tommy's logic was so simple it hurt.

"Some people just refuse to listen. If they won't listen, that doesn't leave much choice."

The muscle in Taos's cheek twitched and his teeth ground together. He watched Samantha's skirts sway as she turned to heap mashed potatoes in one bowl and green beans flavored with bacon and onions in another. She had something to say and it was obvious that she was making him squirm on purpose. He had to gain control of this tendency she had of tuning every situation against him. Taos purposely practiced patience in his dealings with people and used it to his advantage many times.

Why didn't it work with her? Well, maybe it would work, but he couldn't seem to scrape together enough coherent thoughts around her to find out. One look, even one word and she had him playing her game. His gaze bored into her back then slid down over her hips. Closing his eyes, he inhaled a long breath. It would be much easier if she wasn't so . . . distracting. He rubbed his chest where her finger had poked him. He had to stop letting her touch him. It scrambled his brain until all he wanted to do was touch her back.

He'd already decided she wasn't leaving, no matter what, until he found out what she was up to. At least that's what he told himself. But it was more than that. When he came home and she wasn't there it bothered him much more than he'd let on—and not just because of Tommy. But being in the same house presented some issues. They needed to talk about some rules, maybe. Establish some boundaries and distance between the two of them.

Taos half-listened as his son explained the finer points of fishing. Samantha smiled and nodded at the little chatterbox. Taos would pay good money to see her smile like that at him. The lilac dress highlighted every curve and stretched tight over the most interesting parts. He closed his eyes again. A dip in the creek and a stiff shot of whiskey were the only things that were going to help him at this rate.

Tommy jumped down and brought Taos a chocolate cookie. "See what she made me?"

Taos took a bite. Nobody around here had baked cookies since he was a little boy. The sweet treat melted on his tongue. He smiled in spite of himself.

"So you found everything you needed in town?" Taos asked Samantha.

"And then some." Charlie pressed a hand into his back. "'Bout threw my back out loading it all. You'd think she was movin' in for good."

Taos sat forward and looked directly at Charlie. "How much did she spend?"

Charlie glanced at her.

"Not one dime," Samantha piped up. "Of your money, anyway."

"Whose money did you spend?" Taos's voice raised slightly.

"Mine."

"I told you to put everything on my account." Taos stared at his brother.

Charlie shrank under the scrutiny. "Well, she insisted. And I know how much you hate causing a scene and everything, so . . ."

"Why did you insist? I can take care of it." *What the hell?* Was she out to embarrass him in front of the whole town?

"I refuse to be obligated to anyone, especially you." She paused. "Besides, from the looks of things, I didn't think you can spare it."

Darren squelched a snicker and Charlie hid his grin behind his fist. Taos's cheek twitched with renewed fervor.

"And while we're on the subject, this whole house could use a good cleaning, and I intend to give it one tomorrow."

"Sounds like a warning." Darren reached over and grabbed a cookie.

"It is."

All three men looked at her.

"In fact, if there is anything you're attached to I highly recommend you take it with you. Otherwise it'll be cleaned within an inch of its life or thrown out altogether."

Jimbo let out a low bark, eyeing the table through the screen door.

"And that goes for that hairy mutt, too."

"Who said you could just come in here and start dishing out orders?"

She turned toward Taos, a large wooden spoon in her hand. "Let me see if I understand this." She pressed her lips together and narrowed her eyes at him. "I volunteer to scrub this pigsty for you and your brothers, without being asked, or paid, and all you do is complain?"

Silence.

"How ungrateful can a man possibly be?"

"No one asked for your help with anythin-"

"Tough!" she turned back to the stove. "You're getting my help anyway, no matter how undeserving you might be!"

"I think it's nice that she wants to clean the place up a little," Darren mumbled, "Sure couldn't do no harm."

Charlie nodded, "Less for us to do, not that we ever do it. I'd sure like to come home and sleep on clean sheets for once."

"Then it's settled." She glanced over her shoulder, silently daring Taos to say something.

He simmered, trying to plot his next move. She was doing it again. Not only did she think she could just take over his son and his house, she made him look like the bad guy. He needed to talk to his brothers in private. Clearly they had no idea how dangerous it was to let a woman think she runs everything.

As Samantha placed Taos's food in front of him, she balanced herself by placing her hand on his shoulder. He jumped and jerked away like she'd burned him.

Everyone stared. Taos cleared his throat and grabbed his plate. "Thank you," he said.

"Well that was awkward." Charlie raised a brow at Samantha, who smiled.

They were both playing him now. Taos jabbed his steak and ignored them.

Dinner turned out to be a mostly silent affair. The chicken fried steaks were golden brown and fork tender. Everyone watched as Tommy had half a steak, two helpings of potatoes, and a large piece of cornbread before he was full. Finally, the boy leaned over and whispered to Samantha, "That was great, ma'am."

"Why thank you, sir." She put her arm around his slim shoulders and squeezed gently, giving him a quick peck on the cheek.

Tommy blushed and darted up the back stairs to get ready for bed.

"You shouldn't let him get too attached." Taos scowled as he picked up another piece of cornbread. "He'll just be disappointed when you leave."

"It's not my fault he's starved for affection."

Taos paused a moment, almost taking the bait, but then went back to his meal.

"I'm sure he comes by it naturally though." Samantha pushed "Like father, like son. Or so I hear."

"What is that supposed to mean?" His fork clattered on his plate.

"Just that I hear you haven't been to Miss Sadie's in a while." She paused, "It explains a lot."

Taos stopped mid-chew as heavy silence blanketed the entire kitchen. She met his glare with a delicate arch of her brow. Charlie coughed dramatically and Darren's eyes grew round.

"What did you hear, and who did you hear it from?" Taos braced for battle. He called her bluff with a smile that was more a dare. He could easily embarrass her into silence on this subject, then the advantage would be his.

"Oh, you know. People."

Taos's eyes narrowed. *Rumors.* She was bound to hear a whole slew of them in town. There was no way she could know anything about his particular habits with women, or lack thereof, and her evasiveness was proof. He would push until she admitted it right here in front of everyone.

"Who are these people, exactly, and what makes you think they know anything?"

She was nonchalant, even confident. "Mavis and Cinnamon told me all about it this morning when I went to Miss Sadie's. I really don't think they had any reason to lie."

Taos glared at Charlie's white face. The tight grip of humiliation squeezed Taos's throat until his voice was a low rumble. "Did you let her go to that place?"

"*Let* is kind of a strong word." Charlie fumbled with his napkin and flashed a helpless look at Samantha. "She just wandered off while I was loading the wagon, and by the time I found her . . ."

"Actually, I snuck off so it's really not his fault." She shrugged. "As it turned out, I learned a great deal."

"About what?" He bit the words out.

"A number of things."

Taos fought to remain calm. "What things?" He would control this conversation if it killed him. His suspicion returned full force. Had she met up with some accomplice in town? His eyes glanced out the backdoor. Maybe she was ready to spring him on them now. "Well, at least we got a decent meal out of the deal."

Taos tossed his napkin on his plate. "So where's he hidin' honey?"

"We're not back to that again are we?" She heaved a frustrated sigh. "And 'we' didn't decide anything, you did. So it doesn't count and there is another option, as you well know."

No one moved a muscle as the tension mounted. "You are not going to do that." Taos said calmly. He pushed back from the table and stood indicating the conversation was over.

"Why not?" She smiled at him. "And the girls at Miss Sadie's gave me a list of men who might be willing to help me in that respect."

The blood rushed to Taos's head so fast he saw stars. He hadn't lost it . . . yet. And he wasn't going to. She was not going to push him that far this time. He leaned forward on the table as his lips curled into a sneer. "You'll never get a chance to try your little plan. I will make sure you never leave this house."

"Oh, good, because the perfect man is already here." She smiled.

Charlie and Darren stared at each other and then at Taos who chuckled humorlessly.

He rubbed his chin with his hand as he shook his head. "Even if you were the only woman for a thousand miles, I would never—"

She pushed aside the sting of his remark. "Oh, don't worry, you aren't even on the list of great lovers at all. According to the girls at Miss Sadie's, that is." She flashed a sexy smile at his brother. "Charlie, on the other hand was at the very top."

Charlie perked up immediately. "They really said that?"

"Oh yes, they had wonderful things to say about you. Apparently Raven thinks very highly of your, um, skill."

"Really? I can't believe they said that. Right at the top?"

"Number one."

"Enough!" Taos's voice rattled the panes in the window. *She could make angels weep in frustration! She couldn't be serious,* he thought. *And what about Charlie, that backstabbing son of a bitch!* He looked at his brother who was puffed up like a peacock.

He's just dumb enough to fall for it, too. For a brief moment Taos's mind pictured Samantha wrapped in Charlie's arms, and it pushed him to the edge of insanity. He marched around and jerked her up by the arm. "You two find somewhere else to be!"

Both of his brothers jumped to their feet.

"Now maybe you should calm down a bit, Taos." Charlie moved toward Samantha and slowly took her other arm. "We can talk about this."

"You keep your hands off her." Taos pulled her behind him. "Talk is over. Disappear!" Rage oozed from him as his brothers stood perfectly still.

They stared at him like he was a mad man. The same way people in town did. She cooked this up to go against him and in less than two days he had already lost the battle with his own family. He stalked down the hall and up the stairs, Samantha in tow.

"Gee, Pa, am I being sent to my room?" she squealed.

He didn't find her sarcasm one bit funny. "Yes. And you're going to stay there until I figure out what to do with you." He stopped in front of the door to her room and grabbed both of her upper arms. He brought her face within inches of his.

"Well, Cinnamon had a few suggestions of what you could do with me." She pressed her palm on his chest and moved toward him with a seductive smile.

Taos just stared. He thought, no dreamed, about her looking at him with that smile all day. Now, it scared him to death. If she asked him for anything right now she just might get it. Samantha rubbed her hand across his shirt. The movement snapped Taos out of his stupor. He shoved her into the room.

The door slammed shut and the lock clicked. His footsteps echoed down the stairs.

Samantha breathed a sigh of relief, then giggled to herself. Maybe she had overdone it a little, but he certainly seemed convinced. There was no way he'd let anyone near her now. *Mission accomplished.*

She tried the adjoining door. It opened and she moved silently through Taos's room. The large glass knob on his door to the hallway turned slowly. Unlocked. He was so mad he never even thought about it. Well, she certainly had given him a thing or two to think about.

She returned to her room and slumped against her side of the door, emotionally drained and exhausted. It had been a long, eventful day. The last ray of light disappeared from the window as she slipped out of her dress.

The shirt of Taos's she had worn last night still hung inside the armoire. She passed up the new white nightgown and robe she'd purchased and instead slipped the cotton shirt on again. It was soft and comforting. She pressed her nose into the fabric. It smelled like him, and she imagined him wrapping his arms around her, holding her close.

That thought startled her a little, since she had just spent the better part of an hour purposely getting him as angry as possible. It was necessary, she reasoned, and it had been exciting in a way. Even while he was yelling at her, the intensity of his gaze made that strange tingle rumble across her skin. She was a little sorry he wasn't still here screaming at her. What if he was? What then?

The adjoining door to his room squeaked open as she poked her head in once again. He was still downstairs. She sat on the edge of his bed in the quiet as the darkness grew and tried to sort out her tumbling emotions. Her hand smoothed across his pillow and the image of his head lying here in this exact spot gave her the oddest sensation, as if she were made of warm honey.

Lady, if you were the only woman in a thousand miles I would never . . .

The haunting coldness of his words reverberated in her mind and made Samantha shiver. Cinnamon said he would pretty much take anybody. *Am I really that bad?* She had been told she was pretty. Maybe there was a difference in what was pretty and what he wanted. What about the way he reacted when she touched his shoulder? It had been the same when she put her hand on his chest. He liked it; she knew he did. But then a strange expression came across his face.

At first she thought it was fear, but it was ridiculous a man—especially one of his size—would be afraid of her. No, he just wasn't used to anyone touching him. He must have been surprised, that's all. Who could blame him? She had been nothing less than a shrew to him since she arrived. Well, he would be more surprised tomorrow. Not only would this house be scrubbed to bare wood, but now that he believed Samantha's threat and insisted she stay, she could relax and be herself.

Those thoughts sapped the last of her strength and she laid her head on his pillow and breathed him in.

Yours Again

Chapter 11

Taos watched the amber liquid swirl in the bottom of his glass. The leather of his chair squeaked as he propped his boots up on the desk. The alcohol took a little of the edge off, but not much. The house was quiet as most everyone had called it a night.

He heard soft footsteps upstairs that could only be hers. They were like two combatants plotting their next move. *What the hell am I going to do with her?*

Samantha was serious about her intentions, no question. He stared out the window as the last purple glow disappeared over the horizon. She was out of harm's way temporarily, but he couldn't keep her locked up.

Well, maybe he could. The frustration made him want to believe it. He ran his fingers through his hair. It wouldn't work. Just one more battle he would lose. Next thing would be a newspaper ad for a husband or some other such nonsense. Taos envisioned a long line of men with hats in hand stretched clear around the barn, and him the guard dog. He tossed back the last of his drink.

How was it that he sat in this same chair two days ago a different man? Successful rancher, good father. In complete control over his life and those around him. Now he was on a runaway train screaming at a deaf conductor. She was good and deaf, too.

She was the most headstrong, stubborn woman—no, make that *person*—he had ever met. Even a logical argument "didn't count." How could it not count? Logic and reason made the world go 'round. For everyone but her.

Didn't even make the list of decent lovers. How could they tell her that? Wasn't there a code of silence or something with whores? Some kind of confidentiality thing like with lawyers and preachers? He knew he wasn't a bad lover, it's just that it's different with women like that. It's not worth the effort to please someone who's being paid. They probably didn't explain the difference, if they even knew the difference.

She actually went to Miss Sadie's. He couldn't even imagine her in that place. She had more brass than most men and certainly more than any woman he'd ever met. Samantha was full of surprises, but then she had always been. Memories of a skinny little girl floated through his mind. She was all knees and elbows then, and she had attracted trouble like a flame attracts moths. That part hadn't changed.

Come to think of it, she had the ability to cause trouble from the time she was about four. She and Darren were usually in it together, though. The tobacco incident was a prime example. A slow smile crossed his face. He pictured a blond-haired little girl with the brown juice dribbling down the front of her dress. Darren said she told him that real men spit tobacco and they decided to learn together. Darren swallowed most of his and was sick as a dog. Not her though. She learned and could spit nearly as far as he could. Her father, Sam, had threatened to drag Sammy to the woodshed many times, but he never did. Maybe he should have.

Taos poured another drink and sat back, staring out the small window into the darkness. He had watched the train pull away, taking her to Boston nine years ago. The memory still haunted his dreams sometimes. She waved from the window, but her eyes held the deepest sadness he had ever seen. She was the closest thing to a sister he ever had, and it hurt like hell to see her suffer like that. He wanted to run after the train, to stop her from going, but he couldn't. Jake and Mattie had decided New Mexico Territory was no place for a young girl to be, and just like that Samantha was on that train to Boston. Mattie had obviously taken care of her better than a bunch of cowboys ever could.

If only he'd recognized her right off, then things would be different. He would never have touched her lips or caressed her soft flesh. Now that he had, there was no escape from the desire to touch her again. Knowing she was upstairs just a few steps away from his room, his bed, drew his imagination like a magnet.

The sultry invitation she'd presented this evening almost broke down any defenses he had. Her touch lit a torch in his chest, and those sparkling green eyes made promises that it seemed she was fully ready to keep. The scent of flowers was so heavy he could almost taste it. He shook his head. His mind teased and tormented, not caring if he was awake or asleep, sober or drunk. It was a cruel trick that he had no power over.

Charlie appeared at the door. "Is it safe for me in here?"

"I haven't decided," Taos frowned.

Charlie's face broke into a wide grin, "Good." He shrugged at Taos's reproach and slouched into the chair in front of the desk. "Ain't like you to be in the firewater."

Taos took another sip. "She brings out the worst in me."

"I'd say it goes both ways."

"I have to talk some sense into her."

"I remember you trying to talk sense into Sharisse. That was a disaster. What makes you think you can get anywhere with Sammy?"

Taos remembered, too. He'd failed miserably with Tommy's mother. Every conversation had ended in an argument, most of the time over nothing. The last argument, though, that one had cost him more than he could have ever imagined at the time.

With Samantha, he would just have to find the right words and practice his speech. She would come around. "It has to work. It's for her own good."

Charlie's expression conveyed his skepticism. "Hers, or yours?"

"What's that supposed to mean?"

"That maybe you're thinking about her."

Taos grunted.

"Thinking about her . . . and you?"

Taos ignored the comment. "She's dead set on getting her hands on that ranch."

"No, she's not."

"What do you mean she's not?" Taos perked up.

"She told me. On the way to town. She doesn't want anything. She just wants to stay."

"She's lying. She knew you would tell me."

"She has money."

"Then why did she come all the way out here?" Taos asked himself as much as Charlie. If she didn't want the land, and she didn't want the money, then what? He thought for a minute. The answer hit him suddenly like a rock breaking a window. "A man."

"A what?" Charlie laughed. "I think that's the whiskey talking."

"No, it makes perfect sense."

"How do ya figure?"

"She's not planning to go back to Boston." It was such a simple answer, he had never even considered it.

"She can't. That guy, John Larson, Lawton—"

"Lawson?"

"Yeah. He's after her. She's in danger."

"She *said* she was in danger. If she were really in danger, Mattie could have fired him and called the law immediately. There was no need to send her away." Taos leaned forward. "She's damn near a spinster at this point and she has to know the clock is ticking. What if she just ran off and Mattie has no idea where she is?"

"Why would she have to come here to get a man?" Charlie's tone reflected his disbelief. "Don't you think she had lots better choices in Boston?"

"She knew she had to have a husband to get her inheritance and that's what she's here for, she's trying to get herself married . . . to me."

Charlie howled with laughter, slapping his hat on his knee. "You have lost your mind!"

"It's the first sense I've been able to make of this whole mess." Taos voiced his confidence.

"You can't believe what you're saying."

"Yep. I do." Taos got up and paced behind the desk. "She wouldn't be able to get her hands on the ranch without a husband, right?"

"Right."

"Then she wouldn't be able to run it without help, right?"

"Right."

"She said all she wants is to stay here with us for a while and then go back to Boston, right?

"Right."

"Then don't you see, if she tricks me into marrying her, she gets the whole ball of wax."

"Which is?"

"A husband to take her off the spinster list, her inheritance, plus part of this place, and a bunch of men to run the whole thing and send her money the rest of her life. It's a perfect plan."

"Far-fetched is what it is. She isn't that kind of woman, and you know it. Why would she think you would ever fall for that?"

"Cause it worked on me once before."

"She didn't know about what happened with Sharisse until I told her."

"So *she said*. There's one way to find out." Taos rummaged through the drawers of the desk. He found the ink and a piece of paper.

"What are you doing?"

"Letter to Mattie." Taos looked at the pile on the desk. Extending his arm, he shoved the mess to one side. An avalanche of paper slid to the floor. He ignored it and tapped the pen on the table, thinking of what to say.

"But Sammy said we can't contact Mattie or Lawson will know where to find her."

"*She said* he was after her, and *she said* we can't contact Mattie, which means we have no way to verify her story at all." He dipped the pen in ink. "Dear Mattie." He spoke quietly as his pen scratched across the paper.

"You have lost your mind. What if Lawson shows up?"

"There is no Lawson, never was—and even if there might be, Mattie will confirm it for us."

He folded the page and searched for an envelope. He banged the drawers and searched part of the pile remaining on the desk. He finally sat back in frustration and tapped the edge of the letter against his knee.

"What?"

"No envelope. I'll have to buy one in town before I send it." He frowned. If he sent it tomorrow, it would take an easy week or two to get there, another week or two at least to get any reply. Three, maybe four weeks, minimum. Too long. He wouldn't last another few days the way things were going. In two weeks he would be a stumbling drunk or a shotgun groom. "A telegram."

"A what?"

"A telegram. We'd know in just a few days."

"Perfect." Charlie said sarcastically and walked to the door.

"You're not going to say anything about this?" Taos warned.

Charlie feigned innocence. "Me? Why would I want to keep you from making a complete jackass out of yourself?"

"Not a word to anyone."

"I won't have to say nothin'. By the time the door of the telegraph office hits your butt everyone in town will know." Charlie disappeared.

Taos shoved the letter in his shirt pocket. Charlie had a point. Everyone knew everyone's business in River City. Fine. He'd send the letter and wait. He could always ask Mattie to reply by telegram. He pulled out another piece of paper and revised his letter, tossing the first one under some papers. Either Samantha was telling the truth, or she wasn't. If she was lying, they would all know in a few weeks. Then she would leave. His mind refused to dwell too long on that possibility. She needed to leave. He needed her to leave—for his own sanity, if nothing else.

What about Tommy? She had been here such a short time, and he already thought she hung the moon. How did she do that? Of course Taos was a grown man and couldn't stop thinking about her either, but for very different reasons. Tommy was only seven. He was defenseless and she'd already taught him to swim, which made the bond even stronger.

The magic of seven. Such a simple thing to convince a boy that he has the power to do anything he sets his mind too. He wished he'd been there watching her teaching his son to swim for the first time. No doubt Tommy needed a mother. He wasn't much older than Tommy when his mother died. He didn't remember much about her except that she left a very large hole in his life that never went away. Tommy didn't know the difference. Or did he? He was already a changed boy, and he followed Samantha around like a shadow.

What I need is some magic of thirty, and whiskey ain't it. So what was? His mind drifted back to her soft body and warm lips. How her eyes lit up and flashed when she was mad. He stared at the liquor bottle. She made a sober man drunk in a hurry.

He had to admit it was a little incredible to believe that she was after him for a husband. Sharisse made it clear that he was no prize. Samantha would find out soon enough. If she couldn't get him, she just might try Charlie or Darren. He didn't think he could stand to see any man touch her, even a brother. He would just have to manage until he figured out what to do.

Taos poured another glass and thought about what Charlie had said. What if she really just needed his protection like she said? He quickly pushed that idea aside. It couldn't be that simple or that easy; life just wasn't like that. He could feel the warning bells sounding in his head. If he allowed his resolve to crack even the slightest bit, he'd never be able to let her go again. He didn't want to even contemplate what that might mean.

No, she was the bad guy here, not him, no matter what the rest of his family thought. He was also protecting them in the long run. They just didn't realize it right now.

Taos analyzed the situation from every angle, mentally trying different scenarios and what-ifs. The whiskey slowly disappeared as the moon rose. He usually didn't drink much, and the alcohol went straight to his head. Taos shook the growing cobwebs away and climbed the stairs.

Things will look different in the morning.

His room was dark and he didn't bother to light the lamp. He quickly shed his shirt and lay on top of the bed, sleep instantly claiming him. Sometime during the night he dreamed of her snuggled close to him. The scent of flowers drifted though his dreams.

A few hours later as dawn tinged the sky, Taos struggled to consciousness. His mind throbbed with the reminder of last night's detour through a bottle. The dream he'd had was still with him, and he refused to open his eyes. The feel of a slim thigh crossed his knee, and he realized this was no dream. Taos strained his eyes downward to see the top of a blonde head.

Samantha was curled up next to him, her head resting on his shoulder. His body quickly leapt to full alert as she moved softly against him in her sleep. When did she crawl into bed with him? *This is going to be harder than I thought.* His body was way ahead on that one. He hesitated for a moment, then curled his arm around her. Samantha sighed softly and snuggled deeper into his chest.

Taos felt like a drowning man with boots full of water. He should wake her up and throw her out for playing this little game with him. He should, and he would . . . later. Her hand moved across his chest as every hair on his body strained toward her.

Please, God, just let me drown.

He tried to bring back all the terrible things she'd said to him, to rouse his anger and cool his pounding pulse. But it wasn't working. At all. He placed a soft kiss on Samantha's head and rested his hand on her waist. Her warm curves beckoned him. It was irresistible torture. He slid his hand up her side slowly, remembering those warm curves. Samantha's eyes fluttered open and met his.

"Hello, Sunshine," he whispered

Samantha tried to pull away, but he tightened his grip. The realization of where she was dawned instantly, and she seemed mortified to be half-naked in his bed. The shirt twisted around her waist and barely covered her hip.

She summoned a shred of composure. "I need to get up, please."

"If you really wanted to get up, you wouldn't have crawled into my bed in the first place."

"I didn't crawl into your bed. I just fell asleep after you locked me in my room!"

"This isn't your room."

His mouth came down on hers just as she opened it to argue. Her soft lips didn't struggle. They yielded and the temptation was too much. Taos breathed her in, tasted her, and she tasted back. His hand slid down to her knee and up her thigh. He felt soft skin quiver under his touch as his hands roamed freely. Rolling her onto her back, Taos covered half her body with his.

She moaned into his mouth and the pleasure made the blood pound in his ears. He deepened his kiss, dominating her and taking as much as he was giving. He pulled one of her knees up and ran his hand along the curve of her hip past her waist.

The door clicked open as a rooster crowed in the distance, and a small head poked into Taos's room. Tommy frowned at the two people in the large bed.

"Are y'all coming to breakfast?"

Taos and Samantha jumped off the bed as if it had just caught fire. Taos glanced at Samantha then at him. A few more minutes and they wouldn't have had enough clothes on to accomplish that maneuver.

Tommy looked from one to the other.

Taos cleared his throat, "We, ah, we're on our way."

"No you weren't. You were squishing her."

"We were just talking." Samantha took Tommy's arm and led him to the door.

"No you weren't, he had his mouth . . ."

"Tommy! We'll be right down." Taos's voice demanded obedience.

The door closed and Samantha looked at Taos. They were both shaken and not just by the boy's unexpected entrance. She ducked her head and started toward the adjoining door. He grabbed her arm as she tried to brush past.

She whispered. "We'll talk about this later."

"I don't think we need to do any more *talking*. This is dangerous with both of us here, together." He cleared his throat, trying to get his thoughts together. "This is going to get out of hand. What we need are some rules."

"Rules?"

"Yes, like no crawling into my bed." Taos's voice wavered a bit. He already hated that rule. Waking up with her in his bed was the best thing that had happened to him in years.

"Ohhhh, those kind of rules." A smile played at the corner of Samantha's mouth. "Like no squishing before breakfast?"

He smiled in spite of himself. "Yeah, like no squishing."

"Well," she whispered, "that's probably a good rule, especially without the door locked. Any others?"

"We should just give each other some distance."

"I'll consider it, but you know I don't take instruction very well." She said. "You have the same problem, you know."

"Me? I wasn't the one who came in and crawled in someone else's bed."

"And I wasn't the one doing the squishing." She left him staring after her.

Samantha was the last one to arrive in the kitchen.

Darren and Tommy munched leftover cornbread at the table while Taos sipped his coffee. Charlie was nowhere in sight. Samantha quickly set about starting breakfast.

She glanced over at Taos. He held her gaze as a slow, lazy smile crossed his lips. "Mornin', Sammy."

"Morning, Taos." Her voice gave nothing away.

"You're up a little late, Sammy." Darren looked her over from head to toe. "Why is your face so red?"

"We were having a little chat." Taos winked at her and was rewarded with a hint of color that rose to her cheeks.

"What kind of chat?"

"Never mind, Darren," they both said.

The house seemed to get smaller by the minute.

Yours Again

Chapter 12

Charlie had left early for a short stint as deputy in River City while Sheriff Blake was out of pocket in Raton. After Darren and Taos saddled up and rode out, Samantha finally got a few minutes of peace to herself as Tommy tended to a few chores. She watched him running toward the barn, his huge dog loping along beside him.

Her mind strayed back to the way she and Taos had leapt off the bed when Tommy walked in this morning. Samantha giggled to herself. At least it wasn't Charlie or Darren. This morning's *conversation* confirmed one thing in her mind. He wasn't afraid of her, he was afraid of them—together. And he did have a point. This house didn't allow for much space, especially with their rooms right beside one another. But rules? Really! Next thing you knew he would be drawing a line down the center of the house. Of course, that would only last until he realized the kitchen was on her side.

The men had talked this morning about branding the spring calves and warned her the next few days would be long, especially without Charlie around to help. Perhaps it wouldn't be all that hard to comply with Taos's suggestion. She certainly had no desire to give Tommy any more unwitting lessons on the birds and the bees, and she'd gotten what she wanted: a place to hide, at least for now.

As it turned out, Samantha found plenty to occupy her time. The house cleaning turned into a multi-day project. She had no idea so much filth could accumulate in one place. Tommy was a real help, lugging water and keeping her company. Darren and Taos worked hard to finish the branding, coming in at dusk each day bone tired. They fell into bed only to rise before dawn the next day.

Taos stuck to his part of the bargain, though Samantha felt his gaze follow her constantly. It seemed whatever room she was in, he was in. She talked to him, or at him, most of the time. He didn't say much, just watched.

Darren, on the other hand, talked her leg off. It was as if he hadn't had a friend since she left, and she honestly wondered if he hadn't. Only a year apart, they had shared a childhood. Of all the Williams brothers he was truly the most like a real brother to her. She knew he felt the same about her and would do anything for her. She so wanted him to be happy.

Most evenings Samantha and Darren talked and laughed, catching up on the last nine years. Taos kept his silence. He also continued to keep his distance, and so did she. But at night she heard him tossing and turning, chasing sleep and never catching it. She had the same problem.

Tonight was no different. Samantha lay in bed and stared at the ceiling. It had been more than a week since she had felt Taos's touch, and her body almost ached for it. She heard the clock downstairs strike one in the morning. A low rumble of thunder echoed in the distance. Rain. She longed for a cool breeze and the sweet smell of moisture in the air. She flipped the covers back and went to the window. Pushing on the sash she tried to raise it a little, but it wouldn't budge. She banged each side with both hands and it finally moved, but only an inch.

"Need some help?" Taos reached around her and easily lifted the window.

She breathed in the leather-and-spice scent of him. He turned to go, and she reached out and touched his arm. "Thank you. I didn't mean to wake you up."

"I wasn't asleep." He looked at her and frowned. "Why are you still wearing my shirt?"

She shrugged and stared out the window. *Because it makes me feel safe*, she thought.

He raised his hand as if to touch her then let it drop to his side. He walked back to his room and closed the door without a word. Samantha let her head fall forward and thunk on the wooden window sash. How was she supposed to sleep now? She puffed up her pillow so she could see out the window and watched the storm roll toward the ranch. The lightning intensified, and thunder rattled the glass. She drifted off to sleep as the rain began softly drumming on the roof.

Suddenly she was in John's office, feeling his cold touch and vile breath. She stared into the depths of those beady eyes as his tongue flicked across her skin. Her body jerked and moaned in disgust.

Now she was riding, rain pelting her. *Have to go faster, he's following.* The man closed in as hooves pounded the wet ground. A big clap of thunder shook her to the core, and she screamed, "No!"

Samantha sat straight up in the darkness. Her breath came in short gasps and her heart pounded. The door swung open and Taos rushed to her. "What's th-"

She leaped into his arms and buried her head in his chest.

"You're okay, shhh." He comforted her, stroking her hair and holding her tight. "It's just a storm."

She shook her head, "It's not that, it's just. . ."

He didn't let her go, and she didn't want him too. After a few minutes he picked her up and carried her to his bed. He tucked her in next to him. One long arm curled around and pulled her close.

"It's okay. You're safe," he whispered, stroking her hair. Samantha fought fatigue, wanting to enjoy every touch, every whisper, but eventually a peaceful slumber overtook her.

The next morning Samantha stood on the porch as the sun licked the shadows into retreat. She watched Taos saddle his horse and prepare to leave for the day with Darren. The air was cool from the rain, and tiny insects danced in the orange light of dawn. Birds chirped, and the slight, sweet scent of honeysuckle floated on the air.

What if he could tell by looking? Her body fairly hummed with excitement now just as it had when he walked into the kitchen that morning. He had been gone when she woke, and neither one said a word about last night.

The urge to run inside, to hide these feelings, tugged at her, but the desire to stay was too strong. She picked at her fingers nervously and glanced at Taos out of the corner of her eye. There was no doubt she was heading down a dangerous road but she'd given up the idea she had any control over it. It was fun at first to toy with him, tempting him with her jokes and innuendos, but last night, lying in his arms, she had felt safe and at peace. That compassionate, caring person she remembered still existed under Taos's gruff exterior and there was no more denying the fact that she wanted more.

The muscles of Taos's back rippled under his shirt as he tossed first the blanket, then the saddle atop his horse. Her gaze slid down his torso all the way to his boots. Aunt Mattie would have called him a long tall drink of water, and Samantha was parched. The men mounted and headed out. directing the horses past the house toward the back pasture. Taos met her gaze with a slow smile. The curve of his lips sent a warm rush through Samantha, and she smiled back.

Did he think she was pretty? Last night he had held her close, which was wonderful, but he didn't even try to kiss her. He'd liked her well enough when he woke with her in his bed the first time. She rubbed her forehead with her fingers and closed her eyes. What must he think? He hadn't pushed her away, but was she any different to him than the women at Miss Sadie's? His gentle touch and soft lips could wipe her mind of any control she might have and leave her powerless to resist, not that she wanted to.

How do you ask a man what he really thinks? Do they think about things like love, or do they just grab what comes by? She could sit him down and be completely honest and just ask him flat out. He might laugh. Could she handle it if he turned her away? The conflicting emotions distracted, thrilled, and annoyed her as she set about cleaning the kitchen from top to bottom with a vengeance once again.

She practiced the different possibilities in her mind. What if he had the same thoughts and feelings she did? Would they eventually get married? Her heart fairly tripped over the thought of being his wife, of really belonging here—to him. The idea of waking up in his arms every morning was intoxicating. What if they had another little boy like Tommy, or maybe a girl with his beautiful blue eyes?

Samantha paused and frowned. She was just as bad as he thought she was! She'd tried her best to convince him she had no interest in any man, and that had been true when she got here. But now, something had shifted. She'd gone from finding new ways to irritate him to wanting to have his babies in a matter of days, which was ridiculous. She punched the pillow she was holding and then set it on the newly made bed. It wasn't like she was fourteen with some school girl crush. She was a grown woman who knew her own mind—at least she thought she did.

Taos was certainly an adult as well and all man. Her mind wondered back to the feel of his weight on her in bed. She'd wanted so much more and her imagination had worked overtime with the erotic ideas she'd learned at Miss Sadie's. If Tommy hadn't walked in things would have gone much farther. What if they had?

She stirred up another batch of cookies, rolled the dough onto the table, and cut them with an upturned glass. While they baked, she cleaned the parlor again. If this mental turmoil kept up she'd scrub right through the floor. Dust rose in clouds from the chair cushions as she whacked the fabric with a broom.

The office posed the biggest challenge. She hadn't cleaned at all in here yet, and the idea still overwhelmed her a bit. But this is where she felt his presence the most. She stood at the door and stared. Where to begin? The pile on the desk seemed the least intimidating. She stacked and sorted until the papers were in some sort of order.

Bills, cattle receipts, bank deposits, and miscellaneous correspondence. Even at first glance, it appeared to her the ranches were doing well. She looked for a ledger book in the drawers. She found one and blew the dust off it. The date of the last entry was more than a year ago.

She entered each receipt she had piled on the desk, then looked through every drawer, around and behind every piece of furniture, and through every book for other receipts. She carefully added these to her previous entries and totaled them. She frowned and totaled them again. The ranch wasn't doing well . . . It was doing very well. So why did they live like paupers? Her mind struggled for a reason. Why does he not want me to know how well things are going? There was plenty of money. Why would he lie?

He's doesn't want me to know how much my ranch is worth. She tossed out the idea. But it crept back, causing an unmistakable chill in her heart. He wants both ranches. The old Taos wouldn't have even considered keeping what wasn't his, but this man was not the same person—at least sometimes. It was like he was two different people: cold and unyielding sometimes, warm and irresistible others. Was he manipulating her?

Taos said repeatedly he didn't want her, yet he'd given up completely on getting rid of her. It had been a little too easy as he could just have plopped her on the next train to Boston. Was he just pacifying her until he figured out a way to keep her out of his business?

He didn't really want her, did he? Even now she wanted to believe he did. The attraction was just too strong for it to be one-sided, but he'd kept his distance. Even last night with her right there in his bed, he hadn't touched her or kissed her the way he did that first night. She wanted his touch, needed it so badly it was driving her insane. She couldn't go on like this; she didn't want to, and it was high time they ditched those stupid rules.

She turned her attention to the pile of correspondence. She stacked the letters and looked for a place to put them. The drawer with the ink and paper seemed the logical place. She moved everything to the front and piled the papers in the back of the drawer. A folded piece of paper fell from the stack. She unfolded it and read:

Dear Mattie,

Must send Samantha back to you. No place for her here at this time. Please advise.

Taos

Fear shook her. If John Lawson got a hold of this he'd know exactly where to find her. The letter was by itself in the drawer. Maybe he hadn't sent it. Maybe he'd changed his mind. She didn't know what to think anymore. She shoved the letter into her pocket and returned to the kitchen.

She popped another pan of cookies into the oven and slammed the door shut. She paced around the room as they baked, working herself into a frenzy of "what ifs." What if Lawson had already gotten the letter and was on his way. What if Mattie were in danger, too? Taos had no idea the kinds of problems he may have set in motion. By the time Taos and Darren stepped through the back door for dinner, she was an emotional wreck.

Taos was a little startled at the hostility he sensed. Darren didn't seem to notice, and slid into a chair, exhausted. Taos walked over to the pot of coffee and stole a quick glance toward Samantha.

"Whoa boy, it's warm out today." Darren flipped his sweaty hat into a chair.

"Kinda warm in here, too, don't you think, Sammy?" Taos asked. She looked at him as if he were a mosquito she wanted to swat.

He looked back at the floor. They hadn't tracked in any mud, so that wasn't it. He could tell she had cleaned again. Was he supposed to say something? "The kitchen looks great."

"Thank you."

Burrrr! That wasn't it either. "Um, and the cookies smell good."

"Thank you."

He looked closely at her to make sure icicles weren't hanging off her tongue. As she dished slices of ham onto plates he took a seat at the table.

She wasn't upset when they left. He had felt some kind of shift last night. It was as if she had dropped this crazy game she was playing and was just a frightened, beautiful woman who wanted his comfort. He wasn't sure what scared her so bad, but it was real and not just some lighting storm.

Taos had thought of her all day. The way she stood on the porch, surrounded by the orange glow of sunlight. She was beautiful, and it was all he could do not to jump off his horse when she smiled at him. He revisited every minute of last night a thousand times from her soft smooth skin to the way she responded to his touch as she slept.

So what had he done since then? Nothing. Absolutely nothing. He leaned back as she plopped his plate down in front of him so hard the cookies in the middle of the table jumped, and so did Darren.

Why the attitude? Taos wondered, was it because he won? He'd kept his distance and she hadn't. That had to be it. She knew he was in control now and didn't like it one bit. She was flustered and embarrassed that she responded to him the way she did. That was it. He'd always heard that there was a thin line between fighting and loving. He beamed a smile at her.

"What's so funny?" Her voice was sharp.

"Nothin'." Taos picked up his fork and took a big bite. She seemed to be more annoyed by the minute. "Where's Tommy?" he asked.

"He already ate." She reached for the cookies just as he did, and their hands touched. She jerked hers back as if she had been scalded and stared down at her plate.

"He's been tired lately. You must be putting him to work." The soft tone of his voice drew her eyes upward. She was as skittish as a new colt. This was definitely his game. He felt like a man who held a full house and she had only a pair of deuces. He grabbed the coffee pot off the stove and went around the table, filling each cup.

He leaned over and gently touched the back of her arm "You okay?"

"I'm fine." She squeaked and scooted away, her face staining red.

He and Darren talked casually about the work still ahead tomorrow as Samantha finished her meal in silence. He caught her watching him and returned her gaze with a slow smile. She blushed and he found it more and more difficult to concentrate on what Darren said. Although he wanted to completely unnerve her, he was the one getting frustrated. If he kept this up, he'd end up dragging her off to the barn for a roll in the hay—literally.

"There's a dance in town in a few weeks." Darren informed them while polishing off the last of his sandwich. "I thought Sammy might like to get out for a while."

Startled out of his thoughts, Taos glared at Darren, then at Samantha.

"That sounds nice."

She was distracted, something was definitely on her mind.

"I don't think you should be going." Taos commanded.

She ignored him. "When is it?"

Darren opened his mouth to reply, but was immediately cut off.

"No need for you to go, you won't be here long enough to get to know anyone." Taos said.

"Excuse me." Samantha laid her napkin on the table and walked out the back door.

Darren frowned at him. "Do you have to be a total ass?"

"What?" Taos held up his hands innocently.

"Some days you have all the personality of thirty g-grit sandpaper!" Darren stood. "It's a wonder you ever had a woman within t-ten feet of you!" He took the stairs to the second floor two at a time to get away from Taos.

"Damn." Taos felt less than an inch tall. Something just wasn't right with Samantha. It was like she was distant, sad. He didn't like it, not one bit. He thought he had it figured out this morning. She had responded to his touch, smiled at him like he was the best thing on earth, and now this. Somewhere between then and now something had changed, but what?

He wasn't trying to hurt her; she wasn't playing the game right. This wasn't how she was supposed to react. He was supposed to say something to make her mad, and her green eyes would flash that beautiful yellow color and she would go for his throat. She wasn't supposed to fold. This was like playing poker blindfolded.

Yours Again

Chapter 13

She had to leave. Samantha hadn't really thought about it until Darren asked her about the dance, and she had suddenly realized it didn't matter when it was; she would be in Boston by then. Either Taos sent the letter and Lawson would be here any day, or he hadn't and Mattie would soon alert her that all was well. There would be no more reason for her to be here, and she couldn't keep up the charade that she was just in it for the ranch. Either way she would be gone. She'd stalked around the house all day angry at Taos for not trusting her but the truth was she didn't trust herself.

Her feet plodded along the path and Samantha was lost in thought, not caring where they took her. As the sun sank toward the horizon, her heart felt like it had shriveled to the size of a raisin. *Be careful what you wish for*, Aunt Mattie had always said. There was certainly no doubt in her mind where she stood now. Nowhere. The letter proved he wanted to pawn her off just as fast as he could on someone else, and time was short. She closed her eyes and silently begged to see the young man she had known once. The old Taos was pretty much dead and any dreams she had to the contrary were just that: dreams.

She stopped as the fragrances wafted toward her. She was on the edge of the flower garden. The beauty of the spot had a soothing effect, and she wandered along the path until she stood in front of the tiny angel. She knelt and sat back on her feet, staring up at the red-and-white striped petals that covered the rose canes. She should be thrilled at the thought of going home, but instead it filled her with an aching sadness.

A large pink rose suddenly appeared in front of her.

"A peace offering." Taos's soft voice vibrated just above her ear.

Her hands shook as she reached for the flower.

He sat behind her, long legs to one side, leaning near enough for her to feel the warmth of his chest on her back. She felt his breath brush her neck and closed her eyes. She was so tired of talking. To him, to herself. Wondering how he felt or what he thought. She couldn't make heads or tails of her own emotions let alone his. Did she have feelings for him, or just the memory of him she'd held on to for the last nine years?

He slid an arm around her waist and drew her back against him. "People say a lot of things they don't mean sometimes."

"People?"

He didn't answer. Just the warmth of his arm circling her made her feel better than she had all day. She twirled the rose in her hand. The petals were soft and fragrant and she trailed them along her cheek. She imagined his fingers following their path. She glanced back and found him watching her intently. "What kind of rose is this?"

"It's called a cabbage rose. It's the same rose you might see in a painting by one of the Dutch masters in one of your museums in Boston."

"Boston seems a lifetime away from this place."

"You a little homesick?"

"Yes, and no." She glanced at his questioning expression. "I mean, I miss Mattie." She inhaled the sweet scent of honeysuckle that wafted on the breeze from a nearby trellis. "I don't miss the noise, or the traffic, or the people."

"You didn't have friends."

"A few, but . . ." *No one that knew her, or really understood. Not like here.* "The people there are just different, that's all."

"More civilized and citified than a bunch of cowhands, I bet."

"Yes, but that's not necessarily a good thing."

He raised his brows at her statement.

"There are so many people that only care about appearances. They try constantly to be something they are not. With the people here, what you see is what you get, warts and all."

He laughed. "There's plenty of warts."

"It is a very good thing to get back to who and what you are. To find where you belong. I think it's like a wonderful gift."

"I know what you mean," he mumbled.

Was he talking about himself, or was it a reference to her? God knows she hadn't been herself since stepping foot off that train. "How do you know so much about roses?"

"You think it's a strange hobby for a rancher?"

"A little."

"There were some books my mother had when she came here." He trailed a finger down her arm, leaving fiery warmth in its wake. "When I was a teenager, I asked my dad what she was like and he handed me these books. They were about gardening and flowers, roses in particular. He could never talk about her, so I read."

"I saw the books in your office."

He shrugged. "I've added a few here and there."

"I really didn't remember much about my mother either, as far as what kind of person she really was. I just remember her always being there for me. I don't know what she worried about, or what dreams she had growing up." She stared into the distance. "Or even if she liked roses."

"I remember you mother. Claire was beautiful." He thought a minute. "Your dad loved her very much."

"I remember that part. He used to surprise her with all kinds of little gifts, and me too."

"You look just like her you know." He reached up and ran his thumb along her chin.

Samantha curled shaking fingers around his wrist and leaned her cheek into his palm. Her heart pounded as the blood rushed through her ears with a deafening roar.

"Do you miss her?" His voice was a soft whisper.

"Do you miss yours?" She stared up into his eyes, then her gaze slid to his lips. The feeling that welled within her was so intense she could hardly breathe. She felt so close to him, she didn't want it to end. She wanted to be closer, much closer. He leaned toward her and kissed her warmly, tenderly.

Her lips fairly sizzled. The heat radiated trough her body sending tremors all the way to her toes. His arms closed around her and urged her closer. She needed no encouragement. Her body craved the warmth of his and drifted toward him like a boat on a powerful tide. Taos groaned and deepened his kiss as his hands slid down her back to her waist and back up to her hair.

Samantha was beyond thinking about tomorrow or any of the what ifs. She clung to this man and willed time to stop.

After a few minutes Taos pulled away and smiled at her, allowing her to catch her breath.

Samantha was more than a little dazed. Wow! She turned and leaned her back against his chest. He hesitated, then circled her with his arms, his breath hovering above her right ear. Affection seemed such an easy thing for most people to give, yet so difficult for him. It made her crave it all the more.

Samantha gazed at roses. "Tommy told me you planted this garden when he was little."

She felt his nod.

"Most of it I planted before he was born. I have added a few things since then, though."

An unmistakable coldness crept into his tone. Something unpleasant happened here, but what? Curiosity urged her on. "Why did you plant it at all?"

He paused, his voice quiet. "When I married, things weren't perfect, but I thought . . ." He shrugged. "I don't know what I thought, but I tried to make things better."

Samantha stared at the little angel.

"I planted this garden because my wife complained about being out on a dusty ranch with nothing beautiful around."

"Did she like it?"

He grunted and shook his head. "She liked things that cost a lot of money. It was me she didn't care for. She never set foot out here."

"What a waste." On both counts. Samantha sighed. Secretly she was glad. The thought of Taos sharing this place with his wife was extremely distasteful. This was probably the only place on the ranch that was untouched by the shadow of Sharisse's memory. How could a woman cause so much damage? "Charlie told me she wasn't very nice."

"I'll bet." Taos laughed. "Sharisse and Charlie did not hit it off at all."

"Everyone likes Charlie."

"Not her. I think he was the only one who could see her for what she was, and she knew it." Taos paused. "He tried to tell me. They all tried to tell me. But I just wouldn't listen."

"Does Tommy ever ask you about her?"

"No. Why, has he said something to you?"

"No. Not yet."

He was silent, as if deep in thought.

"He'll want to know some day," Samantha said.

"Yeah, I just don't know what I'm going to tell him."

"How about the truth?"

Taos shook his head. "You mean that she hardly ever touched him? Flat out refused to get up and tend him when he cried at night? Or how about that the day she left? She never even looked at him, let alone held him or said goodbye."

"Surely it wasn't that bad, Taos."

He squeezed her arms slightly. "It was."

The white roses with red stripes bloomed vigorously. "What kind of roses are these?" She hoped he'd volunteer information on the little statue underneath so she wouldn't feel as if she were prying.

He looked up. "These are special. They're a type of wild rose."

"Why are they special?"

"It's an apothecary rose, first cultivated by the Persians and Egyptians for their perfume and medicinal value." He smiled. "There's a legend that goes with them."

"What is it?" she asked and glanced back at him. Taos's eyes sparkled as he talked, and she felt his mood lift.

"Once upon a time," he used his best storyteller voice, "an ancient warrior fell in love with a beautiful young maid. While he was away fighting an important battle, she fell ill and died."
"Oh, how sad."

"The warrior returned and was heartbroken, afraid that she would be forgotten. So he decided to build a garden as a memorial to her. He spent years traveling the world in search of a flower that was as beautiful as she had been."

The sound of his voice held her spell bound. A vision floated through her mind of him sitting on the edge of a bed a few years from now, telling this same story to a little blonde-haired girl.

He paused as if checking that she was listening.

And?" she said impatiently.

"He eventually found it: a pure white rose with a yellow center that had an incredible fragrance. He brought the rose home and grew a large garden filled with them."

"So why do they have red stripes on the petals?"

"I was just getting to that part." He purposely teased her curiosity. "Each year the roses bloomed for only a few weeks, and the warrior spent the entire time stroking the petals and remembering his lost love. The thorns pricked his fingers but he never stopped. Every year, each and every petal became striped with red from his blood. When the man died, the roses continued to bloom with the red stripes along the white petals."

He whispered in her ear, "It is said that any woman who wears the fragrance of these roses will never be forgotten."

"They smell wonderful." Samantha reached out to pick one, but his hand immediately shot out and grasped her wrist.

"These belong here, don't touch them." He cleared his throat, clearly embarrassed at his emotion.

Samantha's hand dropped to her side. She had to know. "Why is the angel here?"

He paused a moment, "I suppose you heard rumors of what happened with Sharisse from the people in town."

"Yes, but I think there's more to it than what I heard." She twisted around to face him.

"I'm sure it gets worse with every telling." Bitterness edged his words. "We had an argument. I don't even remember what it was about now. She got hysterical and ran up the stairs. She tripped and fell. By the time the doctor got here, it was too late. She lost the baby she was carrying."

His face turned to stone and the vein on his forehead bulged. "Sharisse blamed me and spread the word all over town that I had beat her and killed the baby."

She touched his arm. "Not everyone believes that."

He gave her a grateful smile and kissed her cheek. "It doesn't matter anymore." He stretched out his arm and gently touched the angel. "She wanted to pretend the child never existed. Didn't even want to have a marker as a reminder. It is a terrible thing to not have even a marker to acknowledge your existence."

A tear slid down Samantha's face as he continued.

"It was a little girl. I buried her here."

Several moments passed as she tried to regain her voice. "What was her name?"

His expression hinted at a deep and unhealed wound. "Sharisse didn't name her."

"I'm sorry, I didn't—"

"But I did."

He twisted the angel and the statue separated from the base. Leaning over, she could just make out the inscription on the tiny stone underneath:

Beloved daughter

Samantha Rose Williams

1880

Yours Again

Chapter 14

Samantha sat on the edge of her bed in the dark listening to Taos move around his room. She waited, watching the light that peeked from under the bottom of the door. Taos had become a complete enigma to her this evening. The man she'd met in the rose garden hardly bore any resemblance to the hard, unyielding persona he's been to this point. She was touched to the core that he'd named his daughter after her, but what did it mean? Did he still see her as that young gangly girl that was nothing but trouble? Or did he see her as she was, a woman ready to be loved?

The jumble of emotions she had toward him were rushing forward and she had no idea how to slow them down. This man had angered her, frustrated her, and excited her more than she believed possible! But most of all he'd made her feel alive. She'd had lots of opportunity to find someone to love in Boston, but hadn't even come close. It finally dawned on her why. She was already in love with Taos—or at least the idea of him. She'd carried him around as her ideal for so many years, no one could ever compare, and she knew that even if she returned to Boston without really experiencing all this situation had to offer, that would still be the case. Maybe she just wasn't meant to find the kind of love her mother knew with a man who loved her back, but she wasn't gone yet.

This might be one of the last nights she would be this close to him, or have the chance to find out what it was like for him to really love her. Even if it was only physical for Taos, she didn't care anymore. She wanted to feel his muscles ripple and heart pound as he loved her and held her in his arms. She would rather go back to Boston with that one experience—no matter how short lived—than settle for a lifetime of regret.

The light in Taos's room finally disappeared. She waited for a few minutes until all was quiet. It was time. Now or never. Samantha took a deep breath and slipped through the door. Carefully she tiptoed to the bedside—she could tell he was still awake. She quickly unbuttoned the shirt and let it drop to the floor.

"Hey, what are yo-"

Samantha clamped a hand over his mouth and flipped back the blanket. She climbed on top of him and straddled his hips, one knee on each side.

He didn't move. Well most of him didn't. She felt his erection spring to life. For a moment she sat there feeling strangely powerful. She leaned forward, allowing her hair to fall across his face, then slowly removed her hand, replacing it with her lips.

She trailed kisses down his cheek to his neck and felt his body tense. Slowly his hands slid up over her backside and around to her breasts. He tweaked and massaged gently. She arched her back and moaned, rocking her hips against his. Taos pulled her close to his chest, kissing her long and hard. The power of his embrace thrilled Samantha. This is what she'd dreamed of, what she wanted. Damn the consequences.

She slid a hand down his chest and into his underwear clasping his throbbing erection just as Cinnamon had instructed. She felt a jolt ripple through his abdomen and reveled in the confidence this knowledge now gave her.

He lifted her slightly and slid a finger into her warmth, massaging with a gentle rhythm. Samantha's thighs tightened and she gave in to the sensation. She focused as much as possible, trying to match his strokes with her hand. He leaned her forward and danced his tongue across her nipple, creating an electric pulse that burned all the way down her body to her very core. She moved on his hand wanting more. She whispered, "Harder, deeper."

With a guttural growl he flipped her over, shedding his underwear, and settled between her legs. Her body felt as if it had been waiting an eternity for this and she urged him into her. He was larger than she thought he would be and she felt a slight burning sensation, which quickly dissolved into pleasure.

Slowly, then with more urgency, they rocked together in unison as he drove into her, their bodies covered with a slick sheen as they strained for ultimate release. Faster and faster, toward the edge of some unknown cliff. Samantha's groin pulsed in spasm as the tingling spread down her limbs, firing into the tips of her fingers. Taos gave one last stroke and released, collapsing onto her.

She smiled to herself, reveling in the weight of his body as he caught his breath. After a few minutes he rolled to her side, bringing her with him. She slid a palm across his chest and he covered her hand with his. She felt his heart pound just as it had in her dreams. This was wonderful. *He* was wonderful, and even if this was their only night together she wasn't going to waste it.

Samantha rubbed a hand across his chest, feeling it tighten at her touch. He almost growled and hugged her to him again, kissing her deeply. The fuse between them lit once again and Samantha was carried away again by his touch. They kissed, touched and loved the night away in each other's arms, and Samantha knew she would never regret this night as long as she lived.

Taos lay awake long after Samantha had finally drifted off to sleep. *What in the hell was that?* She hadn't said a word after they made love, or before, and the few words during were more direction, not discussion. He heard her sneak into his room and thought about telling her to get back in her own bed until that shirt of his hit the floor. The moonlight on her naked body was irresistible, and there was no way he could have told her no at that point even if he wanted to. Which he didn't.

He enjoyed every single second of loving her tonight, but now he wasn't all that sure he wanted to deal with the outcome. He'd done everything in his power to stay away from her since that first night, and truth be told he had about reached his limit in the rose garden. It was all he could do to hold her without taking advantage, and he swore if she crawled into his bed again he wasn't holding back. And he didn't. Not the first time, or second or third. He'd have never guessed she would be such a natural at loving, and now that he knew there was no way he was keeping his hands off her. But why now? Why tonight?

Samantha hadn't been herself all day, and most of her anger seemed to be directed at him, until the lights went out. He had told her more than he'd ever told anyone about Sharisse. Did she just feel sorry for him? Her hair spilled across his chest and Taos pulled the blanket a little higher to cover her bare shoulder. Samantha snuggled into his chest perfectly as if she belonged there, and it felt like she did.

He'd wondered what it would be like to make love to her since he'd tied her up and held her close on the ride home in the rain, but his imagination didn't hold a candle to reality. It had been a very long time since he'd felt any kind of emotion attached to sex and it was powerful. Maybe too powerful.

He hadn't made her any promises and she hadn't acted like she expected any. The idea that she was tricking him into marriage or whatever seemed ridiculous now. She'd wanted this, he could tell, and she'd given herself body and soul tonight. No demands, no expectations. He loved every second, but it worried him. Was she really saying goodbye?

The only thing he could do now was follow her lead. She could come to him at any time, and he hoped this wouldn't be the last time but if it was, he'd have to be happy with that.

Taos sighed. Morning would come soon enough. For now he wasn't missing a minute of her in his arms.

Yours Again

Chapter 15

The next week passed in relative calm. Samantha and Taos hadn't talked about that night, though she could tell he wanted some kind of explanation. She wasn't about to tell him she didn't have one, even though it was the truth.

Sometimes he would pass her in the hall and every hair on her body would lean toward him. He was so close, yet stayed just out of reach. He seemed to go out of his way not to touch her, and it was sending her into a fevered wanting she'd never experienced. She went to sleep each night thinking of the events of the day, then dreaming of his soft lips and warm touch. She thought that night would get him out of her system and allow her to look forward to going home. But just the opposite had happened. She wanted to stay here with him so badly it ached.

She'd awakened this morning and sat in her bed for almost an hour before the sun came up. She wondered what he thought of that night. He hadn't avoided her, in fact quite the opposite;

he seemed to be around the house quite a bit more. He didn't say much, but he listened to her talk about Tommy or his brothers or even the weather. Maybe he was waiting on her to give him some kind of signal.

The letter crossed her mind for the thousandth time as she dressed. The nagging doubt refused to fade, and not knowing for sure left her in limbo expecting John Lawson to jump out of the shadows any minute. The time had come to clear the air.

She paced the parlor most of the day and now sat in a large leather chair. Every possible scenario played through her mind. She practiced her speech until she knew she had the perfect words. Not overly confrontational, just questioning. He might be able to offer a good explanation. It was a glimmer of hope and she clung to it. If the conversation went well, who knew what would happen? Maybe this would break down whatever barrier still stood between them.

Footsteps thundered through the house, jolting her upright. Samantha's heart froze in mid-flip as Taos appeared in the doorway. In two strides, a giant tower of anger was within a foot of her. Her thoughts had focused on him most of the afternoon, but she never pictured their meeting starting like this. Air blew from his nostrils like steam and the vein on his forehead vibrated a warning. He gritted his teeth; his lips curled into a snarl.

"I just want to know why." Eyes of blue ice glittered.

She tried to gather her wits, but they insisted on behaving like naughty children playing hide and seek. The practiced speech fled, leaving her mind grasping for a thought, any thought. A little tremor tickled up her back as she searched for a reason that might explain his anger. Did he know she had found the letter? Had he finally seen the ledger? Did he know she was aware of his deception? Her only option appeared to be to play stupid and hope she could regain some clarity of thought while he explained.

"Why what?" She stepped back.

"You knew what they meant, and you just had to destroy them." He tore his gaze from hers in disgust and stared at the wall, his cheek twitching. "I want you out." He pointed a finger at her. "I want you out now." He turned and took the stairs three at a time.

Samantha gathered her skirts and hurried after him. She rounded the doorway of her room just as he threw open the doors of the armoire. He grabbed fistfuls of her clothing and flung them onto the bed. "What are you doing?"

To think she was going to give him the benefit of the doubt! He was the one who wrote the letter, doubted her and her motives. How could he be so angry that she'd found it? She should be the one angry with him.

He continued to open drawers and add to the pile.

She walked directly in front of him. "I said," her voice was a shrill siren, "*what* are you doing?" She grabbed a lacy garment from his hand.

"Helping you pack." He hissed.

"I'm not leaving."

"Yes you are."

"No, I'm not."

He turned a cold smile on her. "I'd say that in this case, *lady*, size matters and yes, you are leaving." His long arm reached around her again. "Right now."

Samantha's skin turned cold, then flashed hot as her anger built. "What did I supposedly do?" She stepped out of the way as he cleared out one drawer after another, tossing the items behind him in the general direction of the bed.

He ignored her and looked around the room for something to put the mountain of clothes into.

A smile played at the corner of her mouth as he stalked around the room, frustrated.

"I didn't bring a suitcase, you know."

"Then I guess we only have one option." He whirled and tugged on the window sash. It groaned, then slammed open with a loud bang, jarring the glass. She watched, stunned, as he hefted two arms full of garments and tossed them out the window. She stared at his heaving chest as a wayward thought crossed her mind, and she immediately acted on it.

He flinched with pain and stopped in his tracks. "Let go!"

She held on tenaciously to the small tuft of chest hair that poked out of the neck of his shirt.

"Not until you sit down and tell me what the problem is." The calm of her voice amazed her, given the situation. She had hold of Goliath by a few chest hairs and she wasn't about to let go. It certainly seemed to be working better than a sling shot at the moment.

The power gave her a heady feeling and she tugged a little harder. "Now, what is the problem?"

He leaned his face toward hers. "The roses."

"What roses?"

"In the kitchen." He spat the words with all the venom of a rattlesnake.

"I don't know anything about any roses." She emphasized each word.

"I'll just bet you d- Ow!" He grabbed for her wrist as she gave the hairs a final yank. She turned and ran out the door.

The sunlight streamed in through the back door and spilled across the kitchen table. A large pitcher filled with roses sat in the center of the table. She caught her breath as she noticed several stems of the white roses had red stripes. Her jaw dropped. She turned back toward him just as the pain flashing across his face changed to anger.

Hot tears sprang to her eyes, and she stilled her trembling lips with the tips of her fingers. "Taos, I didn't—"

He turned away from her as a small body slammed into his thighs.

"'scuse me." Tommy scooted around Taos and ran to Samantha. "Did ya like 'em?" His face was beaming with a smile that went from ear to ear.

"You did this?" She knelt down in front of the boy.

"Yeah, you said that they was your favorite flowers and all. So I brought some in for you." He frowned at her teary expression. "You like 'em, don't you?"

She clasped his hand and smiled. "Oh, I love them. Thank you." She kissed his cheek and he ducked his head and grinned.

"Son?" Taos's voice was quiet.

Tommy's back went ramrod straight. "Yes sir."

"You know you're never to pick those roses."

The boy hung his head and whispered, "Yes sir."

Taos placed his hand on Tommy's shoulder and turned him around. "You know the rules."

The small head bobbed up and down as his son stared at his shoes.

"You know you have to be punished." More bobbing.

"Oh Taos, you can't." She put her hand on his sleeve. "He didn't realize."

He shrugged her off. "He has to own up to his mistakes."

"Well, this is hardly . . ."

Taos heaved a frustrated sigh. "I have to." He turned an almost pleading look on her. "I will not raise a boy that doesn't accept responsibility for his actions." He struggled to convince her and himself at the same time.

"It's okay, Sammy. I know'd I would get in trouble." A small toe kicked an imaginary rock. "Sometimes it's worth it though, like you said."

He smiled up at her then turned back to his father. "Well sir, I'm ready."

He straightened his small bony shoulders and headed out the back door toward the barn, like a proud martyr.

Taos slid his palm across his hairline. He could feel Samantha's eyes look right through him. He refused to meet her gaze and followed his son out the door. Taos's boots shadowed the small footprints in the dirt, his one stride eating up five smaller ones. He stopped just outside, put his hands on his hips, and stared into the opening of the barn as his mind searched for a solution.

He couldn't punish the boy for wanting to make her happy, but he had to do something. No real damage had been done, but the rules were in place for a reason. It was the principle of the matter. The boy had to learn how to get along in this world without making a mess of things. You did that by following the rules, not by bending them.

He wouldn't be doing Tommy any favors by letting him think that rules didn't apply to him. Still, he couldn't help but feel a little proud that Tommy knew he would be punished and stood ready to take it like a man. He didn't lie, or try to make an excuse. That had to say something for what the boy had learned already. He hadn't done such a bad job of raising him . . . so far.

A lacy stocking tumbled past his foot, and Taos looked back over his shoulder at the house. Dresses, stockings and all manner of frilly unmentionables tumbled haphazardly on the ground around the house. His gaze climbed to the window and rested on a white petticoat flapping in the breeze from the windowsill like a flag. A hand reached out, grabbed the garment and slammed the window shut.

He chuckled to himself. *At least Darren and Charlie weren't around to see this.* The smile faded as he stared at the window. She had every right to be mad as hell. Seeing those roses felt like a stake through his heart. She knew what they meant and so did everyone else. Picking them felt like desecrating his baby's grave, and he'd wrongly assumed Samantha to be at fault. He deserved to be tossed out that window and a lot more. He should have known she would never have destroyed those roses, but he wanted to think the worst. That she didn't care. Why else would she come to him, love him so thoroughly, and then act like it never happened? Being angry seemed the only way to stay halfway sane around her.

Everything about her drew him deeper and deeper: the sound of her voice, the music of her laughter, the light in her smile. He left every morning with the sweet scent of her in his mind and willed the sun to set faster just so he could get back to her once again. For a week he'd fought a constant and relentless battle to keep himself safe, distant, in control of the situation. She must think him crazy, one minute following at her heels like a puppy and the next throwing her out of his house.

The last thing he wanted her to do was leave, and she'd dug her heals in and refused. Thank God. She could have just up and left at any time, still might. The realization sent a chill through him, and his mouth went dry.

If Tommy could take his punishment like a man, then so would he. No matter what she did or said, he would take it. He deserved it. Taos stared at the dirt and tried to arrange in his mind how to deal with Tommy, which was suddenly the least of his problems.

A horse whinnied behind him and his head snapped up. Taos hadn't even heard the rider approach.

Charlie rested a forearm on his saddle horn and grinned. "Did it rain women with those clothes, or just the clothes?"

Taos turned and stalked into the barn with his face burning, Charlie's laughter ringing in his ears.

More than an hour later, Tommy and Taos strode through the back door. Darren and Charlie were well into their meal.

"Straight upstairs, mister." Taos pointed and Tommy took off like a shot.

"You're not even going to let him eat dinner?" She looked at Taos like he was the grim reaper.

He shook his head.

She snatched up the empty plates and set them on the shelf with a bang. "I'm sure you're too upset to eat, too."

"You've already fixed dinner." He watched her carefully as he sat down. "We can't let it go to waste." He reached his fork toward one of the steaks.

Samantha grabbed the platter from his reach and opened the back door. Jimbo whimpered and wagged a hopeful tail. She dumped the steaks in front of the dog, who fell on them, gulping large mouthfuls. The platter thudded back onto the table and Samantha headed toward the stairs.

"Why did you do that?" Taos kept his voice calm.

"You didn't want it to go to waste."

"What am I supposed to eat?"

"You'll just have to chew on that beef jerky heart of yours." She disappeared, and her door slammed a moment later.

The wonderful aroma of the steaks still lingered in the air, and the dog wandered in through the open door to sniff for more. Taos met his brothers' shocked expressions.

"What was t-that?" Darren curled a protective hand around what was left of his steak, as Taos's eyes settled on the meat.

"A trip to the woodshed." Taos grumbled. Jimbo rubbed up against his leg and he reached down and scratched the dog's ears. "Got off kinda light, didn't I boy?" The mutt wagged his tail mindlessly and wandered out the back door.

Darren and Charlie finished eating quickly and took off for a night in town.

Taos went to his office and rummaged through the cabinets for a partial bottle of whiskey. At this rate he was going to have to start buying it by the case. He poured a drink and propped his boots upon the desk. The chair squeaked in protest.

He should go up and apologize, not sit here and drink. It was never like him to shy away from a confrontation. Of course it wasn't like him to apologize either. He would just go up, knock on the door and get it over with. He pictured tears glistening in Samantha's green eyes right before she slammed the door in his face. He tossed down another shot. Nope, he couldn't stand her rejection sober.

Taos looked around the office. He hadn't spent any time in here the past few weeks, and it looked like a new place. Every surface had been cleared and polished to a high shine. He pulled his feet off the desk and wiped away the dirt his boots had left.

It was the first time in a year he had even seen the top of the desk. Jake had always kept everything neat and orderly when he was alive. Taos smiled. His Dad would have liked the woman Samantha had become. The fiery liquid began its numbing effect, and he tossed down another shot.

Thoughts swirled through his mind as he watched the last orange glow of sunset fill the room and cast shadows on the walls.

He slowly pulled open the desk drawers one by one. Everything seemed to have a place, not that he would be able to figure out what she had put where. It seemed she had some kind of system: bills in one drawer, blank paper in another, letters in another. *Letters.*

He sat up suddenly and rummaged through the desk drawers, looking for the letter. Had she seen it? He'd left it on the desk, so she'd had to put it somewhere. Did he seal the envelope? He stopped and tried to think through the fog in his mind. No, he hadn't had an envelope. Had she read it? He searched every drawer, then searched them again. His heart pounded double-time.

He went to the secretary and pulled open drawers and rummaged through them. Nothing. He sat back down and breathed in a deep breath. Calm logic struggled to the surface. It had to be here. If she'd read it, she would have said something. Make that, yelled something. Maybe.

He opened the first drawer in the large desk and methodically went through every piece of paper, every note, every scrap. No letter.

He pushed the what-ifs to the back of his mind and concentrated, opening and searching each drawer in succession. He paused and wiped small beads of sweat off his forehead. One drawer left. His fingers trembled a little as they stretched toward the handle. If that letter wasn't in this drawer, this could be a hole too deep to climb out of.

Chapter 16

Samantha tossed aside the covers and swung her feet to the floor. The thought of Tommy lying in bed hungry crowded out any possibility of sleep. She pushed her arms through the long sleeves of her robe and opened the door. A little snack wouldn't hurt anything, and she might finally be able to relax.

Quiet permeated the entire house as she crept down the stairs to the kitchen. The last light of day splashed across the rug on the kitchen floor. The dishes had been washed and everything put back in its place. At least they had cleaned up after dinner. She poured a glass of milk and wrapped two large chocolate cookies in a cloth.

Her bare feet chilled as she walked back toward the stairs. She paused and looked down the hall. The closed office door offered no clues, but she could feel his presence as surely as if he had reached out and touched her. Hopefully he felt as rotten as she did. Not only had he been overly harsh with Tommy, but he'd destroyed the plans she'd spent the whole day dreaming up to clear the air between them.

She stared at the glass doorknob. This night could have turned out very differently. She certainly wasn't in the mood to talk to him about anything right now and the letter only added to her uncertainty. It seemed like every serious conversation they tried to have only intensified the jumble of emotions within her. She didn't know if she wanted to slide into the comfort and safety of his arms or shoot him, and at this point it could go either way. She forced her gaze ahead of her and started up the stairs. Distance could be a good thing.

Samantha opened Tommy's door quietly. A little sniffle greeted her in the darkness.

"Tommy?" She whispered.

"Uh-huh?"

She placed the goodies on the table next to the bed and lit the small lamp.

The boy rubbed his red eyes and sat up. "Are those for me?"

She nodded and sat on the edge of the bed. Tommy crunched into the treats, sending a shower of crumbs onto the sheets.

Samantha laughed. "Slow down there. I can go get you some more."

He took a swig of milk, leaving a white mustache across his top lip.

"Are you okay?" She brushed his unruly bangs from his face as he nodded.

"It wasn't too bad." He munched another bite. "Didn't know I had a sister, though."

Samantha stared. Taos had told him about the baby? "What about your sister?"

"Pa said she died when she was little and that's why he planted those special roses." He paused "If I'd a knowed that, I wouldn't have picked 'em."

"I'm really glad you wanted to give me something. Thank you."

Tommy smiled. "Pa told me it was nice what I did for you and all, but I need ta ask next time."

"I think that's a good idea. Now maybe both of us will stay out of trouble for a while." Samantha paused. She hated to pump the boy for information, but curiosity got the best of her. "What else did he say?"

"Pa said my sister's name was same as yours."

She nodded.

He must like you a lot."

That comment caught her a little off guard and left her speechless for a minute. "Well, maybe."

Tommy frowned and stared at the remainder of his cookie. "Are you gonna leave?" He turned his big hopeful eyes on her. "I'll do more nice stuff if you don't leave."

"Why would you think I would leave?"

"Nate says my momma left cause she didn't want us. Me or Pa neither one. I like you lots, and I don't want you to leave 'cause we wasn't nice to you."

Tears stung the back of her eyes and she cleared her throat. "You don't have to do nice things to get me to stay." She folded the covers over his chest as Tommy settled down into the bed.

"I know pa's real sorry he threw your clothes out the window."

She leaned over and kissed his forehead. "Don't you worry about that. No real harm done."

She stood and turned down the light.

He was asleep before she got to the door. Samantha stood in the hall and stared at her bare feet. Tommy's words tugged at her heart. She didn't want to leave, no matter if Taos had sent the letter or not. She didn't care. The realization came as a bit of a surprise, and it wasn't just about Tommy. She was thoroughly attached to this place, this man.

She smiled to herself. Who was she kidding? She found Taos frustrating, irritating, and irresistible. Even as angry as she had been seeing her clothes dance across the countryside, it was kind of funny too. This might be the perfect time to clear the air. Besides, he needed to know that Tommy was already hearing things about his mother. Taos needed to talk to him.

Samantha found herself standing in front of the office door in a matter of minutes. She forced the doubt and fear to the back of her mind and rapped her knuckles on the door. She peeked in. "Are you busy?"

Taos slammed a drawer with a bang. Samantha flinched and raised both eyebrows at his expression. He looked like a rabbit trapped in a snare. She recognized the contents of several desk drawers scattered on the floor around him.

"Um, yes. I mean no. Um, I mean, come in."

Samantha stood in front of the desk. He had obviously been looking for something. *The letter.* This worked out perfectly. "Looking for something?"

He shrugged and stared at her.

"A letter, maybe?"

No comment.

"A letter to Boston, maybe?"

"You saw it?"

"Yes." She paused, waiting for an explanation. The quiet pressed in on them as the minutes ticked by, but she waited.

Finally, Taos cleared his throat. "I just wanted to be sure someone didn't send you here for some other reason, that's all."

"You didn't send it. Why?"

He hesitated. "It was right at first, and I didn't know what to make of you showing up here so suddenly, is all."

She weighed his answer in her mind. He seemed sincere, and really who could blame him for being a little suspicious with her showing up unannounced like she had.

"Maybe you should send another." She took a deep breath. "If this is what it takes for you to finally believe me."

"I don't think that's necessary." Juices rolled in his empty stomach as he watched her slip around the side of the desk. The white robe covered her from neck to ankles, but glowed with an almost angelic light in the growing darkness. Dry cotton filled his mouth, and the air seemed suddenly thick and heavy, like the calm before the first thunderclap. She leaned back on the desk and smiled at him. To Taos she looked like ice cream on the hottest day of the year. Her scent floated toward him, an enticing blend of rose petals and summer breeze.

His eyes followed her every move. The robe molded to her graceful form as she crossed her arms over her waist.

Ice cream with curves. Would she melt in his mouth? He closed his eyes for a moment and tried to will his mind into self-control, but the mutiny was already well underway.

"I talked to Tommy. He said you told him about his sister."

Taos stared at her lips as she spoke. They drew him in, mesmerized his heart, stirred his soul. He couldn't seem to resist the urge to touch her. Their fight this afternoon probably put any chance of that on hold for a while.

He clasped his hands to his knees to keep them away from her, but he couldn't help staring.

"Taos?"

"Oh, yeah. I thought it was time he knew."

"Did you say anything about his mother?"

He shrugged. "Not really."

"He's been hearing things in town."

"Things?"

"He said Nate told him that she left because she didn't want you or Tommy."

Taos stared at her.

"You might want to talk to him."

"And tell him what? That what he heard was the truth?"

Samantha shrugged and turned to leave.

He didn't want her to go. "I'm sorry about your clothes." He tried once again to drag his gaze away, but couldn't. "I'll replace any that are ruined."

Silence. Her unreadable expression offered few clues.

"Anything you want. Really."

"Are you alright?" She reached out and placed her hand on his forehead. "You're warm."

If he had been standing, her caress would have buckled his knees. The need to touch her was so intense, he laid his hand over hers and silently begged for one more minute of heaven. If he was just warm, then the sun was made of snow.

Samantha's eyes softened and her lips parted. He didn't need any more of a hint. Taos turned her hand over and pressed his lips to her palm. Her fingers cupped his cheek and trailed down his jaw over his slight whiskers making a run for dawn. He opened his mouth slightly and she leaned in, accepting the invitation.

Their lips touched, then melded together. He tugged her waist gently and she slipped onto his lap, the chair squeaking like a tattletale with a secret. Growing darkness was the only indicator that the world still turned.

A ripple of pleasure followed his fingertips as he traced the slim column of her throat. His lips caressed and nipped at her earlobe.

Sudden movement startled Taos as she swiveled and straddled his lap. His world moved slowly, like a beautiful dream. This was one area he was glad not to control. With most women it was a guessing game as to what they liked or didn't like in bed. But there was something about Samantha's sexual advances that made him feel wanted, needed.

Samantha wriggled on his lap and trailed kisses along his temple. She brushed her hand down his shirt front and slid her fingers between the buttons, popping them open one by one. She seemed to know how she wanted this to go and wasn't shy about taking the lead. He was more than glad to hand her the reins and hang on for the ride.

His hands traveled up both her bare legs and under her robe. She moaned slightly and leaned into him as his fingers rounded her hips. Taos lifted her with him and laid her across the top of the desk.

A shadow of light from the rising moon filled the room. Taos swiftly pulled the robe and gown over Samantha's head and tossed them aside. The breath caught in his throat at the sight of her cream-colored skin in the moonlight. He would never get enough of feasting his eyes on what he could only compare to a sculpture of Venus: perfection, beauty, and passion all rolled into one. It was as if he had to touch her to make sure she was real. The palm of his hand traveled down her chest and across her quivering stomach.

Warmth flowed through his hand from her body, calling to him. No stone sculpture could cause a storm like the one she ignited within in him. He leaned down and trailed feather light kisses down her stomach. Soft willowy fingers ran through his hair as he tugged off his shirt. Taos's lips burned their way across her stomach and hips, slowly teasing, tempting as they went. Her legs instinctively wrapped around his waist, and he swore a silent oath to himself. This would be over in two seconds if she made him any hotter.

Even though Samantha anticipated it, the feel of his mouth between her legs shocked and amazed her at the same time. He teased and taunted until she clawed his hair and moaned like a woman possessed. He stopped and she opened her eyes, dazed and disappointed at the loss. His gaze met her eyes and trapped them as his lips traveled up her body. She watched his tongue dart out and circle one nipple. He drew the stiff peak into his mouth and pleasure washed over her. She arched her back as his lips placed kisses across her chest until her other nipple was captured.

Their mouths entwined once again and Samantha's need blossomed into heated desperation. "Oh please, I want you now," she whispered, her breath ragged. Taos paused and quickly shed the rest of his clothes. As he met her lips once again, Samantha gloried in the feel of his naked skin, running her fingernails gently down his back. She welcomed the pressure as he entered her slowly, carefully. He gathered her into his arms and she clung to him, her body closing around his, grasping him with all she had. He kissed her gently and pleasure swirled into the center of her body. She let out a sigh as the dance began.

He set a steady rhythm, and she followed, giving and taking in perfect harmony. Their bodies merged together in raw emotion, leaving doubt and inhibition far behind. The whiskey bottle on the desk swayed as they strained to a fevered pitch. It finally clattered to the floor and the noise competed with the music of sweet release.

Taos dropped his forehead onto her chest as he tried to force his breathing to slow to a normal rate. He hesitated, then raised his head to peek at her. Her eyes were still closed, but the smile on her face was nothing less than angelic. He could go his entire life and never see anything so beautiful again.

Samantha's eyes fluttered open.

"I'm hungry." Taos said.

She stretched like a lazy cat. "For food?"

Taos grinned and stepped back to pull her to her feet. They both dressed in silence, sharing the same smile, the same look, the same desire. Taos took her hand and led her down the hall and toward the stairs.

She started toward the kitchen, but he refused to release her hand.

"I'd rather starve." He saw the heat flare in her eyes as he pulled her to him.

"Me too," she whispered and followed him upstairs.

Yours Again

Chapter 17

The wagon swayed a steady rhythm as they rolled toward town. Taos watched Samantha breathe the morning air deep into her lungs. She was so beautiful. Her face glowed, and her golden hair caught the morning light, holding it hostage. How had he missed that this whole time?

When he had lit the lamp in the parlor on that first night, he thought she looked like Jimbo after a good roll in the creek. Even the next morning she was just passable, kind of pretty maybe. Now the sun dimmed in comparison. He forced his gaze back toward the road and insisted his attention follow, though his thoughts refused to budge.

What was the matter with her? Women weren't attracted to him as a general rule. Most saw him as a hulking beast and scattered quickly out of the way when he came near. Especially once they heard the rumors about him being a wife-beater.

Unless they wanted something.

Somebody should have warned her off, told her how bad he really was at making women happy. She had loved him last night like there was no tomorrow. If he had died in her arms before dawn, he would have gone a happy man.

The semi-lie he told about the letter weighed heavy on his mind this morning. He should have been honest with her, but still he held back. He needed to tell her now, even though he was bound to get a tongue lashing. She would demand to know why he hadn't said something. He didn't have a good reason, or any reason really.

It made him feel even worse that she was ready to take him as he was. Which, as far as she knew, was simply a poor cowhand who worked sunup to sundown. The least he could have done was be honest. Maybe the fact that he could provide for her would help smooth things over.

His eyes gravitated back to the new center of his universe. He had no idea what she saw in him, but he hoped she kept seeing it. Samantha's eyes closed again as she enjoyed the wind on her face. Taos thought her expression nothing short of heavenly.

How did that Bible verse go? Some have entertained angels unawares? The thought made him duck his head and glance toward the skies. The type of entertaining they engaged in last night might get them both struck by lightning if they didn't do something about it, and fast.

Samantha opened her eyes and looked over at him, the same dreamy expression on her face.

"What are you thinking?" She cocked her head and studied him.

Thinking? He had been thinking, but she jolted him right out of his thoughts. His mind went blank. Taos looked at her expectant face. Nothing came to his vacant brain as he struggled for something she might accept. Oh yeah, lightning. He had been thinking something about lightning.

He cleared his throat. "I was thinking that it looks like we might get some rain."

Samantha scanned the cloudless horizon and raised her eyebrows skeptically.

"Um, later. I mean, a storm can blow up out here in no time."

She shrugged but didn't look convinced.

He wouldn't have bought that one either, so why should she? He heaved a sigh as his eyes flitted across the clear blue sky. The only storm that might be coming was between his ears, provided he could figure out how to string two thoughts together.

Taos slumped down and kept his gaze on the road, mentally kicking himself. No use trying to be smooth, it just came out like he was wearing two left boots, one of which was firmly planted between his lips.

He started to assemble a mental list of logical, practical reasons he could use to convince her she needed to stay. Here. With them. *With him.* His eyes darted her direction and were met by her slow smile, which made him want to stop this wagon and hold her in his arms the rest of the day. *Okay that's one.* The wagon dipped into a deep rut and his attention snapped back to the road. He didn't seem able to look at her and do anything else at the same time.

How would he phrase that argument anyway? *You're beautiful and I can't keep my hands off you.* Who would be swayed by that? No, he needed a better reason. Something concrete. Something practical, that a woman would want.

There were the two ranches. Combining them would solve a number of problems. The water rights would no longer be in question, which would be great for him. Samantha would be taken care of and protected, which would work for her. He could provide her a good life, and he would, too.

He nodded to himself. It was logical, sensible, and offered a solution to a number of problems for them both. He just might have her convinced by the time they reached town. He sighed. Time to screw up his courage and just say it.

He could feel her watching him out of the corner of her eye. He knew she had something on her mind. Suddenly she frowned.

What if she thought last night was a mistake? A cold shiver ran along his spine. It was wonderful. How could she think it was a mistake now? He glanced over at her again. She was staring at the road, but clearly not seeing any of the ruts they bounced across. Taos looked back into the wagon bed where Tommy was sleeping. He didn't stir.

Samantha took a deep breath and said, "I suppose we should talk."

He immediately felt the electric charge leap through the air between them. He prepared himself for what could be bad news. Better to know what the problems were than guess at them.

"About last night?" Taos rubbed the reins with his thumb. Maybe she was thinking the same thing he was. This was not the time to guess wrong.

"What about last night?" She turned slightly and her knees banged into his thigh.

He cleared his throat. "I wasn't completely honest with you last night."

"About what?"

"The letter."

Confusion skipped across her face. "In what way?"

"I sent one." He watched her closely. "The one you read was the first draft." His voice trailed off as her eyes narrowed.

Her shoulders sagged, "Why didn't you tell me that last night?"

"I didn't want to start another argument." He shrugged, "You told me last night to send another one."

"And you said you hadn't."

"I said I didn't think it was necessary to send another," he added quickly, "And I don't, now."

She swung an incredulous expression his direction, "Splitting hairs aren't we?"

"No. I just don't see why it matters. I just did what you suggested."

Samantha sighed and glanced at him. "I wouldn't have been upset last night. And I'm not mad, just disappointed."

He preferred mad. They rode in silence for a ways until he broke the stalemate. "What did you want to talk about?"

"Why have you been pretending like you don't have money?"

He inhaled sharply, pulling dust into his lungs. He coughed loudly. *She knew.* She knew last night. "What?"

"Didn't you see the ledger?" She asked

"What ledger?"

She huffed impatiently. "The one I put all the accounts in."

"I've been working. When was I supposed to look at some ledger?"

Silence descended between them as Samantha gazed at the countryside and he stared at the back of her head.

"So what was last night?" he asked.

She didn't say a word.

Taos reined the horses to a stop under a large tree and set the brake. He climbed down and lifted her effortlessly off the seat. He checked on his son, who was still sound asleep, and took her hand.

"Let's walk." He motioned toward a stand of trees, which would be just out of hearing distance if Tommy woke up. He could tell she had to almost run to keep up with him, but he was tired of these stupid games. Just as they reached the trees, he spun around.

"What is going through that mind of yours?" He was as breathless as she was from their short, angry march in the mountain sun.

"Why are you so certain everyone wants something from you?"

He met her stare, "Because they do, including you. You've been lying since you got here."

"Me?" She spat. "Who lied about being a poor cowhand? Who lied about sending a letter, not once but twice?"

"I had my reasons."

"And I didn't? How come if you lie and have a reason its fine, but if someone else does the same thing they are trying to pull one over on you?"

He stepped toward her as she backed up. "Why can't we just have one completely honest conversation?"

Samantha's dress clung to her. It was distracting as hell.

She swatted at an insect buzzing around her ear. "Fine," she said.

Now was his chance. He pinned her with a stare, "What was last night?"

She pressed her lips together and looked away.

"Sammy?" He put a hand on her arm, forcing her eyes to his.

She hesitated, "It was about not having any regrets."

"And?"

She held his gaze, "And that's it. I know this is coming to an end. You said yourself you sent the letter telling Mattie there was no place for me here."

He sighed, "That was a while back."

"And now?"

There was not going to be any time for smooth talk, which was probably a good thing since he didn't seem to be able to say the right thing.

He stared intently at her. "Now I think that we need to get married." The statement hung there between them.

"Why?"

Was she kidding? It seemed obvious to him that two people who spent a great deal of time rolling around in the sheets should get married at some point, but she seemed confused. Taos didn't immediately answer simply because the obvious answers were apparently not flying with her today.

"Thinking again?"

"As a matter of fact I was." His voice rose as fast as the temperature.

"Surely you've had time to come up with a reason to marry me."

"Because it's the right thing to do," he blurted out

Silence descended between them.

Samantha's expression was unreadable. He shifted his weight, waiting on her to say something. True, it was one of the reasons. Most of the others he hadn't quite sorted out yet.

"Wrong answer." She started back toward the wagon and he fell into step.

"Wrong answer?" He easily matched her strides. "It happens to be the right answer, not to mention a damn good reason for two people to get married."

"No, it's not."

He put his hand on her shoulder and forced her to face him. "Yes, it is." He couldn't think why she was being so stubborn.

"Not for me it's not," The tremble in her voice was slight, but it still it caught his attention. She was upset and it was deeper than this. Much deeper.

He reached out and touched a strand of golden hair that had sprung loose from the knot she'd fashioned it into, "Sammy, I just don't know what you want me to say."

"I don't want you to say anything, Taos." Unshed tears glistened. "When are you going to understand I don't want a ranch or anything you think you have to offer me."

"Then what do you want from me?" This was the most confused he'd been since she'd stepped into his life.

"Everything else," she whispered, and then stalked back to the wagon.

He slapped his hat on his thigh. *What in the hell did she mean by that?*

Taos jammed the hat back on and climbed up into the wagon after her. He released the brake and the wagon lurched forward again. As the horses clomped back onto the road, the silence stretched between them. Something about that conversation felt like the most honest chat they'd had since she got here, and if that were true then he'd been wrong. *About a lot of things.* If she'd wanted to get married, wanted the ranch, money, everything he had, he'd just offered it to her on a silver platter. She'd flat refused.

He had no idea what "everything else" meant, but he came up clueless.

"When did you send that letter?" She asked.

The question startled him a little. "Uh, back before—"

"No." She cut him off. "What date?"

"About three weeks ago, give or take." He glanced over at her. He could see wheels in that mind of hers spinning. "Why?"

"I don't think we should go into town."

"Why not?"

"If John got that letter he could be here now." She looked over at him and then glanced back at Tommy.

His first instinct was to push that idea aside. He'd thought she made the guy up anyway, but something in her eyes, her voice, stopped him cold. He instantly knew she hadn't been lying. But even if the guy intercepted the letter, it would be pushing it to think he could already be here.

"You will be fine." He said, trying hard to convince her. "I want to alert Blake to be on the lookout for anyone fitting his description as soon as we get there. We'll stock enough supplies to last for a bit, then go back to the ranch and barricade the place. Okay?"

She did her best to smile, but he knew she was worried. He reached over and took her hand in his, giving her a little squeeze. They finished the rest of the ride in silence, but every sense Taos had was now on high alert.

As the wagon pulled to a stop in front of the mercantile Tommy hopped out, chattering a steady steam. Taos helped Samantha down.

Taos spoke quietly. "Get anything you think we might need."

She nodded, casting a wary glance up and down the street.

"Stay inside, I'll meet you here in a few minutes."

Samantha grabbed Tommy's hand and disappeared into the mercantile.

Chapter 18

Samantha stopped short as the conversations in the mercantile came to a halt and all eyes turned toward her. She twisted and scanned the air behind her. No one. Clearing her throat, she walked up to the counter, Tommy at her heels.

"Good morning Mrs. Hardin." She flashed a warm smile and held out her shopping list. The whispers were barely audible, yet they were there. The sounds floated toward her, but she couldn't determine what all the fuss was about.

The older woman glanced around the store. Samantha could feel the stares of the patrons boring a hole in her back.

"Good Morning, Samantha." She read the scrap of paper then set about filling the order.

A group of men stood at the end of the counter, deep in discussion. One smiled and nodded her way. She smiled and nodded back then turned her attention to a catalogue lying on the counter. The pages were full of things she had seen every day in Boston, but they seemed out of place and far removed from River City. Small snippets of the men's conversation reached her ears.

"Smitty said Fletcher held a gun on one ol' boy, til he put his campfire out," the man with the long handlebar mustache said.

"Don't blame him, myself," a barrel chested older man added. "If that grass caught fire I'd be done for." Several nodded in agreement.

"It's bad enough there ain't enough water, but a fire would take all the forage too," Handlebar added.

"The stock that didn't die in the fire would starve, then?" Mr. Hardin asked.

"Yup." Barrel Chest nodded. "A sane man would've done sold out and just be laying in the weeds 'til things turned 'round."

"Whoever said cattlemen was sane?" Handlebar laughed and they all joined in.

Mr. Hardin walked down to Samantha.

She looked up at him and smiled.

"You feeling alright, Miss Sammy?" His voice was barely a whisper, but the conversation of the men stopped as if waiting on an answer.

"Just fine. And you?"

He didn't look convinced. "You sure?"

Samantha frowned. She thought she looked all right when she left this morning. Maybe worry about John or the stress of dealing with Taos showed on her face. She leaned toward him and whispered, "Don't I look all right?"

"Oh, no, ma'am, you just look fine." he smiled and some of the men chuckled, "We were just worried about you." He straightened the glass jars of licorice. "Wanted to know how you was gettin' along, that's all."

The whispering started again and Samantha twisted around. Two young women that had obviously been staring at her quickly turned away. The men were staring too.

A sense of foreboding gripped Samantha. Could these people tell what she had been doing last night? She must look different somehow or be giving off some sign that she was no longer what they might call a "respectable young lady." Her face burned red.

Mrs. Hardin stepped out from the back room with a stern look on her face. "Henry, can I speak with you a moment?" Mr. Hardin followed his wife out of sight. Samantha could hear their voices, but couldn't distinguish any words until Mr. Hardin raised his voice.

"She said she was fine, Sarah. You need to stay out of it."

"And I said that I will not have this talk going on any longer, and that's that."

Mrs. Hardin appeared once again from the back room. She cleared her throat and said rather loudly, "I have two of these canisters in the back, but they're different colors." She stared pointedly at Samantha. "You'll need to show me which one you prefer."

There was nothing on the list but the usual supply of staple goods for the kitchen. Samantha raised her brows. Mrs. Hardin jerked her head toward the back and Samantha came around the counter to follow her.

"Henry, keep an eye on Tommy, will you? Maybe a lemon drop or two."

He nodded and bent to occupy the boy.

The older woman motioned Samantha into the tiny office at the very back of the store and closed the door. The room was stuffy and oppressive; the only air came from a very small window that seemed more decorative than functional. Papers peeked out of the drawers and from under the cover of a small roll-top desk. There was one chair and a small stool. Samantha perched on the edge of the stool.

Mrs. Hardin was a little short of breath and took a moment to compose herself as Samantha sat in confused silence. "I'm sorry dear, but I had to talk to you. The town's all abuzz."

"What about?"

"You!"

"What about me?"

Mrs. Hardin took a deep breath and reached over to pat Samantha's hand. "Now, dear, I know I'm not your mother or even family, but I knew your mother and the kind of woman she was." She looked at Samantha like she should know what was going on.

"What does my mother have to do with this?" The wary sensation that grew in the pit of Samantha's stomach gnawed at her insides, intent on burning a hole through her body.

Mrs. Hardin heaved her more than ample chest. "Well I guess I'll have to explain." She twisted her fingers together.

"Please do." Samantha rolled the fabric of her dress between her fingers absently as she watched the woman turn in one circle after another with no room to pace.

"A young, unattached woman just can't live under the same roof as an unattached man for an extended period of time unless they"—she fluttered her hands in the air—"you know, become attached."

Dread hit Samantha head on, like unexpectedly walking through a spider web that stubbornly clings to your face. Moisture coated the palms of her hands and shivers chased goose flesh down her back. "Is that what everyone is whispering about?'

"Some people, Mertie Mae in particular, have been assuming the worst." She flung her hands up like the sky was falling. Maybe it was.

Samantha sat in stunned silence.

"Especially after that story went around that you had been to Miss Sadie's."

Oh no. Not that.

"It is just a rumor, isn't it dear?"

"Not exactly."

Mrs. Hardin's eyes widened.

"It's a long story, but nothing happened there. You must believe me."

"Oh, I do child. But other people aren't so open minded when it comes to these things."

"I have to go." Samantha said, her voice a mere whisper. She wanted to run as fast and far as she could.

Mrs. Hardin placed a hand on her arm. "There's more."

More? She didn't think she could take any more.

"You know about Sharisse?"

Samantha nodded.

"Then you know that she talked a lot before she left. About how Taos had beaten her."

"That's not true." She tried to control her temper.

"Now dear, I know that rumor isn't true, I just thought you should know." Mrs. Hardin stared at her hands. "That's why people are looking at you like they are. They expected to see you covered with bruises."

"That is ridiculous!" She crossed her arms, furious at the speculation of strangers. "This whole thing is ridiculous! Do these people have nothing better to do than talk and gossip?"

"No, they don't. You need to realize that and so does Taos. He isn't helping matters, what with threatening to shoot Sonny Harper and all."

"He *what*?"

"Sonny went out to call on you and Taos told him if he stepped foot on the ranch again he would shoot him dead."

"I can't believe Taos would say that." Well, actually she could.

"He scared the life out of Sonny, who was in here this morning telling how he'd seen women's clothes scattered all across the ground and no sign of you."

Samantha breathed deep. This was getting worse by the second.

"We were worried sick."

Samantha jumped up. "I have to go." She had to find Taos. He could set these gossip mongers straight.

She stepped through the door, but the sound of Tommy's voice stopped her in her tracks. The boy sat on the counter, enjoying a small pile of lemon drops with a group of women and men crowded in front of him.

"Naw, she sleeps in her own room most of the time."

"And the other times?" Mertie Mae was leading the pack, her spectacles sliding far down her hawkish nose. The vultures pressed closer, not wanting to miss one juicy detail.

"She sleeps with my dad, but he squishes her a lot."

The breath left Samantha's lungs as the women in the crowd gasped and whispered. She didn't miss a few of the men covering grins and exchanging winks. If a bridge could be burned any faster, she didn't know how. There was no way to explain, nothing she could say that would appease them. Nothing that was true, anyway.

Mertie Mae crossed her arms and smiled triumphantly at Mrs. Hardin.

"Well, well, well. There's the little strumpet now." Mertie Mae strode across the floor toward them, her two mulish daughters in her shadow. The crowd collectively held its breath. She stopped with the toes of her boots almost touching Samantha's. "So, will there be a wedding or will you continue to endanger the moral fabric of our community?"

Samantha wanted to laugh and cry, but mostly she just wanted to breathe. The air burned her throat and her eyes ached with tears of shame. If only the earth would open up and swallow her in one gulp. As the possibility of rescue dimmed, Samantha's mind lurched into motion.

Run.

The crowd waited in hushed silence as a plan materialized. She needed to distract them and get away. Taos would know what to do. A simple plan, but the implementation part might be a bit of a challenge as they stood between her and the door.

Samantha looked into the faces of people who had befriended her in the short time she had been here. They conveyed every emotion from sympathy to disgust. Every one of them stood awaiting some kind of response from her.

Mrs. Hardin scooted up behind her. "You go out there and hold your head up. Don't let that old battle axe get to you. You just stand your ground and meet her head on. Like a modern day Joan of Arc."

The woman had a point. Attack was her best bet. Actually it was her only bet. *Joan of Arc.* If one woman could face a whole army, then she could certainly stand up to one horse-faced woman.

Hopefully this wouldn't end with her being burned at the stake, though her insides were certainly on fire. Samantha threw back her shoulders and squarely faced Mertie Mae.

"Moral fabric? Is that what women like you use to force men to marry?"

Snickers floated from the crowd and the ring leader turned and stared at them, ending any humor. She glared at Samantha. "It's what keeps our communities from being polluted by women like you. Some cheap hussy out to steal our own good men from us."

Samantha's brow shot up. "And just who do you think I'm stealing him from?" She glanced at the woman's incredibly plain daughters, daring her to name them as even remote possibilities.

"From the *local* women. The *local, God-fearing* women." She stared pointedly at Samantha.

Definitely a tambourine banger. Mavis was right about this type of woman. They wore morality like a shield as long as it suited their purpose. The heat rose up Samantha's cheeks and she clenched her fists at her sides. She resisted the urge to pop her hand across the large hairy mole that squatted on the enemy's cheek.

"I have no need to steal anything from anyone." Her voice pitched higher.

"Aheem!!!"

The crowd turned with one motion toward the sound. Mavis stood by the door, a regal rose in a field of dandelions. She floated gracefully toward Mertie Mae with the barest rustle of silk to mark her movement. "Mertie Mae Morrison, are you giving this young woman a hard time?" The crowd watched in stunned silence as the two women sized one another up.

"We don't need your kind either, Mavis Simpson." The woman's bitterness leaked out like sour milk on a hot day.

Mavis's smile was that of a queen, welcome serenity among absolute madness. "I know that nearly half of the population of this town would disagree with you." Whispers chased through the crowd. "Including your husband."

Guffaws and giggles followed as Mertie Mae's face turned a splotchy red.

"Well, I never!" She pointed her nose in the air with righteous indignation.

Mavis chuckled, "So I hear." She winked at Samantha as the crowd roared. Mertie Mae stormed out of the store, followed by her daughters who ran into, then out of, the door.

Samantha smiled her thanks to Mavis and tried to slip out quietly with Tommy in tow. The patrons of the store spilled out onto the sidewalk to follow. They knew she was going to share this incident with Taos, and heaven forbid they miss any fireworks.

Taos was partway across the street on his way from the Sheriff's office when he saw the approaching mob. His eyes met Samantha's. He stood stone still. She hated what she saw in his expression. Fear, suspicion, anger—what must he be thinking? She suddenly realized that Reverend Miller was running alongside them. Her gaze snapped back to Taos. She saw all the blood drain out of his face, and she could just imagine the comparison of this incident to his first marriage.

Her mind screamed at him to run, to get them out of here and away from this crowd. They could talk in private, and she had no desire to give the townspeople any more fodder for the gossip mill. Instead, he stood silently and waited, as still and immovable as a mountain.

Samantha stopped and tried to catch her breath. "We have to talk." She silently pleaded with him.

The spectators spread out, surrounding them like two prize fighters in a ring preventing a speedy escape.

"About what?" He glanced nervously at the crowd as it pressed closer.

Reverend Miller timidly approached and tried to offer his assistance. "I was told there was going to be a wedding." He smiled, silently encouraging Taos.

Samantha could see the disappointment in Taos's eyes. He'd finally believed her this morning; she felt it. He'd believed her about John, about everything. The warm, compassionate man she'd grown to love had finally shown himself completely, but now he was gone again, replaced by the hard, cold, suspicious man she'd first met.

The mountain never wavered. "You were told wrong. There will be no wedding."

There were gasps of disbelief, and conversation buzzed around them with a multitude of speculation.

Samantha looked at Taos, willing him to put an end to this show and just get them home. "I didn't say I would marry anyone, so you can relax."

Silence descended again.

The thought crossed Samantha's mind at how strange quiet could be. Not even the birds and insects seemed to move. The whole world had ceased to turn just for this moment and her gut feeling was that she would remember this as the worst day of her life.

"There was a misunderstanding about something that Tommy said in the mercantile," she whispered.

The sun beat down as she, and the whole town it seemed, waited. And waited.

"Putting Tommy up to it doesn't make it right." He pinned her with a suspicious stare.

Of all the things he could have said, that one hurt the most. Anger, hurt, and absolute heartbreak rose up. "I wouldn't marry you if you licked my boots!"

She pointed a finger and banged it into his chest. "Don't think for one minute that I couldn't do better, Mr. Williams. In case you haven't noticed, men are a dime a dozen. If you don't want me, I'm sure I can find a suitable replacement in no time!" Amid laughter she walked away with what was left of her shredded pride.

"I didn't say I didn't want you." Taos ground out the words.

She stopped and turned. "You know damn well that's not good enough, Taos."

Yours Again

Chapter 19

Taos sat in one corner of the saloon, alone. Dust swirled under the swinging doors with each gust of wind. Boots scraped the floor, accompanied by the constant jingle of spurs. Small tidbits of speculative conversation floated toward him as he sipped his whiskey.

"Crazy is what it is . . ."

"Would get down and beg for a woman like that . . ."

No one approached him or said anything directly to him. He felt like a leper, which should have been a bad thing. But it wasn't. He was not in the mood to talk to anyone, and if someone had the nerve to walk over and say hello, he just might belt 'em one. The different voices droned on, though every so often one or two comments would seep through his thoughts.

"Out of his mind . . ."

"First in line, that's where I'll be . . ."

"Not only a looker, she's got that ranch and all that beautiful water . . ."

He tried to ignore the conversation, but all that filled his mind instead were Samantha's last words.

You know damn well that's not good enough, Taos.

She was right about that. The tone in her voice made his heart skip a beat. He looked into her eyes and saw overwhelming sadness. The same look he had seen nine years ago when he put her on that train. Reality shook him as he watched her walk away. Sharisse was gone, a conquered demon that had haunted him for eight years. The same thing had happened, but this time he had won and refused to be manipulated. But what had he gained? There should have been excitement, triumph, relief even. But the only thing he felt was a strange emptiness that crept into his soul.

Go after her.

His heart pleaded, but his feet refused.

I'll never run after a woman. This was right. This needed doing. He was getting too attached. It was better this way, better to suffer a little now than a lot in the long run. She'd played a dangerous game and lost. It had cost him too, but now he had to get past it.

The crowd had dispersed, disappointed and disgusted, and here he sat, trying to get answers from the bottom of a whiskey bottle again. Taos concentrated on a small speck of dust floating toward the floor. It kept him from jumping up and releasing his urge to pound someone or something. The hum of the saloon didn't even pause as a slender man walked in through the swinging doors and searched the room with his gaze.

Taos looked him over, anything for a distraction. The stranger was dressed in black from head to toe. His shiny black boots were a dead giveaway: here was someone who didn't trudge around in the mountain dirt. The man approached the bartender, who pointed in his direction. Taos thunked the legs of the chair onto the floor as the stranger moved closer. The way the man moved reminded him of a spider.

"May I join you?"

Taos nodded. The man's accent was definitely Eastern. The smile he flashed made Taos immediately wary. There was something very cold and calculating about this stranger.

"I understand we have a mutual friend, Mr. Williams."

"Who's that?" Taos sloshed the amber liquid in his glass.

"Samantha James."

Taos's instincts snapped to attention. "What did you say your name was mister?"

"I don't believe I said, but it's John Lawson." He removed black leather gloves from his long, slender fingers. His manner was condescending, as if he were talking to an imbecile. "She has been staying with you."

"What makes you think that?"

Lawson reached one hand inside the black brocade vest and pulled out a letter. He held it up with two fingers then flipped it across the table at Taos.

Taos turned the envelope over. It was his handwriting. The letter to Mattie. He swallowed hard. This confirmed Samantha had been honest with him from the start. That one thought resounded over and over in his head like a loud thunderclap.

Taos knew what the man across the table was capable of and what he had planned for Samantha. Fear tempted Taos to reach out and squeeze the man's neck until his black marble eyes popped out and rolled across the floor. He squelched the renegade idea as he plotted carefully.

Lawson forced Samantha to run halfway across the country straight to him for protection. And what had he done? Betrayed her and brought the danger right to her.

He made this mess. It was up to him to fix it. Taos sized up his opponent with a glance. He needed to know Lawson's exact plan and stall until he figured out where Samantha was.

He could buddy up to the man. Taos watched the man sip his whiskey with one pinkie raised. On second thought, he could never pull that off. But if he could get Lawson to think he was nothing but a dumb cowboy, it might buy him some time. Taos affected his best country bumpkin attitude.

"Sammy's a great gal. Know'd her since she was a little squirt."

"I'm her fiancé, Mr. Williams, as well as executor of her aunt's estate. I've come to collect her."

Panic gripped Taos's heart and squeezed tight. He had to remain calm. "Executor?"

"Her aunt Mattie signed the paperwork prior to her incapacitation."

"What incapacitation?"

"Poor woman is on her death bed. Just a matter of time you know."

The man lied like he breathed. All of Taos's senses were on alert. Hell would freeze over before he allowed this murderer anywhere near Samantha.

"I believe Miss Sammy wants to stay out here for a while."

"That won't be happening, Mr. Williams. I'll be selling her assets as quickly as possible"—he smiled a little—"to the highest bidder, of course."

"She won't stand for that."

Lawson's face reflected a man on the edge of losing patience. "If you understood these things, Mr. Williams, you would realize that this is no place for my future wife." He paused to let the statement sink in. "The time of our marriage is approaching, and I came to escort her back to Boston for the festivities."

Wife? The emotion that word drew out of a man was incredible. Less than an hour ago, Taos never wanted to hear it again. Now his mind stumbled over incredible fear mixed with intense regret. If he had believed her right up front, she would be out of reach of the evil this man had planned for her. But he didn't and she wasn't, and it was his fault. The tingle started at Taos's neck and ran down both arms. His knuckles itched to pound the man.

"Just seems a bit odd she never said a word to anyone," Taos ran a finger along the rim of his glass, "almost like she had no idea herself."

"Brides can be a little temperamental, but with adequate instruction most turn into decent wives. I'm sure she'll be no different." Lawson filled his glass again from the bottle on the table. "You can deliver her immediately, then?"

"She's not a horse," Taos growled.

Lawson cast an accessing gaze on him.

Now was not the time to let his emotions get the best of him. Taos shrugged and gave him a lopsided grin. "I mean, it will take her some time to pack and say her good-byes. You know how attached women get."

"I happen to know she was traveling rather light. I'll be waiting tomorrow at the hotel. Say, around nine?"

Taos nodded as the man rose and grasped his gloves.

"Mr. Williams, make no mistake. I am her fiancé, and I will be her husband. No one and nothing can change that."

"What if she changes her mind?"

The spider laughed humorlessly. "I've chased her halfway across the country already. There is only one other place she could hide."

"Where's that?"

"The cemetery." Wicked evil poured from the black marbles that stared at Taos. "You know the old saying, 'til death do us part?"

Lawson almost ran over Miles Barton as he exited the saloon. The lawyer brushed past and looked around frantically until he spotted Taos.

"Taos, thank God." He pulled a handkerchief out of his pocket and wiped his brow as he approached the table. "We have to talk, boy."

"Not now, Miles. I have to find someone." He rose to leave.

Miles grabbed Taos's sleeve as he walked past. Miles had been his father's lawyer, but Taos hadn't seen the man in a couple of years at least.

Miles insisted, "Not later, now. This is important. It can't wait."

Taos towered a good foot and a half over the thin, balding man. He shrugged out of his grip and snapped, "It will have to."

Taos scoured the town for Samantha. No one seemed to know where she was, but everyone had questions about what he intended to do when he found her. Single-minded determination allowed him to dodge the nosey inquiries and continue his search at a frantic pace.

He had just finished combing the livery as a last desperate measure when the music coming from Miss Sadie's caught his attention. It was the only place he hadn't looked. He closed his eyes then caught himself. He had actually prayed that Samantha was in the whore house. Lawson, or anybody else for that matter,

Dee Burks

would never think to look there. He stalked across the distance with long strides. Hopefully, God had a great sense of humor.

Mavis handed Samantha another cup of tea. The tears had long subsided and the two women now sat in silence.

Cinnamon appeared at the door. "He's out front and he wants her."

"I'm not here." Samantha sniffed as the girl went to deliver the message.

"He's been looking for you all over town," Mavis said

Samantha shrugged.

"Seems very determined, don't you think?"

Blowing her nose loudly, Samantha stared at the door.

Mavis smiled to herself. "I'd say you're head over heels in love."

Samantha shot a disgusted look toward the ceiling.

Mavis chuckled, "No doubt about it. You cast a hopeful eye at the door every time someone appears, only to be disappointed that it isn't him."

Samantha ignored her.

"Well, all I can say is that Taos needs his behind tanned for this one, though I would bet he is as upset as you are, dear."

"I don't think so." Samantha sniffed. He'd made himself quite clear in her mind.

Loud footsteps stormed down the hallway and Mavis chuckled. "Well we are about to find out!"

Taos stomped into the room and tugged a stunned Samantha to her feet. "We have to get married. Right now."

Samantha snapped to her senses as her body came into contact with his. She pushed away. "I don't want to get married. And if I did, it wouldn't be to you."

He looked at Mavis. "Send someone for the preacher, and hurry."

Samantha's heart wanted this, but her mind wouldn't let go of the hurt, the humiliation. "Did you hear what I said? I will not marry you."

Taos gripped both her arms and bent down to look her right in the face. "We have to. Lawson's here and if you don't marry me, you will be married to him by morning."

Her mouth dropped open. John was here. It was the nightmare she had imagined and the fear and panic that welled up in her chest nearly paralyzed her. She couldn't run. Where would she go? He'd found her here, he would find her again.

Taos was her only rescue. She gazed at him. His hair was tousled and his face grim with worry—not the expression you might envision on a prospective bridegroom. She focused on his ice blue eyes, which pleaded with her. She loved him with her whole heart. She knew that was true. But how could she let him sacrifice himself and go against everything he had said a few hours ago to save her? Was that love? If it wasn't, could she live with the consequences?

"Ahem." Reverend Miller stood at the door as several people crowded around him, trying get a look. Apparently the word was out.

Taos and Samantha turned toward him.

"We need to get married, right now," Taos said.

"I'd say so, son."

Muffled laughter rose from the onlookers as they filed into the room to get a better vantage point. The Hardins were among the group and Mrs. Hardin gave Samantha's neck a squeeze.

"I'm so happy for you, child!"

"Too bad Mertie Mae isn't here to see this." Samantha breathed.

"Oh, Goodness! I can't imagine. The soles of her shoes would burn completely off if she stepped foot in here!"

The reverend glanced about at the collection of people. His gaze settled on Cinnamon in her red satin skirt with black lace. He frowned. "I don't really think this is the place . . ."

Taos arched a brow at Samantha. He left it up to her.

She squeezed his hand. "This is the perfect place, Reverend. We're both here," she said.

"You have a ring, son?"

A ring? "Uh, we'll just skip that part and go straight to the I dos if that's okay."

Jewelry was the least of their worries right now, and she could tell his patience wore as thin as cheesecloth as time ticked away.

"Can we get on with it?" Taos demanded.

The reverend cleared his throat. "Dearly beloved, we are gathered here in this . . . um . . ." A large drop of sweat rolled down the preacher's brow and splattered on his open bible. "This . . . um . . ."

"Hospital for hypocrites?" Mavis dared, and received a dark look from the preacher.

"Dearly beloved. We are gathered *here*, to unite . . ."

The words ran together as Taos gazed down at Samantha. He expected to feel dread and emptiness. That was how it had been with Sharisse. This was different. He felt as if his heart would burst as he took in every detail. He had to make this right, he wanted to. For her.

"Son?"

Taos woke from his daydream to realize everyone was staring at him. "Oh, uh, I do."

The crowd breathed a collective sigh of relief as several men grudgingly paid off bets.

"Excuse me." Lawson's voice rang out harshly as a hush descended over the crowd. He pushed past several observers and walked directly to Taos. "As you know, Mr. Williams, this woman is my fiancé. As such, I do not consent to these proceedings and will not allow them to continue."

Samantha grabbed Taos's arm and tried to scoot behind him. Lawson's long arm snaked out and captured a slender wrist. He gave it a vicious yank and laughed as she stumbled forward. Gasps escaped the crowd.

"You will not get away this time," Lawson hissed.

Samantha stared up at him. Fear pelted her heart, causing it to beat double time. It was as if the devil himself held onto her arm.

Taos's hand slapped around Lawson's throat and he squeezed. There was something gratifying about digging his fingers into flesh. The sharp point of a gun stabbed Taos's side and he immediately released Lawson's throat and stood perfectly still.

"Put that away." Sheriff Blake had been a silent observer thus far, but now he pushed to the front of the gathering.

Lawson refused to drop the gun to his side and kept a tight grip on it. "Stay out of this, Sheriff. She is coming with me, where she belongs. Now."

He inched backward, waving his gun at whoever might make a move to stop his retreat.

Taos shuffled forward, but the sheriff held onto him. "Don't do this, son."

Taos tried to wave off the man's grip, but he held fast.

The lawman moved closer and whispered, "This room's full of innocent people, and if he starts shooting a lot of them are going to get hurt. Including her."

Lawson inched toward the door as the crowd parted.

"Taos, please. You have to stop him." Samantha pleaded as she tried to pry the man's slender fingers from her bruised wrist.

Lawson raised the gun and pointed it straight at Taos. "Samantha, you will come with me or I will shoot him." He cocked the gun and she complied immediately.

"I'll find you." Taos stepped forward.

"You'll die," Lawson waved his gun around the room once more then disappeared down the hall and out the door.

Taos started to follow but the sheriff stopped him. "I don't like this any better than you do. If you go after him now, you'll just get killed, or he'll kill her."

Taos rubbed a shaking hand across his brow.

"We'll mount up a group of men and take him in open country."

"Now, you have to listen to me." Miles stood breathlessly waving a piece of paper at the back of the crowd. "I tried to tell you. This all could have been avoided."

"What do you mean avoided?" Taos snatched the paper from the man's hand.

Miles looked around as if he were afraid he might be attacked. "You are already married." He backed up as Taos stepped forward. "Have been for three years." The little lawyer held out the marriage certificate like a shield. "Now, it wasn't my fault."

Taos grabbed the certificate as the lawyer continued.

"Your father was concerned that Samantha's land would fall into the wrong hands, and since it contains most of the water for both ranches, he came to an understanding with Mattie."

Taos stared at the paper. Marriage by proxy. Samantha's name was signed at the bottom. So was his. She was his, she always had been.

He tried to concentrate on what the little man was saying.

"Three years ago Mattie agreed to a sum that would care for Samantha for the rest of her life in return for the transfer of the water rights, but the terms of the will stated that Samantha had to marry for that to happen." He seemed to relax a bit as the spectators listened in rapt silence. "The marriage was supposed to be annulled immediately after the transfer, but your father died so suddenly that it was never finished."

The sheriff put a hand on Taos's shoulder. "I think we need to go get your wife, son." The room burst into excited chatter as men headed for their horses.

Chapter 20

Lawson pulled Samantha down the alley to his waiting horse. Her hands clawed at the slender fingers that grasped her mouth in panicked futility. The late afternoon sun beat down on them as they emerged from between the buildings.

His ragged breath hovered just above her ear, his words a harsh whisper. "It's no use trying to fight me."

She kicked back with her heels and tried to twist away from his grasp.

He growled, "I like that spirit, it's just not very convenient right now."

Lawson's arm squeezed her rib cage as the breath left her lungs. Small spots of light appeared before her eyes.

"I will win, you know. I have to. This is the only way, for both of us." He gave one last squeeze as they neared the horse, then let go abruptly to grasp a small rope that was tied to the saddle.

She stumbled forward until the hand across her mouth jerked her upright. Lawson tried to calm the now-nervous horse. Samantha strained to breathe and frantically darted her gaze around the alley. Not a soul in sight. In fact, it was too quiet.

Where had everyone gone? She was surrounded by more than thirty people a few minutes ago, surely someone would help her. She had to make some kind of noise.

A small rock lay on the ground less than a foot away. She inhaled once and glanced at Lawson, who was using his teeth to try to untie the rope. She kicked out as hard as she could. The stone ricocheted down the alley where it plunked up against a metal wash tub. Her shoulders sagged. It was barely enough noise to be noticed at all, let alone alert anyone.

A movement to the left caught her attention. Two cowboy hats poked around the side of the mercantile. One man slipped around the corner and hid behind a barrel. Lawson yanked and slammed her hard into his chest. He aimed toward the barrel and fired one round. It ricocheted off the building.

"That's close enough." He waited. No one moved.

Samantha felt his heart pound against her back. She forced herself to calm down. Lawson was cornered and could end up killing her or someone else just by accident.

"You won't get away with this." Her voice trembled a bit. "You can still turn yourself in."

He clamped a sweaty palm over her mouth again.

"No, I've come way too far. I'm so close." His breath was harsh and damp against her ear. "I have everything in order, everything planned." His fingers dug into her cheek until she tasted blood. "That's the real secret, you know. Plan carefully, take your time."

He reached out and grabbed one of Samantha's fists and looped one end of the rope around her wrist.

He reached out for the other hand. Tears threatened as new fear climbed over her heart. Her elbow connected with his ribs. He grunted and, as his fingers loosened, she tore away and ran down the alley, tugging the rope off and flinging it aside.

Samantha headed toward Miss Sadie's. If she could just make it to the building . . . The footsteps behind her pounded the earth and she tried to run faster. Lawson lunged and caught the hem of her skirt from behind, pulling her down in a heap of calico and lace. She dug her fingers into the dirt and pulled herself forward, kicking his hands away as she went.

"Help! Somebody plea-" The words were cut off as a blow landed against the back of her head, and the world went dark and silent.

"He whacked her on the head!" Skeeter Jackson came to a skidding stop in front of Taos and the Sheriff at the entrance to Miss Sadie's. Tall for a sixteen year old, he looked older from a distance. Freckles scattered across his nose gave away his age.

"How bad is it?" Blake grabbed Taos's shoulder to keep him there.

"Not too bad. No blood or nothing.'" Skeeter dragged a sleeve across his nose.

"Good. You and Jimmy tail him out of town and we'll be right behind you."

Blake turned to Taos. "You can't let your emotions run off with you. You got to let him get to open country. There'll be no place to hide and no risk of a long shootout."

"What about Sammy?"

The old law man rubbed his three-day beard. "I know you don't want to hear this, but it's probably a good thing she's out."

Taos glared at him.

"Now hear me out. Once he gets out of town, they'll probably be riding double on one horse. They can't make very good time."

"He won't need much time."

"If he intended to kill her he already would have."

"There's worse things than dying."

The sheriff nodded in agreement. "We'll have 'em before he can even stop to catch his breath."

Taos nodded.

Shouts from the end of the street drew the men's attention. Sonny Harper rode toward them at breakneck speed on a chestnut mare. He skidded to a stop and threw the blankets that were heaped on the back of the horse to the ground. "He's lit the brush on fire."

People started running as more noticed the smoke rising just beyond the last buildings of town.

Sonny jumped off his horse and grabbed the blankets. "It's at the edge of my place and headed down the valley toward town."

Taos glanced around him as people panicked. All of these people's livelihoods were in danger, and possibly their very lives, and Samantha was in the arms of a mad man. He couldn't let these people suffer for something that he could have prevented. His heart burned for Samantha, but he couldn't go after her until the disaster right in front of him was averted somehow.

Blake and Taos grabbed the blankets and ran to the well right on Sonny's heels. They soaked them with water then rode in the direction of the smoke. A thin orange line hugged the ground, sending billows of white smoke into a cloudless blue sky.

Small groups of men stood next to the leading edge of the fire, beating the flames with the wet blankets. Young boys rode their horses to and from the well, keeping the line supplied with more blankets. Taos waved Sonny down.

"Where's your stock?" He shouted over the fire noise.

"Most of them are down just below the tree line on the south side of Placer Creek." He cast a worried look in the direction of the fire.

"We need to move them. One good gust and this thing will jump the creek and head straight up the ridge."

Sonny nodded his agreement and looked at the line of men. "We can't spare any help."

Taos yelled at two of the boys that were delivering blankets. "Can you two round up a few head for us?"

"Yes sir!" Marly and Devin Ward rode to him. They looked like identical twins, though Marly was a full year older at fourteen.

Taos spoke to the boys for a minute, and then he sent them off and rejoined the line. One hour turned to two, then just as they seemed to be getting control a large gust of wind sent flames over the creek and up the slope.

Several men paused to watch and then went back to putting out the flames around them. Taos raced across the creek and up the other side. He pounded the flames and shouted for help.

Sonny grabbed several newly wet blankets and urged a few men to come with him.

"Just let it go Sonny. It'll burn itself out that direction, we need to focus on the town." Tom Banks leaned against a wagon and drained a large cup of water, trying to catch his breath as a couple of other men brought more blankets.

"There's two boys over there rounding up stock. If we don't get to them, they don't have any way out."

Men pounded the earth with renewed fervor. The terrain posed the biggest challenge. Fire raced across the valley floor and they struggled to follow, trying to keep it from getting into the tree line. Growing darkness offered no help as the fire glowed further and further ahead of them. Small groups of pine and aspen burst into flames, one after another.

Taos stood and stared.

Blake joined him. "We're not going to catch it."

"No."

"Those poor kids."

"They're alright. If they did what I told 'em to, then they're all right. We just have to find 'em." His eyes scanned the darkness. *Where were they?* The fire had already raced across half the valley.

"Hey!" One of the men yelled. "I found one of the horses." They raced to the spot and stared at the carcass which still smoked. There was no sign of a human nearby though. The smell of burnt horsehair filled Taos's nostrils. The animal lay with its mouth open and tongue hanging out and Taos thought this had to be the worst way for an animal to die. Several of the men turned away.

"Saddle's still on," Blake mumbled, "Probably got spooked. The boy must be close."

The group walked a wide circle, peering through the darkness at the ground. None wanted to find anything, but the search continued.

A distant cough grabbed every man's attention.

"Devin, Marly?" Blake called.

"We're over here." Taos watched as the boys appeared out of the darkness.

The men greeted them with much back slapping and cheering.

"You don't have a scratch on you! How'd you get behind the fire?"

Devin looked at Taos. "We did what you said."

"Yeah," Marly joined in. "He said if the fire caught us to find a clear spot and lay down with them wet blankets over us."

"The fire went right around us." Devin held out a hand to Taos. He shook it. "Thanks, Mr. Williams. If we hadn't done like you told us we'd been goners for sure."

The fire raced toward the ridge of mountains and away from town. Blake ordered several men to oversee the last of the effort to distinguish the flames close by.

Blake and Taos finally climbed aboard their horses to follow Lawson.

Sonny rode up next to Taos.

"You outta go on home, Harper, and get some sleep," Blake said.

"I'd like to ride along if you don't mind." He coughed a little, "Half my stock's dead and nearly all the forage is gone off my land." He looked over at Taos. "Sure appreciate the effort, though."

"I'm sure you'd have done the same for me."

Sonny grinned, "I'd like to think so. Anyway I'd sure like to help you find her."

"Appreciate it." Taos nodded.

Blake added, "Not only does Lawson have kidnapping on the list, he damaged a lot of property and damn near killed two kids. The man will be lucky to see sunrise."

Taos agreed, and if he got a chance he would make sure John Lawson never took another breath.

Gray fuzz gave way to dim light as Samantha tried to shake the ache out of her skull. Her groan was stifled by a handkerchief stuffed into her mouth.

Great, another handkerchief. She wiggled her tongue. At least this one was silk and didn't crunch. Thank God for small favors.

The wood floor was cool against her forehead and helped the throbbing in her brain somewhat. She pulled herself to a sitting position. Her hands were bound and her muscles sore and stiff. The pounding in her head intensified as she concentrated on staying upright. It was impossible to tell what time it was from the dim light in the window. It could be evening, she thought, then discarded that idea as her muscles ached terribly. It must be morning.

The small, sparsely furnished room contained only a bed and washstand. It didn't look like a hotel of any kind. A hairbrush lay next to the water pitcher and small framed tintypes hung on the wall. This had to be someone's home, but whose? They couldn't be that far away from River City yet. Unless she was unconscious longer than she thought. Who would Lawson know here?

The fog in her mind cleared slowly. He couldn't know anyone. As far as she knew he had never been west of Pennsylvania. Footsteps clicking down the hall interrupted Samantha's sleuthing and she stared at the doorknob. Her heart raced as the door opened. Lawson stepped inside and closed it behind him.

"Oh, good. You're awake."

He looked calm and poised, as if he had come to take her on a stroll in the park. He walked over and knelt to help her up. Samantha shrank back. His hands were surprisingly gentle.

"You don't have to fear me, you know."

He guided her over to bed. She sat on the edge and pulled away from him. His eyes roamed over her body and an uneasy tremor snaked through her.

"You created this situation. Though I won't hold it against you." He chuckled lightly as if scolding an errant child. "Someday we'll laugh about this little escapade. It's a good thing I came to get you. I hate to think what would have happened to you in this Godforsaken place."

Samantha glared at him as he paced restlessly around the room. Shock was the only thing that registered in her mind. She didn't think she could stand any more rescues in her life. Why did men think it necessary to tie up a woman and gag her in order to save her?

"If you had accepted my original offer we wouldn't be here." He stopped and smiled. "Though this will make a wonderful story to tell our children someday."

"Nmm mommonn hmmonn!" The handkerchief vibrated with the frustration of her muffled words, and Lawson's patronizing smile made her hands itch.

"I shall consider myself lucky to be spared what I'm sure was a very unladylike response." He gazed out the window. "You have a number of habits we will endeavor to work on together. In time you will see this was for the best. You're lucky I'm a very patient man."

Samantha struggled against her bindings. It was one thing to be carried off by an evil man. Yet quite another to be at the mercy of a crazy one. Lawson watched her with detached interest as one watches a mouse try to free itself from a trap.

"Your aunt would like to see you."

Samantha went completely still.

"She isn't dead . . . yet." Lawson sat very close to her

Samantha's heart pounded wildly.

"I never intended for her to get in the way. She just wouldn't go along with things." He shook his head then shrugged his shoulders.

"It can't be helped now. The plan is already in motion." He looked into her eyes.

"If you will agree to accompany me and not try to alert anyone, I'll take you to see her one last time."

One last time. Just the thought made tears spring to her eyes. She stared at the floor. The last thing she wanted to do was cry in front of this twisted man.

"You think about it, and I'll return shortly for your answer." He swept out the door like an actor in a dramatic play. If only it was a play.

Samantha searched for some sense of logic in his thought process. *Mattie.* He was probably lying, just stringing her along so she would cooperate. Mattie must already be gone. Samantha laid herself over on the pillow. Tears rolled down her face. Her thoughts jumbled together except for one: The pillow smelled like old socks.

What if the whole thing was a lie? She popped back up. Why else would he be so desperate unless he thought he might be found out? Hope sprang into her heart. Even if he wasn't telling the truth, what choice did she have? Bound like this she had no way to escape. Her only hope was to gain his trust, to do as he asked.

To a point.

She stared at the ceiling. It was a difficult game to dance on the spider's web and not get caught. Games weren't her strong suit to begin with; she just didn't have the patience for them. She tumbled scenarios through her mind to practice her reactions. She had to be convincing, calm, docile.

Docile?

Okay, not a word previously found in her vocabulary. That would be the hardest part, playing the submissive, passive female. She had to keep her thoughts from showing on her face and her mouth shut.

I'd have a better chance if I left the handkerchief stuffed in my mouth.

That cynical thought almost made her laugh. Taos would love to see this little debut of her acting skill. Her shoulders slumped.

She certainly never dreamed she would leave him standing at the altar, even if it happened to be in a whorehouse.

Now *that* was a story she wanted to tell her children. Make that her and Taos's children. If Lawson hadn't stopped them, she would be married by now and out of his reach. She looked out the window to a view of trees and thick forest. She would have been greeting the day lying in Taos's arms and looking forward to a lifetime of loving him.

She sniffed as one last tear rolled into oblivion. He would follow. Wouldn't he? He had to. He seemed so willing to do anything, even get married, to keep her from Lawson. It wouldn't be long until he showed up to take her back home. Home with him. Where she belonged. In the meantime, she would concentrate on getting away from this evil criminal.

She schemed and planned for almost an hour. When the door reopened, she would be ready for the performance of her life.

Yours Again

Chapter 21

Lawson returned an hour later, untied Samantha and prodded her toward the door. Last night's ride left her more than a little stiff. Not to mention somewhat rumpled.

She paused in front of the mirror. When she was five their dog had carried one of her little rag dolls to the porch. The red yarn hair was caked with mud, one eye was missing, and it was covered with dog slobber. If only she looked that good. He motioned for her to hurry.

She quickly freshened up and then stepped into a large room, which turned out to be the main room of the house. The structure was larger than she anticipated, with a stone fireplace, kitchen, and sitting area on one side and two bedrooms on the other. The furnishings were modest but quite clean and bright.

Samantha blinked as her eyes grew accustomed to the morning light streaming in through the front windows. Convincing

Lawson she would be agreeable had been much easier than she anticipated, and she fully intended to keep up the act. It was easy to be convincing when her life depended on it. Tears threatened as panic took hold of her emotions. Samantha forced a deep breath and tried to focus on one thing: escape.

As she surveyed her surroundings, she saw an elderly couple, bound and gagged, sitting on a bench near the door. The man wore overalls and was nearly completely bald. Though the gag prevented him from saying anything, anger emanated from his stern expression and red face.

The woman sat next to him in a faded green dress. Tendrils of gray-blue hair hung across her face, and she cowered in fear. Samantha pressed her lips together. They had to be in their late sixties or early seventies. How could he truss them up like criminals?

"Breakfast would be nice, don't you think?" Lawson stepped around her and sat down at the long table. Pulling an expensive-looking pocketknife out of his coat, he cleaned his fingernails one by one. The scraping sound grated across Samantha's already raw nerves.

She rubbed her wrists as she met the old woman's frightened gaze. Anger rose immediately and Samantha glared at Lawson's back, struggling to control her voice. The man needed to be squashed like a large, odious stink bug.

Docile, you must be docile. "Of course. I'll see what there is," she said

Lawson's eyes followed her as she moved around the kitchen. She gathered ingredients and sat them next to a large bowl on the counter. Each time she stole a look in his direction, she was met by the same piercing, unwavering stare. Her skin flinched in disgust and her nerves stretched taunt.

Samantha stirred the mix. She couldn't afford to make a move too soon. He had to relax at some point. Catching him off guard was her only chance. If only she had some help. She glanced at the old couple. One woman might not be able to overpower Lawson, but maybe the three of them could do something.

"I think some biscuits and ham might be manageable." She attempted to smile. "If that's all right with you, John."

He nodded. "Just hurry. And make plenty. I haven't eaten anything decent in days."

Samantha's mind sparked a quick idea. "Well, I could fry some potatoes, too, if I had some help peeling them?" She extended a spud his direction.

He snorted. "I'm not kitchen help."

"Oh no, of course not," She feigned concern that she hoped seemed heartfelt. "Maybe she could peel them while I roll out the biscuits." Samantha motioned toward the woman.

Lawson raised an eyebrow. Hunger warred with suspicion, but physical sustenance won out. He nodded in agreement.

Samantha loosened the ropes restraining the woman.

"No tricks." Lawson threatened.

The woman shook her head.

"Oh, I'm sure you have nothing to fear from, uh . . .?" Samantha questioned.

"Lillian." Her voice shook.

Samantha smiled and laid a comforting hand on her shoulder. "You're going to be fine. We're all going to be fine." She looked hard at the woman, who nodded silent support, and then at the man, who jerked his head in agreement. It was a relief that Lawson hadn't frightened them too badly to be of any help. She now had two willing accomplices, but no plan.

The two women walked to the kitchen area and Samantha began an easy chat with Lillian as Lawson watched intently.

"How long have you and . . . ?" She motioned toward the man.

"Ben."

"Ben, lived here?" Samantha spoke loud enough to be heard by everyone as she rolled out biscuits on the counter with her back to Lawson. Lillian stood beside her and peeled potatoes with shaking hands. Samantha watched the knife wobble, barely missing the woman's finger.

"About ten years, I suppose." Lillian imitated Samantha's light tone and spoke distinctly. "It was my sister's place, but her man died and she went back east to care for my mother."

"Where back east?" Samantha smoothed out some flour next to the biscuits and began writing words, her body shielding the movement from Lawson's prying eyes.

"Up near New York." Lillian nodded slightly as each word was formed then erased.

"I grew up in Boston."

"I hear it's lovely in the fall there." She peeled more flesh off the last potato than skin as she tried to decipher Samantha's writing. She set it aside, picked up another, and tried to concentrate.

"Oh, it is." Silence descended. It was difficult to carry on a conversation and write secret messages at the same time. She stared at the rolling pin that looked older than she was. "How long have you and Ben been married?

"Thirty-eight years."

"That long?"

"It was nothing much besides Indians and Mexicans when we came out to this area." Lillian did better on the next potato, and her hands stopped shaking. "Our boys were already grown, and we thought we needed a smaller place and got this one."

Samantha relaxed a bit as the conversation seemed to be calming everyone. "So, how has it gone?"

Lillian raised an eyebrow at her with a slight grin. "Well, it hasn't been easy, but it's certainly been interesting."

Samantha formed then erased the last word in flour and helped pile the now-naked spuds in a bowl.

"We haven't put on any coffee yet." Lillian said.

Samantha's brows raised in question as a near-full pot sat on the stove. Lillian opened a cabinet and pushed aside several jars. She stood on tiptoe and pulled out a can of coffee. She slid her gaze toward Samantha and flicked her palm open to reveal a small vial that she quickly concealed in her skirt pocket.

"I think coffee would be just the thing." Samantha glanced toward Lawson, who was no longer looking at them.

Within a few minutes potatoes were frying, biscuits baking, and coffee brewing. Samantha stared at the pot of coffee. She willed the liquid to boil as the back of her neck overheated with pent-up tension. Her hand absently rubbed the aching muscles there as her mind lined up several escape plans.

"A watched pot never boils, honey." Lillian now stood beside Samantha. "Like you said, everything's gonna be fine," she whispered.

Samantha tried to smile and mouthed, "How long?"

Lawson stood and turned in their direction, listening intently.

"Oh, I'd say it will probably be ready in about fifteen minutes or so. Give or take." She raised her voice a bit so Lawson could hear.

Fifteen minutes for it to work. What then? Samantha looked around the room again. Her focus settled on Ben. They had to get Lawson to allow them to untie him. She walked toward the man and leaned over him so it would appear she was inspecting his bindings.

"Get away from him," Lawson spoke calmly, his eyes flashing a warning.

"He seems utterly harmless John," Samantha laid a hand on Ben's shoulder and felt firm muscles. "Why, he's all bone." The man's eyes showed momentary surprise before his expression hid itself again.

"He hasn't been at all well." Lillian chimed in, catching the drift of the ploy. "Had a hacking cough for weeks now."

Ben coughed under the gag then bowed his head and sucked in his chest, doing his best to look the part of an invalid.

Lawson's gaze roamed over the man, an unnatural stare that seemed to pierce flesh.

"It seems incredibly cruel to make this poor man sit here with his hands tied like this while we eat." Ben coughed some more and Samantha patted him gently on the back.

Lawson gave her a lopsided grin. "You are entirely too softhearted." He moved toward the older man and untied him. "That's just one of the reasons you need my protection."

Samantha flashed Lawson what she hoped was a brilliant smile. "Thank you." She forced herself to brush her fingertips along this arm. "I'm sure you're right about that."

She clamped her teeth together and wiped her hand on her skirt. Touching him repulsed her. At least he didn't touch back. She would rather be licked on the earlobe by a snake.

Ben rubbed his wrists and watched Lawson from beneath lowered lids. "Mother, could you help me to the table? My gout's actin' up from sitting here this long."

Samantha's eyes widened as the man limped to the table, leaning heavily on Lillian. Hope dimmed a little as she watched the old man. It never crossed her mind he might not be able to move quickly. Lawson seated himself and absently ran his long fingers along the blade of his knife as if it were an extension of his hand. Samantha dished up the food.

Lillian nudged her side and motioned to Ben with a grin. The man winked. Relief flooded over her. What extraordinary luck to have accomplices that were better actors than she.

Ben heaved a long breath and rubbed his thigh. "Yep. It's a sad thing, gettin' old."

Lawson's attention momentarily flicked toward Ben.

He slapped his knee. "Old war wound, ya know."

"Which war?" Samantha cleaned flour off the counter.

"Why the big one, Missy. The war between the states."

Ben leaned toward Lawson. "We's out on patrol creeping up on ol' Johnny Reb and trying to keep track of his comins and goins up in the Cumberland Gap area. You been there?"

Lawson shook his head no.

"Beautiful country. Mist settles into the mountains and looks like the breath of God hisself."

"I've listened for twenty years about those mountains." Lillian said. "Don't you think it's about time I saw them, old man?"

"Now this is my story, Mother, and there you go trotting right into it!" He whispered at Lawson, "Woman can't stand not to be the center of attention. For mor'n fifty years she's interrupted every story I ever told."

"That's not true. And it is forty-eight years, not fifty." Lillian smiled at Samantha.

"It seems like mor'n fifty some days," he groused. "Anyway, like I was sayin', we's walking through some brush toward a deserted campsite and all the sudden I heard a crack and felt a sharp burning in my leg. Well, let me tell you, I thought one of them eastern diamondbacks had done had his way with me for sure. I's almost relieved when I found out it was only a bullet."

Lillian flipped over some clean mugs and emptied all of the white powder from the vial into one cup. Samantha filled it with coffee and waited a moment to be sure it dissolved completely before offering it to Lawson. She found it exquisite poetic justice that she was slipping something into his drink just as he'd slipped something into Mattie's in Boston.

The other mugs were filled and they all sat down to eat.

"When will we be leaving?" Samantha asked.

"In a few hours," he said. "Horse needs more rest."

Lawson ate as meticulously as he did everything else, working in a clockwise circle on his plate. Potatoes, ham, biscuit—take a sip of coffee. Potatoes, ham, biscuit—take a sip of coffee. She willed him to drain the cup, or at least take a large gulp, but had to watch as he sipped in between bites of biscuit and potato. Always the same order, never deviating. Samantha shook her head. He must have been a very strange child.

The meal ended quietly. The women cleared the table and washed dishes. They chattered lightly, and each occasionally glanced toward the chair where Lawson had settled himself. Just as Samantha finished scrubbing the skillet, the first bead of sweat appeared on Lawson's forehead and he shifted slightly in his chair.

"More coffee, anyone?" Samantha noticed her tone was a little too cheery. She found it difficult to contain the anticipation of escape. She tried to appear somewhat more subdued as she filled Ben's cup.

Lawson seemed not to notice as he squirmed in his chair for a few minutes and finally bolted for the door. No one moved a muscle. The heavy slam of the outhouse door propelled the remaining occupants of the house into action.

Ben leapt to his feet and ran to the window to watch for Lawson's return.

"What was that stuff?" Samantha asked.

Lillian grinned. "A little potion I used to use when my boys needed cleaning out." She laughed, "He'll be holed up in that outhouse for an hour or better."

"I'll saddle the horses."

"Oh no, you've already done so much to help. I can ride his horse," Samantha started, "and if you'll point me in the right direction . . ."

Ben chuckled. "This is the most excitement we've had around here in years. We're not about to send you off alone, little lady." He winked at her. "'Sides, I kinda want to see how this comes out."

Lillian laughed at Ben and nodded. "He just loves a good adventure." She lowered her voice to a whisper, "And so do I!"

The three slipped out the door and around to the barn, keeping a close eye on the outhouse door. They quickly saddled the horses and set off, trying to keep the animals quiet as they passed close to the house.

The outhouse door swung open and Lawson stumbled out, yelling, "I'll find you, Samantha. You can't get away. You'll pay for this." He stopped suddenly, turned, and ran back to the outhouse.

"We better get while the gettin's good ladies." Ben swung his horse around and set a steady gallop toward River City.

Yours Again

Chapter 22

The wind stirred dust across the set of tracks Taos had followed for the last four hours, mostly on foot leading his horse. The darkness had given way to dawn, but the going had been painstakingly slow.

"At least he left a trail big enough for my mother-in-law to find." Sheriff Blake said. He and Sonny had continued on with Taos, though the darkness had seriously hampered their efforts. All three reeked of smoke from the fire. Taos's nose still burned with the acrid odor of burnt horseflesh. He wiped a sleeve across his nose, but it didn't help.

Taos followed the trail as best he could. As time dragged on, foreboding set into his heart. They could be miles ahead by now, and if they lost this trail there would be almost no hope.

"We'll get along a bit faster with a few hours' sleep. Need our strength, you know," Blake said.

The sheriff had hinted at setting up camp several times, but Taos just couldn't stop. It wasn't about being tired. He was certainly that. He needed to be doing, not thinking. As long as he was doing something—anything—to find Samantha, he wasn't thinking about her. Missing her, needing her, loving her. He couldn't let his mind settle on the mights and maybes. The edge of insanity drew closer with every step. If he stopped, it just might catch up.

"Can't rightly figure where he's headed." Sonny rode up beside Taos. "He know anybody out this direction?"

"Not that I know of," Taos hadn't been able to figure out his direction either. He knew Lawson didn't have provisions for any length of time on his horse and he was headed out into an area still considered Indian Territory by most locals. It was sparsely populated with no towns or anywhere to refresh their mounts. The terrain was steep and heavily forested. Maybe Lawson had stashed supplies and fresh horses nearby. He stared at the single tracks they were following.

"Seems he would've switched horses by now." Blake seemed to read his mind. "It's almost like he didn't have much of a plan beyond snatching her."

That did nothing to ease Taos's mind. If that line of thinking were true, then Lawson was way more than borderline crazy. At least sanity made a man partially predicable on the trail. Crazy was different.

The men fell into silence as they made their way along the trail. The sheriff seemed to resign himself to continuing on, which they did.

When the sun peeked over the mountains, the men stopped at a creek to water the horses. Taos stood next to his horse and leaned both arms on the saddle, watching the sun rise. It had the hallmarks of being a beautiful day, the kind of day when most people would be getting up and going about their normal business.

It's not natural, he thought, *for life to go on normal for other people today, yet fall apart for me.*

"You figuring on which way they went from here?" Blake hung gnarled fingers in his front belt loops and stared in the same direction as Taos.

"Nah, I was just wondering how to make the sun stop rising."

Blake nodded in silent sympathy and wandered off, leaving Taos to his thoughts.

Taos breathed deeply of the cool air. His heart ached for the slightest scent of honeysuckle, but there was nothing. He breathed again, closed his eyes, and laid a hand on his chest as the ache expanded.

Sonny kneeled down next to him and washed soot off both his arms in the creek. He cleared his throat, "You know I'm real sorry about before." He looked up at Taos.

"Before what?"

"About Samantha and all." He stood next to Taos. "Didn't know y'all was married."

Taos's face hinted at a smile. "Neither did I."

Sonny shrugged. "Still, I didn't mean anything by it. Just wanted you to know."

"Don't think nothin' of it, Sonny." Taos paused, "You gonna stay in River City?"

"Might as well. Be just as hard to start somewhere else as it is to start here again."

"How many head are left?"

"Maybe thirty, maybe twenty five." He shook his head. "Less than half and I'll have to sell 'em."

"You won't get any kind of price for 'em now with so many selling out."

Sonny stared at the ground. "Got no way to feed 'em. The fire took near every bit of forage I had left."

Taos thought a moment. "You could bring them over to our place, mix in with our heard. Just 'til things are better anyway."

"Can't take no charity." He looked away ashamed.

"It wouldn't be. You could trade a few head for the grass and water. Course we'd expect you to help with our stock and with the other work on the ranch. What do you say?"

The man's face registered a range of emotions from surprise to gratefulness. "I'd be right grateful to you." He extended a hand in Taos's direction.

Taos shook it and smiled. "You may not say that after a few days. We work long and hard."

"Good. Me too."

The sound of horses' hooves in the distance froze the men in place as each listened to discern a direction. The men mounted and headed full bore toward the sound. Just ahead, three riders rounded a curve in the creek and sped toward them. Taos's attention immediately settled on waves of long golden hair flying in the wind.

Samantha spotted him about the same time and the two rode directly toward each other. They reined their mounts to a halt, she leaped into his arms, and he dragged her over onto his horse.

The old couple reined behind her and nodded to the sheriff.

"I take it they're acquainted." Ben winked at Lillian.

"Yes sir, I say that's a fair assumption." Sheriff Blake grinned from ear to ear as the young couple kissed, oblivious to their presence.

Taos hugged Samantha close as their lips melded together. He'd already resigned himself to the fact that they might not find her—or not alive anyway. He'd been so scared he'd never see her again and now here she was. He had to be sure she knew he'd never let her go again.

After a few minutes, then a few more minutes, then some throat clearing, followed by more throat clearing, the group headed back toward town. The sheriff questioned the older couple as well as Samantha.

Ben's description was the most colorful. "That Lawson fella is a little on the odd side, if you ask me. I mean, if I was gonna grab a woman and run off with her, I wouldn't stop and offer to pay for a room at somebody's house."

"Is that how he got you to let him in?" The sheriff's investigator hat sat firmly in place.

"Oh, yes," Lillian added. "He said his lady was sick and they needed to rest." She thought for a moment. "I am curious about something though."

"What's that?" Blake listened intently as the horses made their way around a small group of bushes.

Lillian glanced slyly at her husband. "If you were going to run off with a woman, how exactly would you do it?"

Ben burst out laughing. "Well, there's two possibilities." He winked at his wife.

The sheriff shook his head in frustration.

"If I grabbed her like that guy did, I'd sure keep goin' and not stop for nothin' or nobody."

"What makes you think she might want you after that?" A smile played on Lillian's lips.

"Hmm." Ben rubbed his chin. "That would be a problem." He paused as Taos and Samantha snickered. "Then I'd have to go to the backup plan."

"Which is?" Taos asked.

"Well, I'd just make her marry me and wear her down over time."

"And you think that might work better?" Lillian laughed.

"Well, Mother, it sure worked the first time." He reached over to her horse and squeezed her hand.

Blake shook his head. "I swear I'm gonna puke!"

The conversation returned to Lawson.

"I don't think you've heard the last of him." Blake's concern was evident.

"If we get married, then he won't have anything to claim," Samantha interjected.

"There's been a development in that area." Blake nodded at Taos. "Well, tell her already son!"

"Tell me what?"

"Um, it seems we're already married."

"No, we're not!"

"Apparently, we are."

"I think I would have remembered if I had said 'I do' to anyone."

"You mean the way I said 'I do' before you left me at the altar?"

Samantha smiled at him. "I don't think you can have an altar in a whorehouse."

"We've been married for three years," Taos said.

Her faced reflected her disbelief.

He nodded. "Really. By proxy. Apparently Mattie and Jake arranged it to ensure the water rights would be safe just in case a drought ever made it a necessity. That's where that inheritance came from. They planned to have it annulled, but didn't get the paperwork taken care of." Taos watched her face as she digested the entirety of what he had said. His heart skipped a beat as her mouth spread into a slow smile then came to a near dead stop as she frowned. This could be bad. She glared up at him.

"We have been married this whole time?"

He nodded slowly as pinpricks ran across his neck and behind his ears.

"You mean, I got on a train and traveled across the country, was tied up and dragged to your house"—their three silent companions stared at Taos, who shrugged. Samantha continued—"put up with your mouth, actually went to a whorehouse for advice"—more stares—"not to mention you throwing my clothes out the window for God and everybody to see."

Taos hoped she would at least take a breath soon.

She pointed a finger at his chest. "Just to be kidnapped and tied up and dragged off by an evil man and then forced to watch him eat potatoes, ham, biscuit, potatoes, ham, biscuit . . ."

Taos shook her shoulders slightly. "You're babbling."

The other two men nodded in agreement.

"I can't help it!" she yelled. "I went through all this for nothing!"

"Well, I wouldn't say *nothing*." He paused, but she remained silent.

She didn't look overly thrilled at him. "Why didn't you tell me?"

"I didn't know!"

She gazed at him with suspicion.

"Really! Miles told me after Lawson dragged you out of the wedding. We were getting married anyway, so what difference does it make now?"

"I don't know." She looked tired. "I just need to sort this all out."

"You'll feel better after you've had some sleep."

She nodded and leaned her head on his shoulder. He held onto her with one hand and guided his horse with the other. His mind ran a big circle around the events of the last twenty-four hours.

They were married. That was a good thing, right? He got the security of knowing she was safe and so were the ranches. Samantha got his protection as well as a family and home out of the deal. Things were tied up in a neat little package.

Still, a strange sense of foreboding hovered over him, refusing to be stifled.

He looked down at the top of her head. *What could she possibly have to sort out?*

Chapter 23

Darren heard the good news about the rescue just as he barreled into town to help. He and Charlie had seen the smoke and spent the entire night rounding up the herd and getting them across the river. The wind could shift at a moment's notice, and the herd would not be completely safe until the water lay between them and any further threat of fire. They decided Charlie would stay with the cattle and make sure they stayed in the clear until they verified all was safe.

The sheriff filled him in on the details, including how Taos had saved the Ward boys. Town hardly seemed like the same place. People who just days earlier had been at each other's throats were shaking hands and greeting each other like long lost friends. Several stopped Darren to tell him how grateful they were to Taos. The wife beater rumors seemed all but forgotten. It confirmed for Darren how fickle people could be.

He made his way over to Reverend Miller's where Tommy was staying during the chaos. The man appeared more than eager to hand Tommy over to his uncle's care.

After five minutes, Darren knew why.

"The bad guy grabbed her and dragged her out. Me and Nate was gonna follow but his pa sent us home." He wiggled a little on the saddle in front of his uncle. "Then the fire came and all the people were running and yelling. Nate's ma started crying then his pa went to help soak blankets at the well." Tommy yawned.

"When did you go to bed?"

"We went up to bed when it got late, but we watched out Nate's window 'til near morning. Nate's ma said they found Sammy and she was safe."

"Yep, your pa took her home."

"So she's my very own ma for real, now? Like the way Nate has a real ma?"

"Yes." Nate was the Miller's oldest boy. Apparently the two'd had quite a time with the excitement of the wedding and then the fire. Still, the frustration of listening to the kid rattle on would wear on anybody. Darren couldn't blame Tommy, the boy was just excited. Really excited, and so was he. Though it didn't tumble out of his mouth like it did Tommy's. He almost envied that ability.

Samantha had been a constant companion during Darren's early years, and the fact that she was now a real part of the family was the best news he'd had in a long time. She was the only female he could talk to without getting his words all mixed up. Even when they were kids, she never judged him or thought him less than bright, like so many others did. He didn't speak to a soul for six months after she left.

Tommy's relentless questions invaded his memories.

"So she'll always be here? And maybe we can go swimming?

Maybe every day?" He paused for a quick breath. "Does this mean I might get a brother?"

Darren groaned. This ride was getting longer every minute.

"Nate has a little brother. They do lots together. If I had a little brother I could teach him stuff I know, like how to do chores, and where to dig for the best worms, and . . ."

The boy continued to chatter, but it got Darren to thinking. If his brother was as affection-starved as he guessed, Tommy might get more than he bargained for. A slow grin spread across Darren's face. That might be just what Taos needed to take a little starch out of his stride. He had a mental image of his brother trying to handle a couple of little girls bouncing on his lap. Darren threw his head back and laughed.

"What's so funny?"

"I was just thinking that you might get s-sisters." He poked Tommy's ribs. "Lots of 'em."

"Naw, I don't like girls much." Tommy shook his head. "They don't fish or skip rocks in the creek or nothin'. They just stand around and giggle all the time."

Darren could certainly agree with that, with the exception of Sammy of course. The house rose into view and it's shadow blocked the sun's last rays. The late hour didn't slow the stream of questions from Tommy. If anything, he picked up speed.

"I'm kinda hungry. She'll be here to cook, too?"

"Mmmm."

"I like the way she cooks. She always makes stuff I like—and makes sure I eat." The small voice lowered to a whisper. "Even when I'm in trouble she sneaks me cookies and milk, but don't tell anyone."

Darren chuckled. Sammy was exactly what this boy needed. Jimbo greeted them with an enthusiastic bark as the two climbed off the horse and headed into the house; Darren was two steps behind Tommy. The boy was off like a shot up the stairs and Darren had just enough time to hook a finger into Tommy's back belt loop and halt his progress.

"What?" Tommy questioned.

Darren surveyed the scene with a shake of his head. There was a shirt on one step, ruffles and lace of some sort hooked over the banister, and a stocking dangling from a lampshade. He swallowed his laughter and tried to sound stern.

"I ought to go first. You never know what might be up there."

The boy glanced quickly around. "You think that bad guy's here?" He whispered with the excitement of the hunt. "We can take him Uncle Darren, just you and me. Why, we'll knock him down and kick him." Little fists flailed air. "And then we can call the sheriff and he'll hang him high." Tommy placed his hands around his throat like a noose and rolled his eyes back in his head.

Darren held out a hand to steady the little body as he nearly tumbled down the stairs in excitement. From what he could see it looked like the bad guy was a distant memory, and what he guessed was upstairs would probably shock a boy into puberty. He scooped up clothes as he climbed the steps with Tommy behind him, closer than a shadow.

Taos's door was closed, and Darren paused outside to listen. Tommy slid through his uncle's knees and pressed an ear to the door.

"Think they're in there, Uncle Darren?" he whispered.

"I think they're asleep." He certainly hoped so anyway as he turned the knob and opened the door just a crack. Samantha's head was resting on Taos chest and his arm was curled around her with his fingers tangled in her hair. Taos's eyes popped open and focused on Darren.

"Pa's awake."

Samantha's head popped up at the sound of Tommy's voice. She grabbed the sheet and tugged it higher. "Really, Darren, can't we have a little privacy?" Her voice squeaked.

"Sorry." He ducked, trying to keep Tommy from running in with his one free hand. "I just wanted to be sure you were all right."

"Are you sure?" Taos's voice was laced with heavy irritation.

Samantha poked him in the side. "We appreciate the concern, and we're both fine. Just tired."

Darren lost the struggle with Tommy and dropped his armload of clothes just as the boy scooted around his legs.

Taos and Samantha both sat up in alarm as the small body hopped onto the foot of the bed.

"Darren says you're like a real ma now, just like Nate has a real ma, and you'll be cooking all the time and we can go swimmin' and fishin' . . ."

Darren scooped up the boy and slung him over his shoulder. "We'll be letting you sleep now."

The door slammed shut on Tommy's chatter and Taos flopped back on the pillows. Samantha breathed a sigh of relief.

"And I want a little brother, too," the voice yelled from the stairs.

She cast an alarmed look at Taos.

He was smiling. "You should tell him we've already been working on that."

"I will not!" She laughed in feigned shock. "Of course, I wouldn't mind continuing to work on it." She slid a hand over his chest. He caught it and kissed her palm.

"I feel I have to warn you, ma'am," he said sternly.

"Warn me?"

"There could be some serious squishing involved." He rolled her onto her back as she laughed.

Samantha ran her fingers through the dark wavy locks that fell just over his ears. "So are you happy with the way things turned out?"

"Well, there's a few advantages to being married." His tongue darted between her breasts.

"Only a few?" she giggled as he tickled her ribs and they got back to some serious loving.

Darren rummaged around the kitchen for something to eat as Samantha's laughter floated to his ears. He leaned both hands on the table and stared out the window. That kind of happiness could drive a single man insane. Jimbo's barking snapped him back to attention and he leaned out the door and hollered for Tommy.

The two of them searched cabinets and banged pots until Samantha finally appeared at the kitchen door.

"What are you two doing?"

Her voice stopped them both in their tracks.

"Cooking." Darren plopped a mountain of lard into the skillet as Tommy jumped down from the chair he was standing on. He ran to Samantha and took her hand.

"You gotta help. He can't do it right." The boy pushed her toward the stove as Taos walked in, looking a little irritated.

"Did you two have to make so much noise?" He glared at Darren. "We couldn't sleep a wink."

"Well it's quiet now that Sammy's down here." Darren grinned. "You could g-go back up and crawl into bed."

Taos grunted and glared.

"Darren," Samantha warned. "You know better than to tug on a tiger's tail."

"Hopefully he'll be g-growling a lot less from now on." Darren squeezed Samantha's shoulders and sat down at the table.

"Not if he never gets any *sleep*." Taos huffed.

Dinner was filled with easy conversation, mostly answering Tommy's thousand and one questions. All three adults were glad to see his eyes finally droop . He was sent off to bed in short order.

"So what about this Lawson?" Darren held his cup as Samantha poured more coffee. "You think he'll show up here?"

"No," Taos paused and thought for a moment. "He's not really a fighter. He's more of a snake belly type. Just tried to grab and run. Don't believe he'd stand and go toe-to-toe."

Darren nodded.

"If he tries anything, I figure he'll wait until she's alone and try to take her."

"So . . . I'm not safe here?" Samantha's question seemed to take both men by surprise.

"You are safe, absolutely." Taos's voice was unwavering and confident. "He's not fool enough to confront both of us at once."

Samantha nodded, but didn't seem totally convinced.

"One of us will be with you twenty-four hours a day." He ran his finger along the back of her hand.

Darren cleared his throat. "I guess that means I have the day shift."

Jimbo's rousing bark outside the door joined their laughter.

"He just can't stand to be left out." Samantha shook her head as the dog's voice slid into a rousing yowl.

Taos closed the back door to shut out the noise as the three departed for bed.

As the light in the kitchen disappeared, a shadow moved into the barn.

Chapter 24

Samantha watched another sunset from the porch—except this time, as Taos Williams's wife. She knew her heart, but did she know his? She'd wanted to belong here, to him, and now she did, but uncertainty still plagued her mind.

Last night she'd dreamed that he'd had a terrible accident and she had lost him. She awoke to the sound of his steady breathing and lay awake for several hours with her hand on his chest, feeling it rise and fall. The fear seemed almost paralyzing. Was this the same love her mother had known?

Things seemed to be getting back to normal, but Taos really hadn't said much. How did he feel about her, about this? He had been so absolutely set against marriage. Had he truly changed his mind, or was he just making the best of the situation?

She replayed the last day in her mind. He hadn't treated her any different than before, except they shared a bed now. She looked at her left hand. He hadn't even mentioned a ring. A small wave of sadness washed over her.

"You coming up to bed?" Taos stood in the doorway.

"I'll be up in a minute."

He joined her on the porch. They stood side by side in silence for a few minutes.

"Taos?"

"Hmmm?"

"Are you happy with this situation?"

"What do you mean?"

She let out a long breath. "I mean you didn't have much say in the fact that we're married, and I just wondered if you were happy with how things have turned out."

"Well, it was kind of handed to both of us, but I think it's turned out well. Are you not happy with things?"

"Yes, I am. I just feel like we went from being enemies to being married in a big hurry, that's all."

"So, are you saying you want to be courted?"

"Well, that would be a good place to start if you'd like."

"No, I would not like. Why should we go through all that when we're already married?"

"You suggested it," Her words were etched with irritation. "I just agreed it might be nice."

"I'm not one of those poetry readers and I don't know anything about courting a woman."

"That's not true." The evening they spent in the rose garden popped into her mind. "You have the ability, just not the want to I guess."

Samantha turned, went up to her room and stayed there. She sat on the edge of her bed and listened as he got ready to go to sleep in the room next door. Her thoughts swirled, circling from irritation to sadness. Irritation at the thought that he wasn't willing to put out any effort for her, though she would do almost anything for him. It seemed a very lopsided trade off.

Emptiness filled her at the notion that he was just making the best of a bad situation. She wanted this place and that man so much, but was she willing to live here under those terms? To love and not really be loved? The hours didn't solve the questions.

Taos waited for her to come to his bed, but she never did. He lay awake for most of the night, sleep finally claiming him as the first light of day touched the sky.

The creaking bed in the next room coaxed Taos's eyes open. A small wedge of light poked out from under the connecting door between them. He stretched and ran his open palm over the sheet next to him. She should be here. She was his wife.

The sound of water splashing and the soft hum of her voice drifted across the distance. He imagined her standing in front of the mirror naked, water trailing from her hands into the washstand. Every part of his body tingled as the sound of the water added reality to his vision. He swore he heard the liquid dance over her face and drip slowly down her neck toward the dark crevice between her breasts.

He groaned, rolled over and pulled the pillow around his ears. Torture. She was determined to push him beyond all possible restraint. She was humming again. The muffled sound sent pin pricks up his spine.

Taos grabbed the other pillow and pounded it on top of the first one, determined not to let it affect him. He drew a deep breath and held it for a moment before letting out a defeated sigh. He wasn't even convincing himself.

He had never been good at courting. In truth, he hadn't really done much of it. Sharisse had flat out chased him, but she had ulterior motives. What he needed was help. Some good advice. Someone who could keep their mouth shut. Names streamed through his mind as possible sources of information.

Darren? Well, keeping quiet was definitely his strong suit, but he had done even less courting than Taos. A cocky grin came to mind. Charlie. Now he had certainly done his share. Must be good at it, too, the way the girls always swooned when he walked by. Charlie would be great with advice, terrible at keeping quiet. The whole town would know he had to ask for advice about how to court his own wife inside half a day.

He knew she was still humming. He couldn't hear it, he could feel it. Like a tiny string vibrating from her heart to his. How could she not feel it? Maybe because she was the one plucking the string and he was the nimrod at the end of it.

Maybe someone married would offer better advice. Blake? He'd been married once, but that had to be over twenty years ago. To hear him tell it he was a great husband. Of course, he never married again. If he was so great, why was he alone? Taos pounded the top of the pillow again. No, Blake wasn't the one to ask. Besides, he had already laughed enough at Taos's expense.

What about the preacher? He and his wife held hands a lot at church. Taos chuckled softly. If the preacher gave him advice, they might be holding hands and nothing else for years. Definitely not what he had in mind.

He rubbed the pillow with his thumb as he imagined tracing the softness of her skin, the smile on her face, as he reached out and . . .

A hand touched his arm. He sprang to a sitting position and shoved a pillow over his lap to hide the evidence of his thoughts. The other pillow tumbled off the bed.

"Are you coming down to breakfast?" She looked at him and frowned, leaning over to place her hand on his forehead. "Are you feeling all right?"

"Uh, yeah." He cleared his throat as he regained control. "I mean, I'll be down in a minute."

She still frowned. "You sure you're all right?"

"Yes!" His impatience turned the word into a near shout as he squirmed on the bed.

She pressed her lips into a tight line. "I was just concerned, that's all." The door slammed behind her.

Great job, Romeo.

Taos threw the pillow in the floor and swung his legs over the side of the bed. He stared out the window at the rising sun. It wouldn't matter who he asked or even if he asked. He wouldn't be able to pull it off. Taos gritted his teeth.

She knew this courting business wasn't anything he was good at. She just wanted to humble him, put him in his place. Well he wasn't about to start getting henpecked this soon. He moved around the room gathering clothes and throwing them on as his temper built to full steam.

The kitchen was alive with activity as Tommy relayed the latest news from the fishing hole and Darren tried to help cook.

". . . And just as the sun peeked up, I saw 'em start breakin' the surface."

"Uh huh." Darren was only half listening as he flipped over a piece of ham sizzling in the skillet. Steam rose and the smell filled the kitchen. Samantha placed the last of the biscuits in the pan and put them in the oven. No one seemed to notice Taos's arrival.

"Know what that means, Uncle Darren?" No response. "Do ya?" The boy tugged impatiently on his sleeve, demanding an answer.

Samantha grinned at Darren, who heaved a long-suffering sigh.

"What does that mean, Tommy?" She asked, ignoring Taos as he sat at the table.

"They's hungry, that's what." He hopped off the chair and scooted it toward the table.

"So am I." All eyes turned to Taos, and at least one brow raised at his tone. "What does a man have to do to get some coffee around here?" His mood was sour and his temper short. Frustration etched his face.

Darren cast a questioning expression at Samantha, who shrugged and fluttered her eyelashes in feigned innocence.

"Have a long night, did ya?" Darren asked.

Taos frowned and grunted at his brother.

Samantha filled a cup with coffee and plunked it on the table in front of him, sloshing brown liquid over the rim. He ignored her until she turned her back, then glared at her.

Darren squelched a chuckle. "Like two cats in a toe sack." His mumbled comment brought a grunt from Taos and a smile from Samantha.

All things considered, breakfast was a quiet affair. Taos's dark mood cast a shadow over the entire house. Even Darren steered clear of him, finished his breakfast in record time, and headed out toward the northern range.

"We goin' fishing?"

Samantha smiled at the boy: egg on his lower lip, a stubborn cowlick in his dusty brown hair, blue jeans tucked into his boots.

"You have work to do first. Better get to it."

Tommy's face fell and his shoulders drooped at Taos's command. He shuffled out the back door toward the barn.

"What is the matter with you?" Samantha grabbed the wet dishtowel that was slung over her shoulder and snapped it across his arm.

"Nothin'." He set his jaw.

"Nothin'?" she said. "Then why are you pouting like a child?"

He rose to his feet, intending to intimidate her. "I don't pout."

She looked thoroughly unconvinced.

"I just don't like being told that I have to put on airs for my wife."

"Put on airs? I just thought it would be nice to have a little courting, that's it."

"I just don't see what it matters now if I pick you a bunch of daisies or not, we're already married. It's not like it's going to make any difference."

Samantha turned and stood perfectly still with her back to him.

Taos shuffled his feet in the silence. He finally went over to the coffee to get a refill and glanced sideways at her face. The pot stopped in midair. Tears streamed down her face as she stared straight ahead.

He put down the pot and cup and reached out to touch her arm, but she flinched away from him. He dropped his hand to his side and just stood there.

When she looked up, her voice was strangely calm. "I thought you understood. I don't want you to go through the motions of treating me like I'm someone special. I wanted you to really believe it." She stared into his eyes then looked away. "You know, you're absolutely right. It's a big waste of time for a man to pretend he loves his wife." She turned and walked out the back door.

Taos felt like a hole had opened up in his chest. How could she think he was pretending? Hadn't he shown her? Been willing to give her what he'd sworn to withhold from any woman? Loved her in their bed like the sun would never rise?

The silence of the kitchen amplified the pounding of his heart to a loud drum beat. His feet were rooted to the floor as his mind raced, then suddenly, soft as a butterfly's wings, he heard something.

He strained to hear the sound again, and there it was. He walked to the open window that looked out toward the barn. It was almost a giggle, like a baby's laugh. He started toward the back door to investigate.

"Taos!"

Samantha's scream stabbed his heart. He grabbed a pistol from the holster hanging on the wall and burst out the door as a loud shot blast echoed from the barn.

Chapter 25

Just as Taos reached the barn, Tommy slammed into his legs.

"He's got her, Pa!" The boy's eyes were wide with fear and he struggled to catch his breath.

"Who's got her?"

"The bad guy. He jumped out and dragged me behind the wagon. Said he'd shoot me if I yelled. He waited 'til she came out and then he let me go and grabbed her."

Taos's blood ran cold. "Go to the house, and stay there!" He shoved the boy in the direction of safety and crouched near the barn door. He peered around the corner, catching a quick flash of white lace in one corner of the dark building.

Tommy crawled next to him, stirring a choking cloud of dust in the process. "He tried to shoot me when I ran, but Momma bit him."

Taos hesitated. *Momma?* It barely had time to register as he realized Lawson had just tried to shoot his son. "Go to the house!"

"You gotta save her Pa." Tommy ran for the house.

Taos gazed through a crack in one of the barn boards, trying to see. A wet nose against his ear made Taos nearly jump out of his skin. He grabbed the dog's thick coat and dragged him to the doorway. "Get him, boy!"

The dog darted inside, barking at the top of his lungs. Taos peered around the corner just as the large black dog jumped and snapped at Lawson's gun arm. Lawson thrust Samantha between himself and the hairy mutt, but the dog darted around her skirts, nipping and biting his legs. Taos cocked his gun and edged forward, trying to get a clear shot as the dog antagonized Lawson.

"Taos!"

The urgency in her voice brought Taos through the opening and to a dead stop as a bullet whizzed past his ear. Lawson clung to a struggling Samantha with one hand and tried to hold the gun steady with the other.

His appearance was disheveled. Hay matted Lawson's black hair and his once-shiny boots were now scuffed and caked with dirt. His face was pale and the black marbles within reflected a sinister mixture of desperation and insanity. Lawson ranted as the gun waved in a deadly arc.

"You'll see. It will be even better this way." He aimed the gun at Taos. "Throw that down, over in the corner."

Jimbo jumped and snapped and Lawson moved the gun from side to side, directing it first at the dog, then at Taos again. Taos quickly realized that he and Samantha could both be shot purely by accident. He did a quick mental inventory of his options. Getting the gun away from Lawson seemed to be the top priority.

Taos held up both hands and dropped his gun a few feet away.

"Kick it over there," Lawson growled.

Samantha squirmed and slid to her knees. Lawson yanked her up and tried to get a better grip as the gun continued to wave back and forth. Her hair tumbled over her shoulders and partially into his face.

"As a widow, you get everything he has too. Then we can make a new start. A new life together. You'll just have to trust me that this is best." He spoke to the back of Samantha's head as the arm with the gun drooped.

Taos stood still and looked for the opportunity to make his move. "Let her go, Lawson."

Samantha twisted in Lawson's grip, trying to kick out. The gun moved upward.

"Oh, no. She's mine. She was always meant to be mine. No cowboy could ever take care of her like I can. You'll see. You'll all see."

Taos darted to one side and shoved the gun away. Lawson's arm snapped back, the gun pointed right at Taos. A shot rang out, followed by another.

Taos smelled the gun powder, heard Samantha scream, then his knees buckled.

Samantha tore from Lawson's grip, falling on her knees at Taos's side. The bullet had cut a path through his left shoulder, and warm sticky red liquid oozed from the wound and dripped into a growing puddle in the dirt.

"I'm fine," Taos whispered.

She nodded through tears and stuffed her handkerchief under his shirt to help stem the bleeding. A new fear gripped her, dwarfing her terror of the last few minutes as his life drained away. The puddle grew, and blood combined with her tears as she pressed her hand against the wound.

"Where did he go?"

Taos's whispered question made her jump, and she looked to where Lawson had been standing. He was still there, though not standing. The gun lay in his hand, but his long slender fingers had gone limp. Lawson's eyes stared into a glassy nothing and blood trickled from a large hole in the middle of his chest.

Taos raised his head trying to look.

"He's dead." Samantha looked toward the door, trying to locate the source of the bullet that killed Lawson, and saved them both. Darren must have heard the commotion and come back to help them, she reasoned. The sun silhouetted a form, but he seemed too far away.

"Darren!" she called.

Taos groaned and motioned toward his brother. The form walked a few feet closer.

A small hand gripped a still smoking gun.

Samantha stared. "Tommy!"

"Tommy?" Taos tried to focus his gaze on his son.

"Yes sir," Tommy came closer. His face seeming to age with each step.

"Where did you get that gun?" Samantha could hardly rationalize what her mind told her had happened.

"It's the 'mergency gun."

The two adults stared at him in stunned silence.

"Well, it looked like a 'mergency to me."

The pounding hooves thundered toward the trio. Darren jumped off his horse and ran to Taos's side, skidding to a stop on his knees. He lifted the handkerchief and looked at the wound.

"Not as b-bad as it c-could have been." He strained to pull Taos to his feet with Samantha's help. "We need to g-get him in the h-house. I'll get D-Doc Bentley." He glanced over at Lawson. I'm glad Taos plugged him with one s-shot."

"He didn't," Samantha positioned herself under Taos's arm and tried to steady him. "Tommy did."

"Is Pa gonna be alright?" Tommy asked.

"He'll be fit as a fiddle in no time, he just needs some r-rest." Darren assured him. He tousled the boy's hair. "You did good, Tommy."

Darren and Samantha half carried, half dragged Taos to the house.

The boy walked toward the still body in the barn. He nudged Lawson's knee with the toe of his small boot. "I'm real sorry, mister, but I didn't have no choice."

Tommy stared at the unseeing eyes. "I thought there would be angels or something." He mumbled and knelt down, laying a small hand on Lawson's shoulder. "Maybe bad people don't get no angels." He started toward the door, then looked back. "I'm sorry you didn't get no angels, mister."

Yours Again

Chapter 26

Doc Bentley snapped his black bag shut and removed his small spectacles, cleaning them with a neatly pressed handkerchief. Taos lay on the bed, his shoulder bandaged, his skin chalky white. Samantha paced at the foot of the bed waiting for the doctor to say something. The room was stuffy and confining. Small tendrils of hair stuck to the moisture on her forehead.

"He'll pull through." He returned the spectacles to their position on his nose.

"Seen worse, young lady." His penetrating eyes assessed her up and down, and he seemed to nod his approval.

"You'll take fine care of him I'm sure," He picked up his bag and started toward the door. Samantha released a relieved breath and stared at Taos.

"He'll be fine, really. Up and working in a week or so." The doctor patted her shoulder and left.

Taos's chest rose and fell with each breath. Samantha moved to the edge of the bed and leaned over, placing her hand lightly over his heart. A small drop of moisture slid down her cheek as she felt it beat strong under her fingers. The arguments of the past few days melted away. She stared at his face willing him to open his eyes. Her tears gathered reinforcements, refusing to stop their mad rush down her cheeks. They clouded her vision. She swiped her hands across her cheek.

"The doc said he was gonna be all right, didn't he?" Darren stood in the doorway frowning at her as she nodded. Darren cleared his throat and shuffled his feet. Tears made him antsy. His eyes opened wide as Samantha rushed toward him and hid her head in his chest. The initial shock gave way to uneasiness as Darren awkwardly tried to comfort her. Not sure exactly what to do with his hands, he finally decided that a stiff pat on her quivering shoulder was the way to go.

"It's gonna be all right." Darren said the words as much to himself as to her. He glanced toward the bed as Samantha sniffled. He had never envied an injured man until this second, and something about having to deal with an emotional female made him think that being shot wasn't all that bad. At least you could be unconscious through this part. His attention snapped back to her when he realized Samantha stared up at him, her brows furrowed.

"Did anyone ever tell you that you offer about as much comfort as a tall board?" She smiled and turned back to Taos.

"Haven't had much practice at it, but I intend to work on it." He shrugged his shoulders. "Why all the water?"

Samantha glanced at Taos. "I said some really terrible things to him the last few days." She sniffled. "I couldn't have lived with myself if, well, you know."

"Yeah, I know," he said as he watched one last straggler slide down her cheek. He felt an instinctive urge to brush it off with his thumb as if it would ease the pain. Instead he shoved his hands in his pockets and stared at this brother.

Darren had been more worried about the things that needed saying. Not that he really doubted that Taos knew how he felt, but somehow the time had never really come to tell him out loud.

"Aunt Mattie always said that at the end of life it's the things you didn't do, didn't try, or didn't say that you regret the most." She stared into nothing, lost in thought.

Darren squinted at her. It was like she could hear his thoughts out loud. Taos and Charlie both told him that she could read minds, but sometimes they exaggerated things. The sun streamed into the window as it marched toward the horizon. There were animals to feed and a section of fence to check before dark.

Samantha started toward the door. "I'll fix you something to eat before you go."

A little chill crept up his back. "Go where?"

"Feed stock and check that fence." Her voice trailed off as she walked down the hall.

"It's a sorry day when a man can't even think in front of a woman." He mumbled and followed her.

A sharp knock sounded at the back door just as Samantha set a plate of ham and eggs in front of Darren. Billy Baker's red head came into view as he peeked through the screen.

"Miss Sammy?" He held a letter and she motioned him inside. The boy stopped and stared at Darren's plate.

"Is that for me?" Samantha asked.

Billy's head jerked back to her. "Oh, uh, yeah, ma'am. Ma said you could come get it like everybody else, but I thought it might be important." His gaze drifted back to the steaming eggs. Darren paused, the fork half way to his mouth, as he eyes met Billy's.

The boy licked his lips.

"Can't eat being stared at." Darren groused.

"Would you like to join us?" Samantha smiled at Darren's irritation.

"Um, my ma might not 'preciate it." He shuffled his feet.

"She won't know if you don't tell her."

Billy grinned and nodded, trying to scoot out of the way as Tommy barreled in the back door.

"Smells like breakfast." A small dirt cloud rose as Tommy whacked the front of his jeans with his ragged straw hat.

"Hey!" Darren frowned, swiping at the dust that now filled the kitchen.

Tommy shrugged, "Fell down."

Samantha gazed at the writing on the envelope. It was from Mattie. She felt a tingle of excitement. The postmark was dated just a week ago and well after John had left Boston. He had lied! She was alive. No matter what was in the letter, Mattie was alive! She slid the precious communication into her pocket and quickly fixed more eggs.

Both boys sat at the table.

"How come you're eatin' with us?" Tommy tilted his head at Billy.

"She said I could."

"Because we feed every stray that wonders through the f-fence, that's why." Darren picked up his plate and cup and went to the porch to eat, away from the greedy stares of the youngsters. He let the door bang loudly.

Billy's eyebrows popped up.

"He's always grumpy when he's hungry." Tommy heaved a sigh.

Samantha had the boys eating large helpings of eggs, ham and biscuits in no time, then hurried upstairs and checked on Taos. He was still sleeping. She sat in a chair in the corner and tore the envelope open. Her heart pounded and excited, happy tears filled her eyes as she read.

Taos opened his eyes and tried to focus. Samantha came into view as she sat and read a letter. She smiled from ear to ear, crying at the same time. He must still be dreaming. The pain in his shoulder distracted him for a moment and he stared at the ceiling, willing it to the back of his mind. Samantha shifted in the chair and laughed a little at something she read. He snapped his eyes shut as she glanced toward him. He peeked with one eye to make sure she was concentrating on her letter again.

She was beautiful. She was mean too. The last few days had been nothing but frustration, only to end up with him getting shot. He was beginning to think that every ounce of human kindness had drained out of her before Lawson showed up again. He'd known prize pigs that were treated better than she'd treated him. Maybe this whole event had changed her attitude. Now was a perfect time to see. He grunted and shifted a little to get her attention. She rushed to the bed, still clutching her letter.

"Taos?"

He groaned and cracked his eyelids open a fraction.

She sat on the edge of the bed and put her palm against his forehead. "Are you awake?"

"Yeah, I guess I am." He tried to make his voice weak and thready.

She grinned and held up her letter. "Guess what! Mattie is alive and she wants me to come home!" She reread the letter silently for the tenth time as Taos stared at her. "She says that she is up and around, and has been worried sick about me."

"Must be nice to have someone care about you."

The tone of his voice surprised her and she looked up at his angry face. "What's wrong?"

He shifted and leaned, struggling to prop pillows underneath him. "I'm shot, and all you can think about now is getting back to Boston." He pounded at the pillows in frustration, using what little strength he had. He was weak as a kitten. "No, 'I'm sorry for getting you shot' or 'I'm sorry I was such a shrew' or even 'Are you hungry?'" He grunted.

Samantha slowly rose to her feet, "I'm not a shrew."

"I beg to differ." He refused to look at her, but stole a glance every time she turned her back.

"You can beg all you want, but it doesn't change the fact that I was merely responding to the ill treatment you were dishing out. Not only that, but you were obviously pretending a minute ago with all that groaning just to try and get me to feel sorry for you."

"I should have known it wouldn't work." His shoulder hurt worse now and he scrunched down in the bed.

"I have been worried sick about Mattie since I got here, and I just found out she isn't dead. Why are you making me feel like I'm the one in the wrong?"

"'Cause you are." It was the only response he could think of. He immediately felt like a whiny little boy. He was glad Mattie was alive, too. But he did not want Samantha running off to Boston when things were not right between them.

"No, I'm not. And as far as you getting shot, it's just too bad he didn't hit you in the mouth."

He glared at her then stared out the window.

"Mattie wants me to come home. Do you want me to go?"

He continued to stare out the window. It was time for her to choose. Taos was her husband, but he couldn't force her to stay. "I won't stop you."

She nodded stoically and headed toward the adjoining door to her room. It closed quietly behind her. Taos felt like he'd been stabbed in the heart.

Yours Again

Chapter 27

Samantha plopped down on her bed and propped her chin in her hands. Part of her heart expected him to call her name. She listened for the better part of a half hour, but nothing. There was no question now. He didn't care enough to court her and getting shot on her account had made up his mind. Mattie was alive, and she wanted Samantha to come home. She stood and looked slowly around the room. This was home. She shook her head and cleared her throat. He would never see one tear. No sir, not one. She was through crying. Samantha threw herself into packing; it was easier to be busy.

Darren pushed open the door and stuck his head into Taos's room. Dark was closing in, and he could see his brother sitting up in bed, staring out the window. The house had a strange quiet to it. He couldn't explain it, but it just didn't seem right.

"You coming in or not?"

Darren walked to the window and stared out into the shadows. "How you feelin'?"

Silence.

"Doc said you were gonna be fine."

"You check that fence?" The tone of his voice told Darren there was more wrong with Taos than a bullet wound.

"Yeah, needs s-some work. Not too much though."

Silence again.

"Could get to it at the end of the week if you're up to it by then."

"Yeah, I ain't hurt too bad." Taos took a deep breath.

"I wasn't too s-sure for a minute there." Darren tugged at the curtain, grappling with uncomfortable emotions.

Taos chuckled. "Takes more than one bullet to kill a Williams."

"Don't go around testing that theory out. I'd miss you around here, you know."

"I know."

Darren breathed a sigh of relief in the now near dark room. "How about some light in here?" He lit the lamp.

"What I'd really like is some food. I'm starving."

"Where's Sammy?" Darren quirked up an eyebrow as he just now realized she hadn't been downstairs.

"She's leaving."

Darren went still. Apparently quite a few things had transpired since he left. "Why?"

"I told her to go."

"You *what*?" Darren looked as incredulous as he sounded.

Taos groaned, annoyed at having to explain himself. "She got a letter from Mattie asking her to come home, and she asked me if she should go. And I said, 'Go.' It's as simple as that."

"That's not all there is to it." Darren knew Taos thought he could make a cow patty into chocolate cake if he laid on enough icing.

The muscle in Taos's jaw twitched as he worked his teeth back and forth and ignored the comment.

"What did you do?"

"She started it."

"I'll j-just bet." The accusation was clear.

"I woke up and all she could talk about was going home. She didn't even care that I was shot." Taos frowned.

Darren rubbed his fist across his forehead in frustration.

"I was protecting her you know. She could have shown a little concern."

Darren shook his head like he was scolding a naughty two-year-old.

"Then, after I saved her life, she had the nerve to say that it was too bad the guy didn't shoot me in the mouth."

"I h-happen to agree with her." Darren started toward the door.

"She never planned to stay, Darren. I just let her off the hook."

Darren stopped, "Are you really that stupid, big brother?"

Taos narrowed his eyes at Darren. One of these days he'd learn what women were really like. "Are you bringing me something to eat?"

"Why don't you chew on those big f-feet you keep putting in your mouth?" The door slammed behind him.

Chapter 28

Samantha breathed in the cool morning air. God's first breath, Aunt Mattie would say. Walking slowly along the path toward the rose garden, she gazed upward as just a suggestion of light appeared on the horizon, mixing deep lavender and pink in an awesome display of creation. It wasn't cold, but she still shivered, hugging her arms around her waist. She rounded the bend in the creek and stopped.

The garden was quiet, the air perfectly still. No insects hummed, no birds twittered in the tree tops, and faint light illuminated the petals of hundreds of roses like tiny Chinese lanterns. Samantha stared, soaking in the scene. She wanted to remember the color of each blossom, the turn of every twig, the awesome presence of peace. She willed the sight to be permanently rooted in her brain. It held more beauty than any place she had ever been, and more pain than any place she could ever imagine.

As the light grew and painted the sky, a faint yellow-pink hue illuminated the tiny angel statue inch by inch. The fabric of Samantha's skirt clung to the tiny rose thorns as she approached. Kneeling, she softly ran her hand over the white stone wings. They were cool to the touch, but warm to her heart. This was where it had started. Here in this garden, with this one secret. This was where she started to love Taos. Not the idea of him she'd carried in her heart for nine years, but the real man he was now. She replayed the many times she and Taos sparred and jabbed like knights of old with their words. They seemed like a thousand tiny paper cuts to her soul, each by itself small and insignificant, but together they left her spirit bloody and bruised.

She rose and dusted herself off. Aunt Mattie always said that if being wrong about a man was a crime, then half the female gender would be in the slammer. The problem was she didn't feel like she had been wrong. It felt like they were still connected even if the love was mostly on her part.

"I may be going, but I'm afraid my heart won't be coming with me." Just saying it out loud, made it seem so final. There was always a way, she knew, if the want was there, but she honestly couldn't see it this time. A brick wall had sprouted between them, where a clear path had stood just days ago. Her efforts had proven futile and she was out of ideas and out of hope as Taos had retreated into his shell again. Her shoulders slumped as she turned to leave.

A slight breeze stirred the bushes and the tinkling soft sound of a baby laughing washed over her. She smiled. Maybe she was crazy, but she suddenly felt lighter and reassured. "If something's going to change I'm going to need some help." The sound faded into the rustling tress and she straightened her shoulders and walked toward the house.

Darren loaded Jake's old trunk full of Samantha's things into the wagon as she pulled on her gloves.

"You d-don't have to go." He paused and looked at her. "He didn't mean it you know."

"He said it, and this one time I'm going to give him what he wants." She glanced toward the barn where Taos had hidden all morning. "He's done a great deal for me, and the least I can do at this point is to honor his request."

Darren shook his head as he loaded the last box into the wagon. "Does he know you're just g-going to your cabin?"

"No, but it doesn't matter. I need time to think, and whether I go to Boston today or a week from today doesn't matter. I won't be Taos's problem anymore."

"Where's Tommy?"

"We already said our goodbyes. I told him he was welcome to come see me over at the cabin anytime he wants. That goes for you too, you know."

Darren opened his arms to accept her hug. Maybe he was getting better at this, 'cause this wasn't bad at all. In fact, he was sorry when she let go. He helped her into the wagon and glanced toward the barn. He knew Taos was watching, but refused to make any appearance.

"Coward." Darren grumbled as he disengaged the brake.

Samantha sat ramrod straight in the wagon and refused to turn and look for him, even though every muscle in her body yearned to do so.

Taos stood in the shadows of the barn until they were out of sight. She didn't look back, even seemed pleased about going. He went back to the house. It was quiet and very empty. Heavy boots scraping along the floor were the only sound as he wandered upstairs and walked down the hall. He leaned against the door jamb to her room. Her presence still pervaded the room, like she had just stepped out of the room, not out of his life. He sat gingerly on the edge of the bed, then laid back and stared at the ceiling. His long legs dangled off the side of the bed. Her sweet scent still clung to the linens. He didn't really think she would leave, not without saying a word—or two or three.

He expected a fight, or at least a struggle. She had given up without even a whimper. It seemed there was some invisible line in the sand that he crossed and she just let him.

He lay on the bed for what seemed hours, then eventually made his way to the study and the bottle. That's where he was when Charlie came home.

"You drinkin' that or just watching it?" He dropped into a chair opposite the desk and whacked his hat on one thin knee, raising a small cloud of dust.

Taos swirled the amber liquid for the hundredth time and ignored the question.

"You know she's over at her place, right?"

He nodded. Tommy couldn't keep a secret if his life depended on it. Taos was relieved she wasn't completely gone yet, but still it was just a matter of time.

"So? Are you going to go get her?" Charlie asked.

"Nobody can make Sammy do anything she doesn't want to do." He let that sink in. "If she wants to come back, she will."

"You're an idiot." Charlie gave a disgusted sigh and left the office.

He had no idea what to say to her anyway, and even if she came back she'd just leave again. He really didn't like the idea of her staying at the cabin alone though. While Lawson wasn't a threat anymore, a woman alone in a remote cabin wasn't a good thing either. He just hadn't figured out how to handle that part of it yet.

He stood and grabbed his hat on the way out. The only thing to do was go back to work. At least there was something he was still good at.

Chapter 29

Samantha stared into the fire and sipped a cup of tea. It was the morning of the twenty-third day since she'd packed up and left Taos. The cabin had been a refuge the last few weeks, but still, she didn't sleep at night. She told herself it was because she wasn't used to being completely alone, but that wasn't really the truth. The second she closed her eyes all she saw was him. His smile, his touch, the sound of his voice.

Darren, Charlie, and Tommy visited regularly and often had dinner at her house. She loved having them over but no matter what, they always asked when she was coming home. She'd run out of excuses, and now things were just plain complicated.

She knew Taos watched over the cabin. On occasion she'd seen him ride by at a distance, and she felt his gaze many times even when she couldn't see him. But not once had he come close enough to speak to her.

It convinced her that she'd been right to leave. He might still feel responsible for her in some way, but he didn't want her around.

The first week she'd cried. The whole week. Every day. Eventually the tears had slowed but even now, weeks later, they would creep up on her every so often at the most unexpected times. Samantha was thoroughly and utterly heartbroken. She spent countless hours staring out the window at her mother's headstone. Her mother had died of a broken heart and Samantha could never understand it. She could never understand the kind of love that could make a woman choose death over life. Unfortunately, now she did. There is pain much worse than actually dying, and only now could she understand how devastated her mother had been when her father was killed.

The weather had turned and the first flakes of snow were falling. She had to make a decision soon. It wasn't practical to stay here alone during the harsh mountain winter, but so far she'd clung to some sort of hope that things would work out. Now, even that seemed far-fetched.

A knock at the door dragged her from her thoughts. Charlie said he was bringing her a surprise this morning, but she had no idea what. She swung the door wide open. Standing on her porch was Mattie.

"Sweetheart!" Mattie rushed toward Samantha with open arms and the women clutched one another, laughing and crying.

The sweet scent of lilac and lavender filled Samantha's senses like a favorite memory. She held Mattie at arm's length and grinned through her tears. "You are the best thing I've seen in such a long time!"

The petite woman placed her hands on her hips and gave her head a saucy toss. "Watch the flattery, honey. You know it goes straight to my head!" They laughed again. "You look tired."

Samantha nodded and ran a hand through her hair. She felt like a piece of old wadded newspaper.

"It's more than that, isn't it?" Mattie's discerning eyes sliced through the brave front.

Samantha whispered. "My heart is tired."

"Now *that* requires some explanation. Paul can make us some tea and we'll talk."

Samantha spotted Paul carrying Mattie's luggage toward the cabin. Once Charlie had them settled Samantha gave him a big hug.

"Thank you so much, Charlie!"

"No problem, honey. Just let me know if I can do anything else for you." He smiled and left, giving the women the time to get reacquainted.

Paul busied himself making tea, and Mattie sat on the bench in front of the windows with Samantha.

They sat in silence for a while, taking in the glorious view of the mountains until Paul brought their tea.

"What happened?"

Samantha's cup rattled slightly as she sat it down. Mattie was nothing if not direct. "Where do you want me to begin?"

"At the beginning, of course."

The story trickled at first, then gained strength until it became a torrent of emotional rapids. Mattie grinned as Samantha told of being tied up and "rescued" by Taos, then went into a full belly laugh at her description of the "instruction" under Cinnamon's tutelage. Tommy's swim lesson, the rose garden. Everything leapt forward. As Samantha talked, Mattie watched her closely. She could almost put her finger on the moment she realized Samantha was desperately in love with Taos. The girl's voice softened and her eyes took on a faraway expression. Mattie remembered that feeling well. It was like warm honey flowing over your heart.

"Oh, and by the way," Samantha narrowed her eyes at her aunt. "Why didn't you tell me I was married?"

It was Mattie's turn to squirm. "Well, there wasn't time. You had to go so suddenly."

"I mean before that."

"I was going to, but the time never seemed right. It was just a paperwork snafu anyway."

"That's no excuse."

Mattie leaned forward and waited until Samantha leaned toward her. "Sweetheart," she whispered. "You're a married woman."

She grinned smugly at the frown Samantha wore. "There. I've told you. Does that make you happy?"

The woman's smile was infectious and Samantha couldn't help herself. "Yes, that makes me happy." She paused and took another sip of tea. "Or, at least it did."

"Would you have married him anyway?"

Samantha laughed, "Yes. I almost did."

"When was this?"

"Shortly after John Lawson showed up. Taos asked me—no, make that *told me*—that we had to get married. So he dragged the preacher over to the whorehouse . . ."

"He what?!" Mattie choked on her tea. "You better start over."

Samantha recounted every detail as Mattie dabbed tears of laughter from the corners of her eyes. Lawson's mad dash to the outhouse had Mattie begging Samantha to stop.

"I declare, my stomach's going to be sore for a week! I don't think I ever laughed so much in my whole life." She waved a white handkerchief to fan her face as Samantha grew quiet.

They sat in silence until finally Mattie asked, "Do you regret what happened?"

The question surprised Samantha, and a quick answer was on the tip of her tongue, but she couldn't let it go. Did she regret it?

"Well?"

Samantha sat her cup on the table. "I was just about to say yes, but that wouldn't be true."

Mattie waited as the girl organized her thoughts.

"You wouldn't think it would be very pleasant to be tied up and gagged, kidnapped, rescued again, and forced to the point of marriage, but it changed me somehow." She met her aunt's knowing eyes. "If I could redo the whole thing, the only thing I would change would be the last day."

"When he told you to go?"

"Yes. I only left because I thought he would come after me."

"That's a very dangerous game, Samantha. What if he doesn't?"

"I don't know. I just don't know." But she did know. This wasn't home anymore, he was home.

Mattie poured more tea for them and they both enjoyed the evening. It was astonishing to Mattie that Samantha had left Boston a few months ago a head strong girl and had suddenly become a grown woman. She knew Samantha would go to him, she had to. The older woman smiled to herself. Of course, if that boy had any sense he would be on her doorstep on his knees.

Yours Again

Chapter 30

The bright sunlight of early morning cast a tall shadow as Taos marched toward the hotel in town. He'd come to pick up a very special item from the mercantile and wanted to stop and have something to eat before heading home. He missed Samantha in every way possible and had taken to avoiding his house. A lot. He worked, but even much of that time he spent riding near her cabin hoping to catch a glimpse of her now and then. He didn't really sleep much these days, and he definitely drank way too much.

He'd lost weight, and meal times were especially hard. His brothers and son ate with Samantha several times a week, but he knew he wasn't invited. Well, she probably wouldn't refuse to feed him if he showed up. She fed every stray. But he knew he couldn't be around her and not sweep her into his arms, whether she wanted him to or not.

Actually he'd considered doing just that. His kisses had melted her heart before, but this time was different. If he pushed her too far she just might run all the way to Boston, and he couldn't even think what his life would be like then.

"Going somewhere, Mr. Williams?" Mavis strolled up beside him, having to double step to keep up with him.

"Yup." He kept walking. He needed to think, not talk. His politeness was forced. "You going somewhere?"

She nodded. "Going for a quick bite before I catch the stage to Cimarron at 9:15."

He stopped in front of the hotel restaurant. Damn, they were really busy this morning. People waited on benches just inside. He decided to wait outside to avoid them as much as possible. "Don't you want to wait inside with the others?" He asked Mavis. Maybe she would take the hint.

She smiled. "I create enough talk without having to be within earshot of it."

He snorted. "Bet that's right." It was out of his mouth before he realized it. He abruptly faced her. "I mean, uh . . . I mean I didn't mean anything . . ."

She let him stumble through the half apology. "That's quite alright. When the day comes that I don't stir up talk, then I'll be upset."

"Yes Ma'am." He shuffled his feet, trying not to smile.

A strong wind swirled snowflakes around them.

Mavis frowned, "Well, unfortunately it looks like I'll have to brave the crowd or freeze to death."

He nodded his agreement and stepped inside as well.

The hostess sat people wherever there was an empty seat and Taos surveyed the possibilities. It was either a woman with a hat that looked as if it contained half a dead flower garden or a salesman with his suitcase of wares within easy reach to pitch to his dinner mate. The hostess was completely distracted, trying to figure out what to do with Mavis. It was a touchy situation because they couldn't seat the town madam with just anyone. Taos spotted a couple getting up from a table and motioned for Mavis to join him.

"To what do I owe that very timely rescue, Mr. Williams?"

"Desperation."

She glanced over at the woman with the strange hat. "Too bad you didn't choose her. You could have at least discovered what milk cow she got that hat off of."

Taos grinned, then laughed out loud. Several people turned and stared.

Mavis glanced at him out of the corner of her eye. "Mr. Williams, I believe you were in need of a good laugh."

"Yes, Ma'am, I was." He twirled his hat in his hand. "So you're on your way to Cimarron today?"

Her eyes scanned the patrons and she lowered her voice. "Yes, I have to see an old friend."

"I didn't think y'all made house calls."

"We don't." She paused, "But now that I think about it, there might be a market for such a thing." She winked at him. "I'll think about it." She smoothed her navy silk dress across her knees. "Actually, it concerns one of my daughters."

"Daughters? I thought there was just Cinnamon."

"No, there is another one. What about you?"

Taos took the hint to let it go. "I had to pick up something over at the mercantile and then I'm heading home."

"You're not going to see Samantha?"

Of course she knew. Everyone in town knew Samantha had left him. The silence lengthened between them.

They ordered their meal and the waitress brought them coffee.

"You know, there was a time when I had a chance to choose." Mavis focused out the window. "I was young and stubborn, and I thought that to love someone was weak, and needy, and I wanted no part of it."

She definitely had his attention.

"I thought independence was everything."

Taos nodded. He prized his own independence highly, and so did Sammy as far as that goes.

"I wanted to take care of myself and not feel obligated to anyone, so I did and I'm not."

He had to admire her spunk, if not her chosen profession. "Then you got what you wanted."

After a minute she sighed. "Yes and no."

He hated it when women talked in circles. "It can't be yes and no. It has to be one or the other."

"Life isn't that simple, Taos. That's why there's that old saying about be careful what you wish for. Oh, I'm certainly independent, but also quite lonely."

"You have lots of, um, friends."

"That's business, and knowing what I know now, I would trade it all for the privilege to love and be loved by one man."

She paused and waited until he looked at her again. "It's a very precious thing, and you don't realize it when you're young." She held his gaze. "Youth does that to you. Gives you that optimism that there will be a multitude of opportunities. You never think that you might only get one chance."

She snapped her fingers. "Just like that the chance is gone and you spend the rest of your life trying to find it again."

They lapsed into silence again, each immersed in their own thoughts. Taos rubbed his knuckle across his lower lip. Something he could only describe as a nervous chill gripped him. One chance, one opportunity. How many women would he get the chance to tie up and drag home? His expression started as a smile as he thought about how he dragged Sammy home that first night, then quickly faded to a frown. He had lived thirty years in this town and not so much as one woman of interest had crossed his path until she showed up. What if thirty turned to forty and forty to fifty?

They ate most of their meal in companionable silence.

Mavis said, "Can I ask you something?"

He nodded.

"Do you love her?"

He knew the answer immediately, but hesitated. "I, um, don't take change very well."

Mavis smiled, "Your life has already changed. You're just too stubborn to admit it."

"I guess I am a little on the stubborn side," he shrugged.

Her expression turned stern. "I can tell you exactly what being stubborn gets you, Mr. Williams. And that's alone."

He stared into his coffee.

Alone.

It was such a tiny word to hold what promised to be an entire lifetime of regret.

"Samantha loves you, you know."

He shook his head. Mavis had no idea how things had been between them.

"If she didn't love you, she'd be in Boston."

Taos couldn't afford to scare her off. He knew his best bet was to stay away. Mavis probably meant well, but he'd already made up his mind how to approach this and he was going to stick to it.

"Do you remember how Samantha's mother died?"

The question surprised him. "Yes. She never got over Sam's death."

"She died of a broken heart, Taos. And Samantha is headed down the same path."

He frowned. That wasn't true. Was it? He thought about Claire, remembered her sitting in that rocking chair day after day. Not eating, wasting away. Was that what had been happening at the cabin? Surely not. Charlie or Darren would have said something. He wasn't about to let that happen to Samantha, and he suddenly had a desperate urge to see her—and not from a distance this time.

Mavis paid for her breakfast and then snapped her pearl-rimmed purse shut. "I must be going." She looked at him. "You should be going too."

He nodded and threw some money on the table. "Yes, I've got somewhere I need to be."

Chapter 31

Purple faded into a toasty yellow as the sun rose above peaks that were now capped with snow. Samantha knew in her heart this had been a mistake. A big one. Sharing the whole series of events with Mattie had made her realize how desperately she missed Taos. She had been up since three o'clock, turning possibilities over in her mind, trying to come up with a good solution. One that would dispel her ever-growing depression, yet salvage some remnant of pride. Unfortunately, there was only one way to fix this. Go home.

Her bags were sitting by the door, waiting, ready to go. It was time for pride to sit down and shut up for once. She would just go back and explain that she had reconsidered. Maybe he had, too. If that didn't work then there was always groveling. She grimaced. Maybe groveling was too strong a word. Ladies didn't grovel, they pleaded. At least it sounded better. Yes, definitely. Tommy needed her, and so did Taos if he would just admit it. If reason didn't work, then she would cook her heart out and crawl into his bed every night, whether he wanted her there or not. It had worked the first time.

Mattie's head poked out of one room, her hair still cloaked in her pink cotton nightcap. "I thought I heard you up. It's awfully early."

Samantha nodded.

Mattie cleared her throat. "It's where you belong now, with your family."

She nodded again and pressed her fingers to her lips as they started to tremble. "Mattie."

"Yes?"

"Thank you so much for . . . well, everything."

Tears slid down Mattie's cheeks. "You're very welcome, sweetie." She gave Samantha a hug and disappeared to get ready for the day.

Samantha heaved a big sigh of relief as excitement enfolded her. *Home.* She was going home.

Breakfast was an exhilarating experience. The two women talked, laughed, and shared their hearts. Maple scones dripping with butter and strawberry crème crepes disappeared as fast as Paul placed them on the table.

Samantha popped another bite of scone into her mouth and savored the buttery treat. "Paul certainly outdid himself this morning."

Mattie giggled a little.

Samantha noticed a decided shift between Mattie and Paul. The way his eyes followed her every move and how he touched her arm ever-so-softly when he spoke to her. That clipped British tone softened almost to a caress when he spoke to Mattie these days. She knew love when she saw it.

Samantha had hardly slept a wink last night, and this morning she was very tired. Maybe making the decision to go home relieved some of the anxiety she'd had the past month. Paul and Mattie were at the kitchen table laughing about something and she slipped into her room. A quick nap would do her good. She glanced in the mirror at the dark circles under her eyes and frowned. Taos seeing her like this wouldn't be her first choice either. She sprawled out on the bed and pulled a quilt over her shoulders. In a few hours she'd be in his arms, this time for good.

Just as Taos raised his hand to knock, the cabin door swung open. Mattie plopped a hand on her hip, "About time you showed up."

He stepped inside and nodded a greeting at Paul. "Where's Sammy?"

"Sleeping."

He frowned. It wasn't like her to sleep during the day. But if she was the having the same problem sleeping at night that Taos was, it made sense.

"What are you doing here?" Mattie asked, as she tried to hide a smile.

He thought for a minute. "I came to get my wife."

Mattie grinned at Paul then stepped aside.

Taos cracked the bedroom door open a bit. Golden hair spilled across a bright white pillow.

He sat quietly in the chair next to the bed and watched her sleep. She was turned toward him, with one hand resting on the pillow. She looked so beautiful, but he could see the shadows under her eyes. She didn't look well, and he knew Mavis had been right. He couldn't wait one more minute. Now how was he going to convince her to come home?

Taos reached over and ran one finger softly along the back of her hand. He would not leave without her. He dropped his hand away from hers and exhaled his frustration.

The only thing he really knew to do was hold her close and show her he loved her. That he understood and that was the only thing he'd ever done right with her. He set his hat on the dresser, then removed his coat and boots. Carefully he slipped under the blanket. The minute he touched her, she rolled into his arms and his soul leapt to life. It was as if he hadn't really had a pulse since she left.

Samantha looked up at him. "I need to say some things to you."

He stilled, "Like what?"

"I love you and I want to go home."

His heart jumped up and flipped over, while his mind filled with caution. Nothing with this woman was this easy. *Stay calm.* "I came to take you home."

She nodded. Why did she still look so sad like it was some kind of death sentence? He just did not understand her. She wanted to come home. He wanted her to come home. Why was he the only one happy about it?

"You don't seem too excited." Maybe she thought she was stuck with him now.

"I only left because I wanted . . ." Her voice trailed off.

"What? What did you want?" God knows he had no clue.

"I just wanted you to want *me*. I wanted you to come after *me* and take *me* home."

He suddenly had the urge to strangle her. "That's what this is about?" He shook his head. "I can't believe you left me and came over here for a month because you don't think I want you. That is ridiculous!"

Her temper flared, "Why is it ridiculous to want to be loved?"

"I do love you!"

She stared, stunned. "Why didn't you say something?"

"Why didn't *you*? All you've ever done is yell at me and run off. Is that supposed to be love?"

"Yes."

Blood pounded in his ears and he dropped his head back on to the pillow. "This is not how I planned for this to go."

"You had a plan?" She flashed him that smile. The one that held a lot of promises.

He felt heat flow through him. *How did she do that with just a smile?* He pulled a small velvet bag with gold tassels out of his pocket. "I got you something."

Samantha took the delicate bag and ran a thumb across the velvet. "You were going to bribe me?"

"Well, not right off."

Her brows popped up.

"See, first I was just going to try some big speech."

She chuckled.

"Yeah, exactly." He pointed to the bag. "That was my backup plan."

"And if this didn't work?"

"I was going to tie you up and carry you off."

"And if I called for help?"

"Oh, don't worry. I was planning to gag you too."

She poked his ribs and opened the bag, holding her hand underneath to catch what she poured out. A ring tumbled into her palm. She gasped. It was exquisite: diamonds and emeralds set into a wide gold band.

"You never did get a wedding ring." He watched her slide it onto her hand and wiggle her fingers. The light made the stones sparkle.

"What if none of your plans had worked?"

"I would have begged." He looked into her deep green eyes. "I can't even breathe without you."

"I missed you so much." She kissed him softly. "Promise me you will never let me go."

He smiled. "Now, *that* I can do."

He wrapped her in his arms and covered her mouth with his, kissing her for all he was worth. He wanted Samantha to know she had every bit of love he had to give, now and forever.

Epilogue

Shortly after Taos and Samantha returned home, Mattie and Paul left for an extended tour of Europe and married in London before returning to Boston. To hear Mattie tell it, theirs was a love for the ages, and Samantha was delighted for her.

A few months later, Mattie sent a newspaper clipping from Boston with the headline, *"Littlest Gunfighter in the West"* and a story that contained the exploits of one Tommy Williams. It told how he'd save his whole family with one shot in the wild and woolly New Mexico Territory at the tender age of seven. The story made Tommy a bit of a celebrity in River City, and he loved every minute of it.

Taos and Samantha quickly settled into life on the ranch. Large snow accumulations that winter eased the drought, and by spring their grassland was supporting a much larger herd. Madeline Elizabeth Williams was born that spring, one of four children Taos and Samantha would eventually raise on their ranch. To Tommy's disappointment, three of those four children would be girls.

Yours Again